LIFE AFTER COFFEE

LIFE AFTER COFFEE

Virginia Franken

LAKE UNION
PUBLISHING

Published by Lake Union Publishing, Seattle

www.apub.com

Amazon, the Amazon logo, and Lake Union Publishing are trademarks of Amazon.com, Inc., or its affiliates.

ISBN-10: 1503939375
ISBN-13: 9781503939370

Cover design by Janet Perr

Printed in the United States of America

For Ella Mermaid and Max Morris,
King of the Salmon

CHAPTER 1

Bacon. Peter always cooks bacon for breakfast on Departure Days.

We all know you can't really compensate two children for their mother disappearing on a six-week work trip with three rashers of thick-cut streaky and an elephant-shaped pancake—but my husband is giving it his best shot anyhow. I have no idea how he makes the pancakes. Some secret technique involving a turkey baster and a couple of measuring cups. The man's a modern-day hero. I just wish he could display his culinary gifts whilst *not* wearing *The Apron*.

The Apron.

It was a gift from my mother two Christmases ago. My husband, bless him, didn't read a thing into it. I, however, having known my mother almost thirty years longer than Peter has, saw the gift for what it was: a bold-faced comment on the gender roles within our marriage. Mom's from England and likes to make her remarks on our unconventional setup nice and indirect. So indirect that most people would miss it. Not me, however.

"Oh, well done, Amy, dinner smells wonderful!" was the first thing she said as she walked in the door on her last visit.

"Don't look at me. Peter cooked it."

That Christmas The Apron arrived. And now Peter wears it when he cooks bacon, which he always does on Departure Days, emphasizing the "untraditional" element of our relationship just when I'd most like to gloss over it. Let me explain: The Apron is not a navy-and-white-striped cotton affair with white ties. No. It's hot peach, made from some sort of faux silk, with "Kiss the Cook" printed on it. Peter wears it so he doesn't get covered in bacon-fat splash back.

Despite the emasculating apron, and the fact that his fuzzy-wuzzy beard could use a healthy trim, Peter is looking straight-up handsome today. He is classically beautiful, all heavy dark brows with a strong, flat nose sitting between a pair of broad, rosy cheekbones. Roman centurion meets Colin Farrell. I would quite like to have kissed the cook (plus a whole lot more) this morning, but I didn't get the chance. Things move into hyperdrive on Departure Day.

The first rule of Departure Day is: you do not talk about Departure Day. We both know that if we started really thinking or talking about any of this, it might trigger an emotional landslide that'd bury us so far under we'd never be able to find our way back up. The only reference to my leaving so far today has been a *potentially* sarcastic "And she's off to save the world again" from Peter after the alarm went off this morning. In the past I *have* saved some people's worlds, or at least their livelihoods. I'm a buyer. A coffee buyer. And where do you buy coffee beans? Developing nations. I source the good stuff. Organic, high-quality, high-altitude, tasty. And I make sure my farmers get well compensated for it, better than if they'd gone with some faceless conglomerate anyway. But what happens to those beans after I've purchased them? They come to America, where they get ground up and served in fancy stores to fancy folks. Peter doesn't see the farmers I've helped. Or the desperate worlds they live in. He just sees the latte art, the skinny jeans, the baristas with earlobes you could drive a train through. And I may be wrong, but I think to him it makes my job seem not that worthwhile.

Of course, I could be working for Doctors Without Borders, on the cusp of finding the frickin' cure for Ebola, and it wouldn't make it any easier for my family that I'm about to leave them for six weeks to travel to the depths of the Ethiopian cloud forest.

And despite the not talking about it—of course the children know. The North Face backpack propped up against the bedroom door says it all. And the bacon.

Violet, the youngest, is sitting on my lap nibbling the edges around her elephant-shaped pancake. She's been attached to my side ever since the backpack came out of the closet. It's been a long three days. She's even insisted on joining me when I take a shower, just in case I've figured out a way to vamoose myself down the drain. At this moment she's busy entangling her hand into my hair. I shuffle her butt right up close to my body and squeeze her tight into a tiny ball of toddler.

I try to finish my pancake. Peter made me one in the shape of Africa. I watch him as he flies around the kitchen, rinsing dishes, scrubbing down surfaces. He was not like this when I met him. What has happened here? He darts out of the kitchen and a few moments later we hear it: nervous vacuuming. The carpets are never cleaner than in the days leading up to one of my trips. Poor Peter.

I gently untangle Violet's hand from my hair and slip her off my lap. I don't have much time left. I drain the last of my coffee and dump the cup in the sink. I'd better go weigh my backpack again for the last time to see if it's surreptitiously gained a couple of pounds overnight—I swear it happens.

"Mommy?" My exit is blocked. It's Billy, the just-turned-five-year-old. If he were just one day younger, he'd have been ineligible for kindergarten this year. Peter was all for starting him, but I put my foot down and we're sending him next year. I won Peter over with the argument that he'd have a better chance at getting on sports teams if we held him back, but my secret reasoning is this: if he starts school one year later, I get one year more of him in my life before he disappears off to college. And maybe somewhere over the course of that extra magical year, I'll somehow make up for all the time I'm missing with him now. However, Billy's attitude toward me recently has been less than pleasant, and I'm starting to wonder if Peter's idea might actually have been the better way to go . . . I brace myself.

"Y-es."

"Do you know how many inches there are between the sink and the dishwasher?"

"I do not."

"Twelve."

"Is that so?" I ask, rather flatly.

"Twelve inches. I measured it with my ruler."

"Your point being?" Billy's not one of those kids who likes to spout random facts just for the thrill of it. Billy always has a point.

"Point being, why don't you move your arm the extra twelve inches and put your cup *in* the dishwasher?"

"Um . . ."

"You know, things are pretty hard for Dad when you leave. He has to do everything by himself. The cooking, the driving, my party . . ."

"The vacuuming," adds Violet.

"The least you could do is clean up after yourself *before* you go. Especially as you're going for such a long time. What do you think would happen if you came back six weeks from now and that cup was still sitting there?"

"I dunno. It would be dry?"

"Nope. It would be moldy. There would be so much mold it would fill up the sink, then fill up the house, then break down the front door and start oozing down the street."

"Are you sure about that?"

"Positive." In case you skipped the reference to my missing his birthday party earlier, I didn't. I've got a feeling that's what's really at the bottom of this "can't you move your arm twelve inches" business.

"Listen, bud. Do you know how sad I am that I'm missing your party today?"

"No."

"Well, I'm very sad. I'm super sad. But you know I don't have a choice, right?"

How am I supposed to properly explain it to him? That I've thought *and thought* about how I could do this differently since he was six weeks old and I boarded a plane to Guatemala with engorged boobs and a hole in my heart that never resealed. Almost five years later and I've still got no answers.

"Don't worry about it. I'd rather you were gone than Daddy," he says. The vacuuming stops and he runs off to find his father. No one has the ability to slice my heart in two quicker than my son when he puts his mind to it. But surely he doesn't really mean it? He's just hurting, right? I watch his white-blond head disappear upstairs.

"Mommy?"

"Yes, Violet."

"When you leave us to go away, do you go to heaven?"

"No! If you go to heaven, you don't come back. Mommy always comes back."

"You *sometimes* come back."

"What? When did I not come back?" But for the first time in three days she's left my side and has run off after Billy. "Wait, Violet! When have I ever not come back?!"

I hurry after her. I have to clear this up—she's the last one on my side! I follow Violet upstairs, but before I get to her I see the cat from next door on top of my open backpack, tail up, poised to deliver a hot stream of urine over my freshly laundered and folded clothes. Three days from now those clothes will be unrecognizably caked in mud, sweat, and mosquito repellent, perhaps even donkey poop, but somehow that all seems so much more sanitary than suburban diabetic-cat pee.

"Banksy, no!" I leap toward my bag, but a millisecond before I get there, Billy scoops the cat up, half balances him on the sill, and then lightly tips Banksy out the open window. "Oh God!"

I power hurdle over the top of my backpack, thrust most of my body out the window, and somehow manage to grab a wad of fur and fat right in the center of the cat's back. Banksy would not survive a fall from the second floor. I haul him back in the window, his demented cat claws rotating a thousand miles a minute.

"Billy! What on earth were you thinking?"

"He was going to pee on your clothes," he says, all the explanation that's needed in his preschooler's mind. Banksy has clawed his way up my body and is painfully balancing himself on my shoulder.

"For God's sake, Billy, you could have killed him! That means DEAD forever. No coming back!" Maybe it's the spiteful nip of cat claws in my skin, or maybe I'm still rubbed the wrong way about the whole dishwasher discussion; whatever it is, it's completely crushed the delicate balance of emotion that is Departure Day, and I am *yelling*. Violet's little face starts to scrunch up till she looks just like a cartoon duck and then she starts to wail. Billy pushes past me and zooms down the corridor toward his room. He doesn't want me to see him crying.

"Billy. I'm sorry! I love you—" He slams his bedroom door and I feel the shock waves in my knees. What's wrong with me? I'm supposed to be the grown-up here. I pull Banksy off my shoulder and he shoots off under the bed. One more soul traumatized by Departure Day. I scoop up Violet and she wraps herself around the front of my body, her feet hanging down almost to my knees. I give her cheek a kiss and one plump tear rolls down to meet my lip. I love this girl.

Peter walks in and picks up my backpack. "All set?"

"Already?" Surely I've got more time.

"You're gonna be late." He smiles. I'm notorious for trying to eke out the last droplet from the last microsecond of Departure Day. I suddenly realize with a welt of guilt that Peter didn't get to take a shower this morning. Parents of under-fives can generally only shower by special appointment, and I snuck one in while he was making breakfast. He was supposed to go in after me, but it didn't happen. God knows when he'll get to take one now. Possibly tonight if he's not too walking-dead exhausted.

Given the crushing pressure our relationship comes under every time I take one of these epic work trips (and there are plenty of them), it amazes me that Peter and I are still together. Because as I watch the families of the other green bean buyers I know get ripped in two under the weight of "you're never here," somehow our marriage remains intact. Sometimes I wonder how we've done it, but that would require thinking—which, I already told you, I don't dare do. But if I had to give it a flicker of a thought, I'd say it's because Peter is able to do all this. Most spouses can't. Or just choose not to.

I check the alarm clock by the side of the bed. Peter's right, I am suuuper late. I've got to go. Like, *now*. I can feel my brain and my heart automatically freeze over. That's part of the routine. I can't think or feel when I'm saying good-bye. It only makes the kids more hysterical when I cry, and that helps no one. Plus, it destroys the illusion that I'm okay with this situation. That this is the life I purposefully chose. What else is there to do? I give a quick nod to Peter and we walk out to the car in silence.

I carefully lower Violet to the ground. Peter hugs me in close and we touch our foreheads together for a split second. I look into his eyes, but he's already looking down toward Violet. This is our bastardized version of a Hawaiian kiss. Prior to kids, it used to be our standard kiss good-bye before one of my trips. Foreheads touching, staring deeply into each other's eyes, our breath and tears all mixed together. These days it's a quick head bump and on to the next thing. We look more like a couple of fighting stags than Hawaiian lovers.

Violet knows that the head bump means my departure is imminent.

"Mommy. NO." She sounds so deeply scared that it's all I can do not to hold on to her just as tightly and run. Run away from this situation.

"I'll see you soon," I say to Peter and kiss Violet hard on the top of her head. Peter and I have both learned from experience that there's no happy way out of this. The end result is always a screaming, distraught child. The only choice we get in the matter is whether to rip off the Band-Aid quickly or slowly. Today it has to be quick.

"Let's do this," says Peter. And we do. Just like we've done one hundred times before. He grabs her around the waist, I firmly detach her arms from me and then swerve to avoid her legs as they come windmilling out from underneath her. Half in defiance, half trying to grab me and pull me back toward her.

I get in the front seat, put on my seat belt, and then I hear her. "Mommy! One more hug. Just one more hug. *Please!*" I go to start the engine. And then I pause. Am I really doing this? I'm an idiot. I get back out of the car. Back over to the nucleus of two fusing bodies that is Peter and Violet. I lift her out of his arms and I squeeze her for all she's worth. One final, strong hug. I kiss her cheek as hard as I dare, clenching my teeth to absorb the magnitude of the kiss I really want to give her. And then I hand her back over. And we do the whole windmill-limb thing from scratch. She's even madder the second time around.

Halfway through it all, I turn again and I leave.

I start up the engine, silencing the sound of Violet's meltdown. Without looking back I drive off down the street, her screams still reverberating at full volume around the inside of my head. And I know it's the only thing I'll hear all the way to Africa.

As soon as I turn left at the end of the block and I know they can't see me, I start to cry. Heavy, body-shaking tears. This is also part of the routine. It's also strangely therapeutic: I've never handed my passport over at departures without having froggy eyes that look like a pair of golf balls.

Suddenly my whole body goes light with panic. Billy. I didn't say good-bye to Billy! I can't go back and do it for the third time. Peter will kill me. Plus I've left it so late already that I would miss my plane for certain. Oh God. I am a terrible mother. As the traffic lights turn red, I pull to a stop and just let it go. Hard-core sobbing. Double bubbles in my nostrils. The works. I'm trying to force myself to take some breaths in when I feel the driver in the car next to me watching. How bloody rude. My car is my own private biosphere. You may be able to see in through my windows, but that doesn't mean that you're allowed to look. I've stopped myself from staring plenty of times when some guy's been cleaning out his nostrils with the end of his pinky or singing like he forgot that he did actually leave the shower this morning. I glance over. He catches my eye and mimes a "roll down the window" sign. Really? No one's actually had roll-down car windows since 1992. Snot trails now at upper-lip level, I lower my window. What does this man think he can say to me that's possibly going to make my life any better between now and when the lights turn green?

"I'm trying to find the 210?"

"Huh?"

"The 210 Freeway?"

"Oh."

"Do you know where it is?"

"Um . . . Sure. Straight on past Glen Avenue, then make a right at Fair Oaks. No . . . I'm sorry, I mean Sunset. The signs will tell you to go straight on at Washington but don't do that. They've closed it halfway down for roadwork, and you'll only have to turn around and come back up again."

"Okay," he says. The lights turn green and he's off. He didn't even offer me a tissue. And come to think of it, I'm not sure I have a clean one. Or even one at all. Sleeve wipe it is. Oh, like you've never done it before. Someone behind me gives a hearty honk. I slowly raise the window and start off again, taking enough time to make my point that I consider the honk, under general circumstances, to be very rude indeed.

My life is officially ridiculous.

By the time I'm about halfway to LAX I've managed to calm myself enough that I'm no longer a hazard on the road. It seems to be helpful to distract myself with all the dire logistical consequences of me actually not making my plane today, and so I focus on that.

My phone starts ringing. I glance over. It's my boss, Dexter. There's probably some last-minute change to my travel itinerary. Why can't he text like a normal person? I nearly drive off the road trying to hook up my hands-free device. Eventually all wires and pods are inserted where they should be.

"Dexter, what's up?"

"Amy. Thank God. Listen up. I need you to come in, now."

"Come in? I'm barely going to make my flight as it is!"

"I know. Just . . . I need you to head back."

"What's going on, Dexter? If I miss this flight, it's going to throw the whole trip into chaos."

"You're not going to be flying out today."

"Why?"

"I'm not talking to you about this when you're driving. Just come the fuck in. *Please.*"

"Fine." I hang up. It must be serious if Dexter's using the P-word. He and I are as rude as possible to each other at all times. It's our thing. I cannot think of one possible plausible reason why I'm being called back to home base right now. This trip was the big hope for saving Mateo's Coffee from a severe financial pummeling.

Right now, scattered around the planet, there are acres upon acres of coffee bean crops devastated by rust. Not the kind of rust you find on a secondhand pickup, the kind of rust that's been the fungal blight of the Arabica coffee bean since the very start of the coffee trade. This latest strain is everywhere. We're in the middle of a rust epidemic of unprecedented size.

The world's coffee traders are panic buying what little Arabica there is left, sending prices through the roof. The big guys—whose customers don't have a particularly discerning palate, or really any kind of palate—have resorted to mixing large percentages of Robusta beans into their products. The cheaper, shitty, bitter stuff. They're riding the fine line between cutting it with just enough Robusta that they can still keep a jar of Nescafé at only a moderately increased price and not so much that it becomes undrinkable. At Mateo's we don't have that option. We're about quality. In fact, that's all we're about. We make coffee for the people who've had the fortune/misfortune to stumble across the good stuff. After you've had real black, there's no going back. However, that doesn't mean our customers will be willing to pay twelve dollars for a cup of coffee as opposed to the rather cheeky eight they already pay.

I was headed to Ethiopia today because Getu, one of our farmers there, said he'd discovered a varietal of bean that was so far immune to the epidemic. And not only that, he sent us a few beans to try for ourselves and they tasted like heaven above.

This bean was going to be our way of evading the whole "death to the gourmet coffee world" situation. Without this bean you don't need an MBA to figure out that our business model is more or less screwed. We'll never get through this. Most small roasters won't. I've been on the trail of various rust-resistant beans since the beginning of my career: looking for a bean that could be mass-produced but wouldn't need to be continually doused with fungicide, which ruins the soil and also is very hard on the human body. Whoever gets this bean gets the coffee scoop of the century. It's the fucking holy grail of coffee beans.

So why in sweet Jesus is Dexter calling me back to the office?

CHAPTER 2

"You mean I'm fired?"

"Laid off, technically speaking," says Dexter. Call it vanity, but I feel like he should be looking a lot more upset than he currently does. "But yes, they both amount to the same thing: you don't work for Mateo's anymore."

"What about this company Fuckers?"

"Ruckers."

"Don't they need a buyer?"

"They already have their own, Amy. Armies of them all over the world."

"Don't they need another one?"

"I've no idea, why don't you check their website?" Dexter and I have always treated each other with playful disrespect, but this tone is new. This is the tone of a man who knows he really should give a shit but is finding it somewhat of a struggle to do so. Emotionally uninvested, I think you could call it.

"So how much?"

"How much what?"

"How much cash did you get for this ungodly transaction?"

"The correct term is *buyout*." I pause and watch him wrestle with his answer. "Two point four."

"Million?"

"Well, yes. Not billion."

"You could have got more."

"No, I couldn't have. The company can't sustain itself long-term the way things are run right now. The profit margin just isn't there."

"But what about Getu's Yayu?" I ask. It was the solution to this very problem.

"Why take the risk if I don't have to? The interest from Ruckers is here *now*. The Mateo's name still means good quality *now*. Third-wave coffee has to make way for fourth wave, which is probably going to taste like shit. But in the coming years, as good coffee becomes a fading memory, the name Mateo's will still keep people buying. It's just simple marketing."

"You're literally selling out."

"I prefer to think of it as buying in."

"Smart people know when they're making a mistake, Dexter."

"Accepting two point four million for a business that's almost bankrupt is not a mistake," he says. *Fair point.* "I've made this business into a phenomenon—our customers have always had the most excellent of everything. But we can't do that any longer. The money just doesn't work that way now. If I don't do this today, the whole setup is going to fail."

"Don't you care about the coffee anymore?" I ask.

It's this change that's the hardest of all to understand. The coffee used to be Dexter's primary obsession, the fundamental focus of his life. He'd wax lyrical to anyone who would listen (and there were plenty lined up) about coffee as an art form, about the intense, vibrant beauty of the moment it could create. How it could be the antidote to all the sadness in your life, perhaps all the misery on the planet. For if everyone in the world started their day with the right type of coffee, perhaps we could make it work. Perhaps we, all the tribes of the human species, could finally all just get along, bonded through our mutual love of a perfect moment.

He'd generally go on in this vein until someone stopped him. It was normally me.

"I do care. I just care about my family more." That's a shift. "Don't you want to start putting your family first, Amy? I thought you'd be stoked to spend some extra time with your kids."

"Well, forgive me if my lack of a million-dollar payout is putting somewhat of a damper on my outward jubilation." Which is clearly a segue for Dexter to start talking about my severance package. I've put as much sweat equity into Mateo's as he has over the last fourteen years. And much more literal equatorial sweat for sure. He's looking at me with that same irritating nonchalance, and he doesn't seem to be taking advantage of the segue opportunity. I'll have to do it for him.

"What about my severance pay?"

He's caught off guard. He has the decency to tint a little pink.

"Well, Ruckers didn't really extend that payout to—"

"I'm not talking about Fuckers; I'm talking about you and your plus-size bank account already racking up the interest on two point four million as we speak."

"The money hasn't come through yet. When it does I'll . . . um, have my accountant . . ."

"Don't lie." I expect a wide-eyed denial. It's not forthcoming.

"Amy, under California law I'm not technically obliged to—"

"Fourteen years of me putting my personal life on hold, of missing my kids' first everything—traveling to the places you were too scared to go to. I've crapped out tapeworms taller than you and I've got a foot fungus I picked up in Nicaragua that I'm never going to shake. *Never.* My foot guy says his lab can't even identify it. An entirely new species of fungus is going to live between my toes from now until I die, and you're telling me that you're not *technically obliged?*"

"Well, I'm not." And there it is. Two point four million dollars about to wire itself into his account and he isn't "technically obliged" to give a shit about me any longer. And he knows it. And now I know it.

"All this time I thought we were working toward something together here, but I'm just another commodity to you, aren't I? There's no difference to you between me and a bag of underpriced Kunga. You just take what you need and use it all up till it's gone. I'm a human being, Dexter. I've got kids too. How can you live with yourself, you complete cheapskate?"

"Amy, I'm sorry." To his credit he does seem slightly more sorry now.

"I'll take your apology in the form of a check." Silence. "Nothing? Okay, good-bye then, Dexter. Enjoy your gains from exploiting me and all the dozens of poverty-ridden farmers you've completely let down, you colonial dickhole. Actual children are going to go hungry because of what you've decided to do today."

"Amy!" Below the belt. He deserves it.

"Enjoy your millions."

I kick his stupid plant on my way out. I always hated that rubber plant—just like Dexter, pretending to be something more than it is in its pretentious organic rattan weave pot.

Screw every part of this.

I've got a birthday party to get to.

CHAPTER 3

Driving away from downtown, the cloud of silent calm that seems to have sat on top of my brain for the last ten minutes is starting to disperse too quickly. I try to claw it back, but it's no good. I'm beginning to panic. What. The. Fuck. Are. We. Going. To. Do?

Obviously I'm going to have to get another buying job as soon as possible. But with Arabica prices still on the rise, I'm sure Mateo's is not the only roaster being bought out right now. Most will just go under. There's going to be a glut of buyers on the market and even fewer jobs than normal to go around. Certainly nothing else in LA. There are only about fifteen small roasters in operation on both coasts. Outside of that I'd be buying for the big chains, and I've heard enough about how they operate to know I wouldn't fit in there. The first time I saw warehouses full of old-ass beans being gassed with fungicides, rats running in and out as they please, I'd be out.

Damn it. First things first. Okay, so obviously it's a complete disaster that the only income in our household is no longer going to be coming *in*. But . . . there *is* an upside to being unexpectedly thrown into the pit of unemployment today: I'm going to make it to Billy's birthday party! Better than that, I'm going to see my kids again. And *even* better than that, there is no dark-black moment of departure on the horizon. This is a first. This changes everything. I've never had this in my life before. As I zoom back down the freeway, I swoop through the emotional arc from complete fear to extreme joy. And then all the way back again. I manage to distract myself by thinking about practicalities. The party is an hour and a half in. Will it mess Billy up for life if I turn up at this point? Will he forever presume that in the future when I say I can't make something, I'll actually show up right at the end? It *really will* mess him up for life if I turn up halfway through his party with a "Hey—Mommy got fired. Happy fucking birthday, kiddo!" Not good. Obviously I don't want to miss it. But everyone's going to want to know why on earth I'm not on a plane.

I'll just have to wing it. Tell the kids I missed my flight. How wrong can it go? They'll be over the moon to see me. It'll be like the best birthday surprise ever.

I'm here. I park in the driveway outside the garage. I'm a little surprised that my spot's still open and that Peter didn't direct a Prius party parent into it. Maybe he just knew. I let myself in the back gate. Everyone's assembled on and around the side deck. Must be almost cake time. I slip in at the back of the crowd. I'll make myself known after Billy's blown out the candles.

The mom I'm standing next to makes smiley eye contact. She's all stylish black wrap, snub nose, smooth swept-up hair, and sparkly blue eyes. I instantly know her as one of those women who can chat with people. Anyone—doesn't matter who it is, she'll be able to bypass all the "getting to know you" formalities and slip straight into decadent "we've been friends for years" mode. I really admire that trait in people as I'm so, *so* lacking in it. I'm painfully awkward for at least the first six months of knowing someone. Maybe this woman will be so friendly, it'll completely disguise my social failings and we can do things like have coffee dates where we bond over the banal-yet-wacky adventures we have with our children! Maybe this woman can be my first mommy friend.

I don't have mommy friends. Okay, I don't have *any* friends. No "snort your wine back up through your nostrils 'cause you're screaming with laughter" friends, anyway. I've been doing this circling-the-globe thing since Mom put her foot down, made Dad get a job with an insurance firm in London, and moved the family from Indianapolis to suburban England. I was eleven years old. Quite the culture shock for a midwestern tween, I can tell you. Female friendships have been one of the many casualties. I always thought the friendships would bloom once I had kids and got settled in one town, but so far that's not been the case. Partly because when the other women are standing at the school gates bitching about Common Core math, I'm likely to be inching along some perilously narrow mountain pass, high on quinine and fighting off the latest round of dengue fever. Yeah, my gig's not all *Dora the Explorer* meets *Romancing the Stone*, by the way. Life at the equator is *brutal*.

"Which one is yours?" asks Snub Nose, still smiling. I gesture toward Violet, who's running past in the middle of a pack of girls. The woman doesn't pause long enough for me to politely return the question, which is probably for the best as I'm sure I'd forget to ask it. "Did you see that cake?" She laughs. I give a half nod. Yes, I saw it. I made it. "It's hilarious! I'm sure the father cobbled it together himself, so sweet that he's trying."

"Right." What can I say? I insisted on making Billy's cake this year. I think I was hoping that the act of baking a birthday cake would inch me closer toward bona fide. Three rectangular blocks of Lego. Easy. But it turns out that trying to transform three rectangles of sponge into replica Lego is not that easy at all and it just ended up a mess. Like some Ninjago battle had been fought amongst ancient Lego ruins. What Ms. Judge The Cake doesn't know, of course, is that if I'd just let Peter make it, it would have been perfect.

"Of course, the mother's off again on another business trip, if you can believe it. Right on the morning of her kid's birthday party! How could she? Have you actually ever met her?" Again, no pause here for me to insert that I *am* her. And in case you're wondering, no, I didn't especially plan to be flying out of the country and missing my son's fifth-birthday party today. It just worked out that way. Like large sections of my life, it was beyond my control. "Maybe she's not real. Maybe the dad's actually on his own, and she's just someone he's made up to keep those Cheerful Cheetah class single mommies at bay. There's at least two in there quite clearly after him."

"Oh, surely not!" I say. I'm shocked and instantly worried. I had no idea Peter was being hit on by a flock of women at preschool.

"Well, who can blame them? He *is* gorgeous. Can you imagine jumping in the sack with that every night? Yum! If my husband looked like that, I wouldn't be packing my bags and heading off to Indonesia every chance I got."

Okay, this has gone far enough.

"I'm sure she doesn't really want to leave her family behind."

"Nah. I know the sort. People live their lives exactly how they want to live them. Anyone who says anything different is just making excuses."

Up on the deck I can see Peter has finally got Billy to stand still in front of the cake and has lit all the candles. There's a pretty, youngish woman standing very close to Peter holding the cake knife and plates. She looks very . . . inserted. Just as soon as everyone's finished singing, she grabs Billy and kisses him on the top of his head. I have not come home a minute too soon. I muscle forward and manage to get a picture of Billy blowing out the candles. He sees me.

"Oh, hi, Mom," he says, as unfazed as if I just came back from the bathroom.

"Um, hi."

Not exactly the ecstatic reunion I was hoping for. The other parents around the birthday ring are looking at me in shocked silence. I get the feeling my party absence has been a firm topic of conversation and now everyone is confused. And worried that I've overheard them.

"Oh, you're Billy's mother," says Pretty-and-Young. *Yes, I am, lady, so get your hands off.* "We thought you couldn't make it today."

"Yet here I am." That came out a sneak more hostile than I meant it to. I catch Snub Nose's eye and half mouth, "Sorry," though really, if you feel like applying logic to the situation, she's the one who should be apologizing to me. Peter comes back out the door holding a stack of napkins.

"Babe!" he says, running across the deck and pulling me into a hug. *That's* more like it! "What happened, did you miss your flight?"

"Something like that," I say. I instantly see worry in his eyes. He knows. "Let's get this done first," I whisper.

From behind me comes a high screeching sound like someone just stepped on a puppy, and before I can turn around Violet has shimmied up my body and attached herself to my back, making small whimpering noises. I try to loosen her little hands from around my throat and she digs in even harder. She's crying now. "Mommy, Mommy. You're not dead! I knew you weren't dead!" *Dead?*

In front of our still-assembled audience Peter has to pull Violet off my back and reattach her to my front so I'm not strangled by her choke hold. She nestles in just like she did when she was a baby. I've got to admit, it's a little delicious. Within the sea of faces, I see *one* that I recognize.

"Amber! How are you?" Heavily pregnant for starters. Last time I saw her she was nursing a newborn. I suddenly realize that I haven't seen Amber in quite a while.

"Oh, hi, Amy. Yeah, we're good." I open my mouth to ask her how old the newborn is now and when the next one is due, but she gets there first. "We've actually got to head out now, but it was so good to see you." Something flat in her eyes tells me she actually doesn't think it was that great to see me. I manage to shove a party bag her way before she escapes, and like some kind of suburban Pavlovian bell has been sounded, once the first guest gets going, they all follow after. I run out of party bags two kids from the end and dole out two wooden spoons instead. Their moms give me the stink eye. I know what's going on in their heads: Really, I drop forty bucks at that crafty toy store in Old Town and you serve me a battered Lego cake and then give my kid a wooden spoon? Unacceptable.

Within ten minutes the house is cleared. Good riddance. This is why I don't do social. Billy descends upon his gifts. So many, opened in such a blur. I'm barely paying attention and I've no idea which is from whom. Looks like we'll be skipping the thank-you cards this year. But have we ever done them any year? Don't know, because with a creeping fear I'm starting to realize that I don't know much about how this day-to-day parenting thing works. At all.

CHAPTER 4

While I run Peter through the outline of our impending doom, I keep one eye on Billy as he sits on the couch. He's yet to properly acknowledge my return. Billy's a miniature male version of me with his white-blond hair, pink skin, and permanently concerned expression. He's also a true iChild, always engrossed in any one of the multiple iDevices littered throughout our house. They can go right at the top of the list of things to be sold off. I'm all for restricting screen time to one hour a day. Peter always laughs when I suggest that.

After I've finished telling Peter about the financial Armageddon that's about to engulf us, he barely looks bothered. I'm a little surprised. Does he not get it? One hundred and fifty thousand dollars a year just walked out the door, possibly never to return. But then Peter always has been a "fuck up now, worry about it later—way later" type of guy.

"So. What do you think?" I ask. Maybe I need to reiterate the whole "driving our family into the arms of Mistress Poverty" thing again.

"I think it's great. Perfect, actually," he replies.

"Excuse me?"

"You're tired of traveling all the time, right?"

"Right."

"All you ever talk about is how you're missing out on the most important time of your kids' lives and how you'll never get it back."

"Right."

"Well, now you get to see them all the time. No more work. The kids are now yours, round the clock."

"R-ight . . ." I prepare to launch myself back into Mistress Poverty, the sequel. He obviously didn't hear me the first time around.

"So let's swap. I'll earn the money and you stay at home with the kids. Isn't that what you wanted?"

"Well, yes. But how are you possibly going to replace my salary, Peter?"

"I've all but completed it."

"Completed what?"

"My screenplay."

Jesus, Mary, and Joseph.

"I'm just tidying up the final draft, but I know that this is The One, Amy."

The One. We've been talking about The One ever since Billy was born. The screenplay that he would write that would be so brilliant, so timely, so awe-inspiring that Hollywood would forget that Peter tried to sue Paramount Pictures for changing a story line on a script he'd already sold to them and welcome him back with open arms and heart. It's not going to happen. Not because Peter isn't talented— he is—but because he's barred from setting foot on the Paramount lot ever again and so by default from every other major studio in Hollywood too. Unless Peter isn't telling me something, as far as I know the ban has not been lifted.

"I don't want to add any additional pressure, but you are aware we're under something of a time crunch?"

"You know what they call people like you, Amy?"

"Hardworking? Helpful?"

"Dream squashers."

"Peter, I'm not trying to squash your dream. Just maybe persuade it to squeeze itself to the side, just a little bit, so you can earn some money doing something else and we can eat some food next month."

"I'm going to HushMush and I'm not coming back till this thing's done." He's been working on this screenplay at coffee chains across the city for the last five years. I don't see him completing it in the next five hours.

"All right—see you next year, then."

Oops. Peter snatches up his keys, practically rips his laptop out of the wall, and heads for the front door.

"Billy, Violet, this is your mother, who you may remember from such events as both of your birthdays in 2015 or perhaps Christmas Day 2014—oh, wait—you actually weren't there for those were you, Amy? Never mind, I expect you guys will make your own introductions."

And with that he slams the front door and I am alone with both of my children for the first time in months, if not years, if not *ever*.

As you've seen, my husband can't take criticism. Not a lick. Not a word. Not even a sentence that seems like it might be going in the direction of very vaguely observational. It's why he's unemployable as a writer. Unemployable in general. It's too hard for him to hear that what he's done is not perfect the very first time he does it. He won't play by the Hollywood rules so they won't even let him on the field. It's a shame, because he's a bloody good writer and we could surely use the money. Especially right now.

Violet, who's let go of her cat-claw hold on my leg, is standing there staring at me with her huge eyes. In this light they're deep indigo. And no, we didn't know that our daughter was going to end up with eyes that were almost purple when we called her Violet. I stare back at her. She is so beautiful that "beating them off with a stick" isn't going to cut it when she's older. Peter and I are going to have to keep her in a smooth-sided cloud-high tower surrounded by a team of elite ninjas. She has her father's looks, my personality. As far as I'm concerned, she's a perfect person.

"It's nice to meet you, Mommy," she says, and holds out her tiny white hand. I give it a formal shake.

"Nice to meet you too, Violet O'Hara." I know, I know—at least we didn't call her Scarlett.

"It's O'Rara, actually. Princess O'Rara."

"I hate to break it to you, but it's O'Hara and you're not a princess."

"I am. I'm Sleeping Beauty, Princess O'Rara. Daddy said so."

"You mean Princess Aurora."

"O'Rara." She gives me a hard look. "Mommy, you are wasting up my time."

Now maybe I've been working with guys too long and have completely lost touch with my femininity, but I just can't get on board with the whole preschooler princess thing. I've seen what happens to Violet when she puts that tiara with pink twinkles on her head and starts singing to herself in the mirror. She turns from a minime into a minimonster. Self-worshipping, high-handed. She puts Billy in the role of servant and tells him to tidy up her toys. And he does it! It's a terrifying transition. Number two on the list of things to disappear after the iDevices—any and all princess paraphernalia. I don't know why Peter let it go on for this long.

Well, as of today there's a new sheriff in town.

"It's Violet O'Hara, and to prove it to you, we're going to put your tiara in the Good-bye Box," I say.

"What's the Good-bye Box?"

I'm thinking on the fly here. "It's a box . . . that we put things in that we're going to say good-bye to."

As she stops to think that one through, I take my opportunity and make for her bedroom. I grab the tiara. Now what? I had planned on putting it in the trash, but the fact that Violet's gone even paler than normal means I'm probably not going to get away with that. Violet close at my heels, I go into our bedroom, empty out an old shoe box, plop the tiara inside, and put the box on the top shelf of the closet. At this point I've got a definite feeling that this is *not* going to end well for me. I'm either going to have to back down, thereby demonstrating to Violet that I don't mean what I say, or I'm going to have to deal with some kind of explosive . . .

"NOOOOOOOOOOOOOO!"

And there it is. An hour. The tantrum lasts for a full hour. At the end of it she's screamed so much that she can't talk. And then for good measure she throws up all over herself—and incidentally all over the traditional shrug a farmer's wife in northern Sumatra wove for me—but anywho . . . And did she get the tiara back?

Yes.

How else would I have stopped the tantrum? Okay. Beginner's mistake, I know. But cut me some slack. It's day one here. After systematically ignoring, coaxing, bargaining with, and threatening Violet for an hour—when it all comes to its anticlimactic close—I realize I have barely even said hello to Billy since I returned. Maybe I'll have more luck scaling back on his iPad use than Violet's tiara use. I doubt it. Billy's the "difficult" one. My looks and his father's personality. Not the winning combination.

He's not in the living room. Or the den. Not the kitchen or the bedrooms. A quick scan of the backyard reveals he's not there either. Oh fuck. One hour and eleven minutes in and I've already lost one child. I run into the backyard and yell, "Billy, Bi-lly!"

I go back into the house and start yanking open cabinets, the cutlery drawer—anything with a handle. I've already descended into blind panic. My breath starts coming in cold, edgy gasps. I stagger outside again and scream from the center of my soul, "BILLY! BI-LLY!"

"Hi."

I look down. And there he is. Safe and sound. A shovel in one hand and a pail in the other.

"Where did you go?"

"I disappeared."

"I noticed that."

"And then I came back again. Just like you, Mommy. It's a magic trick."

"Billy, I always say good-bye before I disappear. You have to tell me next time you're planning on doing that or it makes Mommy very panicky."

"You don't always say good-bye."

"Yes, I do."

"No, you don't. You didn't this morning. You just left and didn't say anything." Oh God. I am a terrible mother. *A terrible mother.* From inside the house there's a high-pitched scream. Violet!

She's standing in the middle of the kitchen, tiara still on, holding a bowl and a spoon.

"Violet, what is it? Are you hurt?"

"I want applesauce."

"Applesauce?"

"It's snack time. I want applesauce."

"Violet, you cannot scream like that and expect that—" She belts out another scream. Even louder. I grab the applesauce, rip the lid off, spill it everywhere, manage to smear it over my glasses, dump the rest in her pink bowl, and the noise ceases. I'm going to have to talk to Pe—

"Mom."

"Yes, Billy."

"I need the password to download this game." I look at the iPad I'm being offered. On it is a game icon featuring a bloodlusty-looking Viking.

"Why don't you play with one of your new toys, Billy?"

"More applesauce," says Violet.

"Or you and I could just play real Vikings together instead," he says.

"Real Vikings?"

"We could make a ship and swords and some shields and sail the Seven Seas."

"We could do that." I pause. I open another packet of toxic-looking applesauce. Honestly, why does Peter buy this crap? I take stock: I am more mentally and physically exhausted than I have ever been in my life. Plus I have to unpack, cook some kind of edible dinner, straighten this house out, apply for unemployment benefits, and start hunting for another buying job before whatever feeble offers are out there get snatched up. I don't have it in me to play Viking warriors today. I already hate myself for what I'm about to do and say, but I do and say it anyway.

"Mommy's had a very hard day today and I'm really, really tired. Why don't I download that Viking game now and tomorrow we'll play real Vikings?"

"Okay," says Billy. And from the way he says it, it's suddenly clear that this was his angle all along.

By the time I've installed the Viking game, Violet is back in her room singing to herself in the mirror, twirling around and admiring her reflection. Billy immediately descends into cyberspace, his tiny mind saturating itself in the blood of a thousand virtual Vikings. The house is thrashed. I still have a smear of applesauce obscuring my view. I have failed. I go to wipe the sauce off my glasses but am interrupted once more by Violet's shrill tones.

"Mommy! Come and wipe my butt! Knowing better than to ignore a demand when Violet's wearing the tiara, I race to the bathroom to find her in downward dog, bottom offered toward the sky. There's poop on the seat, the sink, her butt, her hands, the floor; I think I even see some on one of the pink twinkly bits of the tiara. I was supposed to be halfway to Addis Ababa by now. Instead, I'm unemployed and slipping around in my daughter's shit while my husband sulks at a corporate coffee shop.

Still. This is just day one. Things can only get better from here—right?

CHAPTER 5

You'd think it was as difficult as birthing triplets vaginally the way he's talking about it. Stand back, everyone: Peter has completed a first draft. He has *produced*. Considering he's been kicking this thing around for five years and then has managed to pull it all together in less than a week, it actually is something of a minor miracle. I am moderately impressed. Who knows, I might be even more impressed if he'd let me read it. But, of course, that's not going to happen.

It's late. Violet's already in bed and Billy should be, but he's not left his dad's side since Peter swaggered through the door fifteen minutes ago. I pause. He seems so jubilant from completing a first draft, maybe now's the time to bring up my Portland dream job. In the twenty-three minutes of spare time I've had over the past few days—in lieu of scraping the applesauce off my glasses or brushing my hair—I opted to take a look at what buyer jobs might be out there. As far as I can tell there are two jobs in my field right now. In all of the United States: two. One based locally buying for the Penny Bean chain—you know I'm not interested in that one. The other is my dream job, working for Stumptown in Portland. What's so great about Stumptown? Put simply: because of the collective obsessive desire of the people who work there, their coffee is the best.

The best. And they don't care what they have to pay to get there—they simply pass the cost on to their customers who don't care either because they want the best too. If I worked for Stumptown, unlike working for Mateo's, there would be no limits on how many times a year I could fly to and from Ethiopia or how much I could offer to pay a farmer for a pound of beans that I thought was exceptional. Like my Yayu. If it was the best and I had to have it—it would be mine.

So have I put a call in to the owner? No. Why not? Because I know Peter would never leave LA. Even to suggest it would probably cause the argument of the millennium. For Peter, living in LA is all tied up with the idea that somewhere, somehow, he's still a successful writer. Never mind that he hasn't earned anything worth mentioning to the IRS in over five years—in his mind, he's still in the game. Or perhaps he's taken a small halftime break, but he's about to get right back into the game—any moment now.

If we move away, he knows that's it. The end. He can't pretend he's taking a sabbatical anymore. His screenwriting career will have come to the close of its life cycle. It should be plainly obvious to him that it already has. It's obvious to everybody else. Perhaps he could handle Portland? Don't writers thrive in murky, depressive weather? Couldn't he write a bleak-yet-witty crime novel or something? Maybe I'll take my life in my hands and suggest it. I'm going to go for it.

"You know, there's an opening at Stumptown that I saw."

"Stumptown? But they're in Portland, right?" So he does listen to my ramblings about the coffee world.

"Daddy, can you read me a bedtime story?" Billy asks. That's the first time he's voluntarily mentioned bedtime in his entire life. The mere hint of a suggestion of anything to do with bed over the past week has been enough to send Billy into an instantaneous meltdown.

"Later, Billy," says Peter. I wish Billy would ask me to read him a bedtime story and look at me that way with his wide-eyed stare. A tinge of "this isn't fair" flutters up and I squash it down. "I can't do Portland, Amy. Not now that I'm getting close."

"Close? Close to what?"

"Selling something." At least he has the good grace to avoid eye contact when he says it.

"Selling something? You've banged out a draft in a week and—"

"I've been planning it for five years!"

"Remember, you have to let people read the words that you've written before you can actually sell something. I'm sure no one's going to buy it on your good name alone." Okay. That was a little low. I'm expecting a backlash, but it doesn't come. Wait, what's going on?

He wants something . . .

"Actually, I was thinking maybe you could ask Matt to take a look at it." Matt? He wants me to make contact with *Matt* for the furtherment of his career? My face must be transmitting exactly what I think of his horrific idea, because he quickly starts trying to justify his request. "Amy, I already called Nico—he doesn't want to know. No one does." This is bad. If all his contacts are still feeling burned, then Peter hasn't got a hope of selling this to anyone. He's back on the outside again. "I've got to find another way in."

Violet pads out into the kitchen. She's a light sleeper, just like me. Wordlessly she crawls up onto my lap. I kiss the top of her head. She's three years old, but she still smells like a sweet sleepy baby to me.

"Why do you think I could get hold of Matt even if I wanted to? He was scrubbed from my address book a long time ago."

"Mommy, what's an address book?" Billy asks.

"It's a book that people used to write phone numbers and addresses in. Before we had iPhones," I tell him.

"You mean like in the olden days?" asks Violet.

"Yes. The olden days. My address book is from the olden days and so is Matt."

"Who's Matt?" Violet asks.

"Mom's old boyfriend," says Billy. How on earth does he know that? I swear that kid's got surveillance cameras around this house.

"He's not exactly hiding under a rock. Just call Colburn Entertainment," says Peter.

"Just like that?"

"Why not?"

"Not that I'm intending to call, but even if I did I'm sure he wouldn't deign to speak to me."

"Then you don't have anything to worry about, do you? Just try, Amy. For me."

"Daddy, if you sell a screenplay, will you be working all the time?" asks Billy.

"That's the plan," says Peter.

"But who will look after us?" says Billy, his eyes wider than ever.

"Your mother, of course."

"Hurray!" says Violet.

"But she doesn't know how!" objects Billy. The kid's got a fair point. "It was Wacky Wednesday at school today, and she didn't believe me and made me wear my regular clothes. Everybody said I just looked *normal*."

"Normal was what everyone aspired to when I was in school," I say.

"*And* she made me wear the shirt with the scratchy label."

"Ooh," says Peter. Insisting Billy wear the shirt with the scratchy label (because it was the only one that was clean) has been my biggest parenting faux pas to date. If I had known it was going to cause as much drama as it did, I would have trashed the thing long ago. In hindsight, it was cutting the label off and then insisting he wear the shirt that sent things irretrievably off the rails. Apparently, the stub of the label was *even more* scratchy.

"And then yesterday she made me eat cabbage sandwiches for dinner."

"Cabbage sandwiches?" Peter looks alarmed.

"They were kale-and-lemon panini." See, I'm trying to make healthful meals for my family. Plus, I'd never tried out the panini maker I got from Peter's mother two years ago. Granted, they turned out kind of awful.

"You can't feed a five-year-old a kale sandwich, Amy."

I'm about to tell him that I'm sure somewhere in this vast world, there is at least one five-year-old child who has, at some point in history, consumed a kale-and-lemon panini—when Billy does something truly awful. Standing behind Peter, he opens the laptop, performs a few deft keystrokes, and then closes it again.

"Billy, what did you just do on Daddy's laptop?"

"Nothing."

"Yes, you did something—I just saw you." Peter grabs his laptop and pulls it open.

"He deleted it. He deleted the screenplay."

"No, I didn't!" yells Billy.

"Goddamn it, Billy, *why would you do that?* That was all of Daddy's work!"

"Because I hate you!" This kind comment is targeted directly at me. Granted, the kid's had a lot to deal with recently with a complete caregiver flip-flop; granted, I did insist on dressing him "normal" on Wacky Wednesday; and yes, I did more or less hand off his care to his father when he was just six weeks old, but still . . . his words hurt so much I feel like he just plunged his little hand inside my rib cage and squeezed my heart for all it's worth.

Violet somehow immediately senses my emotional devastation and starts sobbing, her tiny fingernails digging into my neck skin.

"What's wrong, Violet?" Peter asks.

"I don't know! I just feel sad."

What's she going to be like when she's a teenager? What's *Billy* going to be like? He's already dropped the "I hate you" bomb and he's only five. My kids are hormonally deranged and it's all my fault. I'm sure there's a study somewhere that proves that the lack of constant physical presence of a mother causes the chemical balance of the brains of under-fives to disintegrate. Well, here I am: sitting in the middle of the chemical fallout. And all in the pursuit of the perfect cup of coffee.

When Billy was born, I should have moved us all into a one-bedroom rental, pledged a sacred vow never to get on a plane again, and taken a part-time job at Macy's. Would that have made me a better mother?

Both Billy and Violet are crying now—and I'm not far off myself.

"Okay. Calm down, everyone. I've got another copy. It's not gone forever."

Oh yes. I forgot. Peter hasn't relied on hard drives to retain any information since the "spilled cup of Kenyan Karinga" incident of '06. He always e-mails himself everything he writes. He was way ahead of the rest of us as far as cottoning on to storing stuff virtually. I kinda wish he'd have reminded us all of that fact about three minutes ago, as I might have responded to Billy's act of sabotage with a little less of a dramatic edge.

"Billy, I want you to apologize to your mother."

"No! I *do* hate her." Doesn't look like this situation is diffusing anytime soon. It's one of the most insane things about family life. One minute everything's borderline calm and then one seemingly tiny thing happens and everyone's screaming at each other, as emotionally distraught as if someone just beheaded Mickey Mouse on live TV. And then someone (usually Peter) will say the right thing or a sufficiently novel distraction will come along, and we'll all be bouncing along again like the Get Along Gang. It's psycho.

"He doesn't have to apologize, Peter."

"Yes, he does." Of course he does. We can't let our child think it's okay to go around screaming at people that he hates them every time they reprimand him. It's just that . . . well, I'm kind of feeling like a child myself right now—or at least an emo-esque teenager—and I don't want him to apologize unless he *wants* to apologize. I want him to genuinely retract his statement. I want to know that he loves me. Unconditionally. I want to know that he'd love me even if I fed him cabbage sandwiches for a month and then went on a yearlong work trip and didn't even return with a gift. Aren't all boys supposed to love their mothers more than anything on earth? Isn't that a thing?

"It makes Mommy very sad when you say that you hate me. I know I don't always do things the same way Daddy does, but that doesn't mean that it's okay for you to say those words."

"I hate you." Now he's just using it as a weapon. He knows. He knows he's killing me slowly every time he says that. He wants to kill me. He wants me to give up so he can get his father back on the job. I'm hanging on to my mature parent persona by a rapidly fraying thread here. If he says it one more time, I am going to lose my shit.

"You say that word again and there will be no iPad tomorrow."

"I hate you!"

"That's it. No iPad." This, you understand, is the ultimate punishment. Ultimate. He'd rather get a lifetime ban from Disneyland than not get his iPad for the day. And I know why. It's because he's bored. And it's all my fault. If I were the kind of parent who woke up with ideas for one hundred and three fun-yet-educational activities up my sleeve every day, he wouldn't be so overwhelmingly attached to his tablet. He'd be overwhelmingly attached to me instead. But I'm not and so he is. And removing it is my only weapon. And I know to Billy it's a weapon that's as painful as me hearing "I hate you." And I'm using it on him.

"Now I *really* hate you," he yells, and kicks the kitchen table with his bare foot. This, of course, hurts him and he falls to the floor screaming. I shift Violet off my lap, run over, and try to rub his foot. He pushes me away.

"No!"

I think I'm going to start crying real tears now.

"Come here, bud." Peter scoops Billy up off the floor and sits him on the kitchen table.

"Daddy," he cries, his huge green eyes spilling over with tears. He's looking up at his father and his face says it all: *How could you let it come to this?*

"Let's take a look." He lifts up Billy's foot and wiggles each of his toes one by one. Within a few seconds of basking in his father's full attention, Billy's tears turn off as if by magic. "Well, nothing's broken it seems. But there is, unfortunately, one big problem."

"What?" says Billy, entranced.

"I'm very, *very* hungry. And it appears to me that these feet are made of extremely delicious cheese."

"No!" Billy squeals, with delight this time. Peter then proceeds to do a big song and dance of eating Billy's "cheesy" feet. He actually has a song that he seems to have specially composed for such occasions as this. Everyone knows the words except for me. Violet then, of course, asserts that her feet are even more delicious and insists that they get eaten too. Peter obliges.

"What about Mommy's feet?" Peter asks. "Do you think they're delicious too?"

"I bet they're the most delicious of them all!" says Violet. I'm touched.

"I don't. I bet they're just stinky. Like old lady's feet," says Billy. He's completely serious. I've never been so devastated by someone's assessment of my feet in all my days.

"Billy, why are you so mad with Mommy?" asks Peter. I'm not sure if I want to hear the answer to this or not. Billy stares downward. He knows he's in the hot seat now that his father's asking the questions.

"Because she said I couldn't have the iPad."

"You said 'I hate you' before all that!" I snap.

Any outward act of my being a calm and caring parent evaporated around the time of the foot slight. If Peter came over to try and eat my stinky feet, I think I'd just kick him away. Why am I sinking down to their level like I just stepped into a pile of juvenile-behavior quicksand? I'm supposed to rise above all this. That's what my mother's been telling me my whole life: "Amy, just rise above it." That's what *she's* been doing her whole life—the second half of it anyway. It seems as if I've yet to rise. Are these parenting skills that you're supposed to pick up along the way, or was the ability to remain reasonable in the face of provocation supposed to be gifted to me right after I finished labor?

"Look. You can have the iPad tomorrow, Billy," says Peter.

"No, he can't!"

"It's fine," says Peter. *Officially undermined.* "Billy, you can have the iPad if you'll just tell us why you're saying such bad things about Mommy." Billy pauses for a moment. He clearly doesn't want to talk about this. Yet he clearly does want access to his iPad tomorrow. I suppose it is quite clever the way Peter's turned it from a stick into a carrot.

"I don't care about Mommy being here and getting it all wrong. That's not why I'm mad."

"Then what is it?" asks Peter.

"I miss you, Daddy. You haven't been here to play with me. It's just boring without you. When are you coming back to look after us again?"

"Soon, bud. Very soon. Just give me a bit more time, okay? Mommy is so excited to hang out with you guys right now." Yeah, I'm practically doing somersaults. "Can you say sorry to her, please, Billy?"

"Sorry," he says, too quickly, avoiding eye contact. I know he doesn't mean it, but Peter doesn't seem to be after a genuine statement here. He just wants to diffuse this thing. And he's doing a better job of it than I ever could—as evidenced by the last eight minutes of my life.

"Now give your mother a hug." Billy slumps over, gives my midsection a hollow embrace, and then heads off toward his bedroom. I feel like the kid picked for the team only after the teacher insists someone call her name.

"You okay?" Peter asks me.

"No," I answer.

"I know," he says, and comes in for a head bump. We lock eyes deeply for zero point three seconds.

"Daddy! Come and read me a story," yells Billy. And the moment is broken. Like so many of them before this one.

No one tells you about all of this in the birthing classes. They should. In fact, they should probably do a seminar when we're all still in high school on how parenthood's guaranteed to run your relationship and your mental health straight through the shredder. But then the birthrate might start dropping even faster than it already is and fifty years from now there would be no one left to pay the government its precious taxes. This is all a conspiracy.

And now it's two in the morning and all of this trouble is still floating about in my brain. Around the midnight mark I started to wonder if I was permanently angry as a kid myself, if I ever put my own mother through all this drama. I don't remember it being that way, but I expect I had a skewed view of the situation. I do remember general tears, fuss, constant arguments—accusations of my being "emotionally volatile"—but that wasn't until I was a teenager. Maybe I should ask her what kind of a child I was. Maybe Billy's generalized rage toward me is just par for the course for Jansson stock? Mom and I have had a rather distant relationship since the kids came along and I didn't quit my job. Every conversation became laced with hints that my constant circling of the globe was practically child abuse, and eventually I just stopped calling. She's never approved of the untraditional situation. Not that "traditional" worked out any better for her.

I close my eyelids tighter. These kids are going to be up in four hours and counting. I've got to sleep. Peter's busy not-so-gently snoring. Violet has her head in his armpit and her feet on top of my stomach. It's no wonder I'm wide awake. A fragment of some past advice I read on insomnia comes to mind: if you can't sleep, get up and do something else. It's ten in the morning in England. Mom will be at work so I can't call her. I'll e-mail instead.

I gently push Violet's feet to the side, slip out of bed, creep to the laptop, and open it. After a few moments of indignant whirring—turns out that, unlike me, my computer *was* sleeping—we're ready to go.

From: coffeegirl2000@earthlink.net
To: Libby_Jansson@hotmail.com

Hi Mom,

How's life in sunny Yorkshire? Any new "English cuisine" recipes for me? If you want to send one now, there's a chance I might actually be able to cook it these days because I got FIRED. Yup. Fourteen years of doing everything for that cock monkey Dexter and he sold off the company, hoarded the profits for himself, and threw my livelihood into the dumpster. We are screwed. Utterly screwed. We've got next to no savings, Peter's as allergic to work as he ever was and to top it all off, the kids are totally thrown out of routine by my actually being in their lives and now both hate me. Especially Billy who's being an uber-shit.

As you've often vaguely hinted, I've always been a failure of a mother. But I feel as if my one saving grace was an ability to provide for my family. Now I'm not even doing that anymore, I'm not sure where I fit in. I think maybe I've missed my chance to be a proper part of my family, to be a proper mother. I

think I might have missed my chance to ever
have their love at all.

Anyway. When you get a minute, maybe you
can draw on your own personal experience
of a lifetime of handling bullshit and let me
know how I'm supposed to cope with all this.
Cheers!

Your darling daughter,
Amy

Well.

I obviously can't send that diatribe.

As much as Mom disapproves of my career, she'd go hairless with
worry if she found out we'd lost our only source of income. There's no
point in dragging her down with me into the poop pot of hell that is
currently my life. Especially as she's in no situation to provide any help,
financial or otherwise. Besides, between her all-consuming job at the
county council and my father, she's got enough going on.

My mother's been basically living life from inside a shitstorm
since 1997 when—within one glorious year—my dad lost all his
money, renounced his US citizenship, developed hard-core arthritis,
and moved them from their leafy north London semidetached to an
ex-council house in the depths of Yorkshire—and not the nice part. I
never got to the bottom of what happened to Dad's cash. I was told
that tax laws were technically not broken, but from what I can gather,
he'd authorized loans to a couple of firms in the States and had bent
regulations to the point of being obnoxious. He hasn't been back to
the United States since. I don't think he dares. These days they're
broke. They seem happy enough, considering all they've been through,

but I think the news that their only child and two grandchildren could be about to starve to death might send them both into a mental death spiral. So what's the point?

I quickly delete the e-mail before I have some kind of brain spasm and hit "Send." In its place I send something written in my normal brand of upbeat/vague that I always use for my parents.

From: coffeegirl2000@earthlink.net
To: Libby_Jansson@hotmail.com

Hi Mom,

How's life in sunny Yorkshire? Any new "English cuisine" recipes for us? Things are much the same as ever here. Peter's had some time recently to work on his screen-play so we've got fingers and toes crossed for that one. Billy's and Violet's legs both seem to get two inches longer every time I look at them. Both are as crazy as ever. But that's kids—right!? I know I can't have been all peaches and cream—or maybe I was . . . ? Thanks for Billy's Paddington Bear—he loved it. Sorry I didn't get many pictures of his party. Anyway—hope you and Dad are well and his knees aren't giving him too much trouble.

Miss you both!
Love,
Amy

Now that I've purged the need to dump all my problems onto my mother, my brain clears, and for one glorious moment I can breathe.

And then someone extremely worrying rushes into the blank space: Matt Colburn.

Matt and I began dating just before his meteoric climb upward, just after he started writing and producing *Real World Vampires*. Matt jumped right on the whole vampire/supernatural thing just as it was taking off. Despite what he says in interviews, he never had a flicker of interest in anything remotely supernatural before the show. He's more of a social scientist than a writer or producer. His ability to scope out trends a millisecond before they take off is uncanny. After our relationship finally finished, he produced three hit movies, migrated right to the top of the entertainment world, and stayed there. I like to think that the two events were not related. That's how I met Peter, stalking Matt at Comic-Con trying to find out if the reason he'd finished with me so abruptly was to start seeing someone else. It was: his future wife. I don't know if that makes it better or worse.

Matt ended our three-year relationship in a three-minute conversation when I called him up from a farm in Brazil in the middle of a trip. He announced that what we were doing was no longer practical; that he needed me to make a choice between him and my job, then and there. I wavered for one point two seconds and then chose the job. By the time I got back to LA and wanted to talk it through properly, he was seeing Kimberly. The problem with Matt and me was that each of us was always the most important person in our own lives. I wasn't willing to ditch my coffee career/obsession to accompany him to premieres and be his mental support hotline/punching bag when he went through one of his self-flagellation episodes. I wasn't willing to be physically there for the larger percentage of the year. And he wasn't able to go for weeks in a row by himself.

In the end, I suspect it was in some part the sex that finished our relationship. It was just so damned good that the pauses in between became almost unbearable. So we ended, and I married Peter on the rebound. Not to slight my marriage to Peter. We've hit the skids a little since the kids have come along, but who doesn't? And honestly, Peter's a much better match and a more supportive husband to me than Matt ever would have been. With Peter there's a connection that was completely missing in anything Matt and I had. You quickly get the idea from watching *Real World Vampires* that its creator and writer isn't the most nuanced of people. (And, by the way, shouldn't that be *Real-World Vampires*? Maybe they thought a hyphen would confuse their target audience.) Personally, I always thought the show was slightly exploitive of the mentally ill. Each week Matt's crew would profile some sad soul or even a group of unfortunates who sincerely believed they were actual vampires. Fascinating, disturbing, compelling. Matt jumped on the wave of reality TV right as it appeared on the horizon, and he rode that thing all the way to shore—making plenty of money as he went.

It's getting cold so I crawl back into bed. I see my glasses on my nightstand. I should take this golden opportunity to try and get some of the applesauce off the lenses. I walk into the bathroom, pick up a dampened Spider-Man washcloth, and gently rub at the applesauce. It's not coming off. Whatever toxic mess of chemicals is in that sauce seems to have bonded with the lens. I rub with a little extra vigor. Big mistake—the lens pops out, straight onto Spidey. If it took me four days to get around to wiping sauce off my glasses, when am I going to find time to get them fixed? Is it still legally permissible to drive if I close one eye? I dig through the medicine cabinet and there at the bottom is a tube of Krazy Glue. Two minutes later and the lens is back in place; however, there is now a semitransparent trail of glue running across the center of the lens.

Looks like by trying to make things better, I just made everything incrementally worse. I take this observation as a signal from up above that, likewise, it's probably a really bad idea all around to call Matt.

But you know what? I think I'm going to do it anyway.

CHAPTER 6

Peter is watching the kids and I've been allotted fifteen minutes in which to call Matt and convince him to read my husband's script with a view to either buying it or passing it on to someone else willing to plonk down the money for it.

I have the number for Colburn Entertainment, scrawled on a Post-it, in one hand and my iPhone in the other. Should I even make this call? It would be completely easy to tell Peter that I left a message with Matt's assistant and then just give a series of "oh well, such is Hollywood" shrugs as time passes and the "phone call" is not returned. That's a rather devious and dishonest way to approach things. However, if there's a simple way to avoid making this call, I should probably take it. Now that I'm confronted with the moment, speaking to Matt—if I get through—is going to be super awkward. What do I say? "So remember the last time we spoke and you told me unless I ditched my career in order to support yours, we were over? Turns out the guy I opted to marry instead is—in direct contrast to your stupendous success—a colossal failure of a writer. So, even though we haven't spoken in almost a decade, could you do me the kind of favor you probably wouldn't extend to ninety-nine percent of the people you meet and please read, and potentially buy, his screenplay? Oh yes, and no one in Hollywood wants to work with my husband because of his bad/litigious attitude—but you probably know that already."

Well, it's just not an easy conversation to have, is it? Plus, I'll completely look like a stalker, like I've been waiting with bated breath for the past nine years for an excuse to call him. It'll look like I never really forgot about him. It'll look like part of me still wishes it were the olden days, that things had worked out differently. But Peter needs this. No one else is going to do him a favor, and in all honesty Matt's probably his best way in. We both know that. Peter is a good writer, and who knows, if he's written something interesting enough, Matt might take a risk on him. And, of course, the truth is, I want to talk to Matt. I want to know that his marriage bores him stupid and that—no matter how it looks to the outside world—his career success hasn't made him happy at all.

Should I? Shouldn't I? My fingers apparently have made the choice on my behalf as they appear to be tapping out his number. Looks like I'm doing this. I take a deep breath. It doesn't help. My finger shakes as I plug in the remaining digits. My heart's ramming my breastbone like it wants to break free from my chest, free-fall down to my phone, and physically stop my finger from dialing. Too late. It's ringing. I don't know if I'm actually going to be able to get a word out. Too quickly someone picks up.

"Colburn Entertainment." An image flashes into my mind of the impossibly hip twenty-two-year-old girl on the other end of the line. Legs and arms at adolescently awkward angles, her pink pudgy lips all sulky and sultry.

"Um, can I speak to Matt Colburn, please?" I can hear that I sound like a nervous mess. Ms. Sultry probably gets a hundred people a week trying to bluff their way into speaking with Matt. She'll hear my tremble and think that I'm a wannabe.

"Is he expecting your call?" The way she says it clearly indicates that she already knows the answer is "nope!"

"Not exactly."

"Do you have a referral?" Eh? From my doctor?

"No. Can I just leave a message for him?"

"Sure," she says, and somehow I doubt my message is ever going to make it into Matt's hands. But that's fine with me. I've done my duty. I leave my number, hang up, and mentally mark the close of the entire sequence of events. However, before I've even reached the bedroom door, my phone rings. Well, damn it. My arms and legs start to vibrate again. I pick up my phone and stare at the screen. Now that I see the number, I can't believe I ever forgot it. It's Matt's cell. I drop the phone, then pick it up and answer.

"Hello," I say.

"Amy?" Just two syllables out of his mouth and it's like I've stepped through a fold in time. Nothing's changed. He's exactly the same person. We're in exactly the same situation. I've just had him on pause all these years. I should not have made this call.

"Matt. How are you?" I go for formal. For "let's act as if we've never seen each other naked—ever."

"Amy? What's happened? Why are you calling?" He's not joining in with "formal," and his tone's gone straight to intimate. Conspiratorial. This isn't helping my emotional system, which has gone from being flashflooded with adrenaline to saturated in oxytocin.

"I'm actually calling to ask you a favor," I say, trying very hard to keep the flirt out of my voice. Unfortunately, if there was a curly cord attached to this phone, I'd be twirling it between my fingers right now.

"Where are you?" he says. There's an urgency to his tone that I vaguely recognize. I'm not sure what the emotion is behind it. Regret? Lust? Passion? I'm possibly projecting here.

"I'm at home, in Pasadena."

"Can we meet?" he asks. Meet? I wasn't expecting this.

"It's okay, Matt. I don't want to take up too much of your time." Going for ultraformal now. "It's Peter O'Hara. My . . . husband. He's written a screenplay, and I was just wondering if you'd take a look at it."

"Oh, you were, were you," he says teasingly. He thinks I'm lying! He thinks I've engineered this whole setup in order to get in touch with him.

"Yes. I was. Will you look at it?"

"Sure."

"Great. What's your e-mail?"

"Hold up a minute. If I'm going to spend the time reading your husband's screenplay, then I want to see you in person."

"Can we Skype?"

"No."

"Why do we need to meet?"

"Because now that I've heard your voice, I want to see you." That urgent tone again.

"Are you sure it's a good idea?" I ask. It seems a pretty pertinent question at this point.

"I think it's the best idea I've had in about a decade." Well, I can't say I'm not flattered. But I have to draw this to a close.

"I'm going to messenger it to your office."

"You do that and I'll put it straight in the trash." *Bastard.* Maybe I'll just hang up. Pretend none of this ever happened. "Don't hang up the phone, Amy." He's not as psychic as he seems. Hanging up on Matt when the conversation wasn't going the way I wanted was always my thing.

"Come on. I'm surrounded by a bunch of Hollywood jerk-offs all day. It'd be really cool to talk to someone real for a change."

"One of the little people."

"Don't be like that. I know things finished weird between us. I miss you, Amy. You were a laugh. Let's just meet to say hi. What have you got to lose?" *Everything.*

"When?" I ask.

"Soon. I'll call you." And with that he hangs up. The lack of "good-bye" somehow seems to make everything even more implicitly shady. Perhaps I'll hand him a printout, we'll all have a good *laugh*, and that'll be the end of this episode of *Real World Exes*.

Perhaps. In the meantime I'd better go and share the glad tidings with Peter—and check that there's some ink in the printer.

CHAPTER 7

It's a quarter till six. Day fourteen. Peter's already left for HushMush. Smart guy. He knows if he's still around when the kids wake up, he'll never get away. I'm clinging to the side of our mattress in order to accommodate Violet's body, currently dominating the middle of the bed in an X shape. Most of the night was spent in an unhappy H with Peter and me on the outside and Violet the horizontal line connecting our bodies. It's not a configuration that lends itself to restful sleep.

The last few days at home have been a complete disaster. I've yet to unpack my backpack or find my way to the grocery store. I still haven't had time to pick that line of Krazy Glue off my glasses. Any day my new contact lenses will arrive in the mail. Apparently, right now they are in some depot in Ohio where they've been for about a week. However, until the glorious day that they arrive, I'm committed to glue-obscured vision. The only positive thing I can say about the last few days is that we haven't been to the ER, though the police have been called on us, so we didn't totally avoid involving emergency services within the first two weeks. I don't know who put in the noise complaint to the cops. But I have my suspicions that it was my overly wholesome next-door neighbor—Lizzie.

Lizzie thinks I am a lousy parent. She's never said a word to that effect, but the thoughts are coming so loudly from her brain that she may as well have a permanent thought bubble over her head: *Amy O'Hara's such a bad mother, I'm worried she'll have a detrimental effect on my children simply by osmosis.* Quite frankly, after the last couple of weeks I'm considering donning a wooden placard around my neck: "World's Worst Mother. Have Mercy."

So far this week I managed to induce a massive bout of diarrhea in my firstborn when I ignored his observation that Daddy never gave him cheese and forced him to eat a cheddar sandwich. What? We'd run out of peanut butter and I thought he was just being fussy. I completely forgot that he was lactose-intolerant, probably because I'd never actually witnessed an episode before. You can be reassured that the fact is now *burned* into my memory. I had to bribe him with three new game downloads before he'd swear not to tell Peter about it. And a "fun" trip to the pool didn't go that well either. Turns out that reports of Violet's progress at her swimming lessons had been vastly exaggerated, and when I rather enthusiastically threw her up in the air and into the pool (*she asked me to!*), she sank to the bottom like a stone. Luckily, the seventeen-year-old lifeguard was on the ball. On the same day that I nearly drowned my daughter, I also let both kids burn to a crisp. I'd been diligently applying sunscreen to them all afternoon only to realize—after they both started turning a scorched, raw pink—that I'd been slathering them with my very expired SPF 4 self-tanner from back when I cared more about tanning than skin cancer. On top of that, I can't seem to cook a single thing that they both like to eat. I keep forgetting to put Violet down for a nap after lunch, which means she keeps drifting off while standing up and then falling over and hitting her head. All in all, far from the whole experience finally bonding us together, *both kids* now hate me and keep asking when Daddy's coming home. Well, Billy still hates me, Violet's as clingy as ever—yet still manages to scorn me at the same time.

I too am wondering when Daddy is going to put in an appearance. Peter's not saying anything about anything. Just disappearing before dawn, coming back after the kids are in bed, and then hunkering down in the office for yet more quality time with his MacBook. I am hoping that by virtue of sheer hours spent in the company of his laptop, his screenplay is being polished to a blazing shine. If questioned, he neither confirms nor denies this hope. Peter's been pretty introverted the few moments we've seen him during waking hours—only opening his mouth occasionally to stop Billy and me from killing each other. It is, in fact, a complete relief to have one mouth in this house that stays more or less shut in my presence. Between the screaming, the whining, the crying, the talking, the laughing, the fake laughing, and the foot thundering, I think the decibel count alone is enough to send me running back to the workforce. Because here comes the admission, the admission that would have Peter straight to dancing the "I Told You So" jig if he and I were having in-depth communication these days: Looking after the kids all day is hard. Harder than sourcing coffee beans in countries without plumbing. So there.

"Mommy." There's a prod-prod on my back. Perhaps keeping my eyes closed as a sign that I'm "sleeping" will somehow cause Violet to spontaneously develop empathy skills. She'll think, *Poor Mother must be exhausted. What a time of it she's been having recently. I'll entertain myself until she's rested enough to make my breakfast.*

Prod-prod. "Mommy!" As I roll over to face her, I am confronted with a small pile of sand. How? And why? But at two weeks in, I've stopped asking those kinds of questions. Out loud, anyway.

"I'm a baby lizard and you're the mommy lizard."

"Right."

"The baby lizard wants milk."

"No 'please'?"

"Milk."

I grab my glasses and go to pick at the glue.

"Miiiiiiiilk!"

I resign myself to limited vision for life, don the glasses, and make for the kitchen. And yes, a better parent would explain to their child that unless they ask nicely, there will be no milk at all. I am not that better parent.

"Mommy! Walk like a lizard!" I've no idea how a lizard walks, but I do some kind of lizard waddle and that seems to satisfy her. Over the last few days I've learned that there's no point in refusing to walk like a lizard/sing like a snowman/slither like a pink worm—a happy one. You just do it—without question. Or there will be big trouble.

Violet and Billy both demand caterpillar pancakes for breakfast, which apparently is a firm favorite from Peter's range of food-art specialties. I pretend I don't hear them and serve up jelly sandwiches cut into wonky stars. That's as special as it gets from Mommy.

"Mommy, you're a weirdo," says Billy. "Sandwiches are lunch food." Kid's got a point, but the truth is, it's difficult to compete with caterpillar pancakes by serving up Special K—which is about all we have left in the pantry. My other big concept is to serve scrambled eggs and put a happy face on it with ketchup, but I think I'm going to save that idea for a grand lunchtime reveal one day. Plus, we're currently out of eggs. The domestic side of things, in general, seems to be rapidly falling apart. Peter transformed from "clean freak" to "typical male" the moment I got back from the airport, and no one appears to have stepped into the breach. The dishwasher's permanently full, we've been using paper towels instead of toilet paper for about a week, the floor tiles are starting to get kind of sticky, and there's a long smear of what could possibly be turd over the back door that's been there since last Tuesday.

From behind me comes the sickening sound of Violet's favorite pink cup tipping over and the milk inside spilling out over the table. This seems to happen a lot. I go to grab the paper towels, remember they're in the bathroom, and grab The Apron instead. Turns out faux silk doesn't absorb milk that well. Even so I do my best with it, then I ball it up and push it firmly to the bottom of the trash can. Peter's not going to be wearing it anytime soon, and I'm certainly not donning it in his place. Bon voyage to The Apron!

Two hours later I'm persuading both kids out the front door and into the car. Things usually mellow out incrementally after I've dropped Billy off at preschool.

"Amy!" Awesome. It's Lizzie. "How have you been?" The clouds haven't burnt off to reveal the morning sunlight yet, but even so Lizzie's skin seems to gently glow in what morning light there is. Much like Cleopatra used to bathe daily in the milk of seven hundred asses, I suspect that Lizzie takes daily baths in the juice of seven hundred pressed organic vegetables from the most local farmers' market possible. She's that wholesome. Her hair is geometrically perfect. She's an ensemble of flawlessly round circles, from her round blue eyes to her rounded tiny hips. Lizzie always reminds me of a ripe coffee bean, patiently waiting to be plucked from the tree. Small, round, rosy, perfect. She looks like she put more thought into her outfit this morning than I've put into my entire life plan.

"You know. Working," I say. "Hello, Odessa." Odessa—Lizzie's daughter—wasn't blessed with her parents' perfect genes. She has reedy hair, she's shy and fearful, she picks her nose, and has been known to eat whole patches of grass from her front yard. I've no idea what's with the name. Maybe the poor child was conceived in Odessa—I never asked.

"Oh yes. All that travel!" She makes a face when she says "travel" that looks like the face someone would normally use when they say "eating fecal matter for dessert."

"Where are you guys off to?" she asks.

"We're just dropping Billy at preschool and then . . . we're going shopping," I improvise. I need an excuse for the fact that I'm driving Billy to school when it's only six and a half blocks away.

"Shopping? But you're still in your jammies."

"Well—that's why I need to go shopping. I gave away all my clothes."

"Really?"

"Yup." That should shut her up. The average individual would clearly see that I'm being facetious—driven to it in response to her endless questions. But she opens up her mouth to talk again. "Actually, we're running late so . . ." I poke Billy toward the car.

"I just needed a moment of your time to discuss . . . an issue." Great. Last time we had to discuss "an issue" it was Billy peeing through a hole in their fence and right onto her husband's leather Hush Puppies. I never did reprimand Billy about that. I was actually quite impressed he had that kind of aim, and besides, no one should be wearing Hush Puppies in the year 2016. I don't care if they had a second coming in the nineties; they were dorky then and they're even dorkier now. That said, most days I dress in what could only be described as "United Nations chic" and until very recently wore a leather friendship bracelet that I'd been sporting since 1998, so what do I know?

Lizzie beckons me conspiratorially to the side. "It's Billy again, I'm afraid." She's talking about him as if he's some kind of problem child.

"What is it?"

"He's been taking sand."

"Sand?"

"From Odessa's sandbox."

"How would he even get to Odessa's sandbox?"

"Through a hole."

"A hole?"

"That he kicked through our fence." Okay. I'm a little shocked at this part.

"I'm sure he didn't kick a hole through your fence, Lizzie."

"He did. I have the footage." Lizzie whips out her iPhone, pulls up some kind of kid spy app, and plays me the footage. It's grainy, but clear enough to see a little foot kicking and pushing through the fence, then Billy scurrying across their backyard, shoveling sand into his pail, and hurrying back to home turf. I don't know what to say. This explains where he's been hiding, and it partly explains the piles of sand I've been finding everywhere. My firstborn is a vandal and a thief.

"Um. Wow. Sorry?" I manage.

"Don't worry about it. I'll get it fixed and send the bill over." A bill for fixing her fancy fence? That's the last thing we need right now. I consider asking Peter to fix it, and then I remember that high-heeled Lizzie probably has more hands-on experience fixing fences than he does. Peter isn't handy. His three brothers are. But they're in Boston, with no plans to visit.

"Okay, fine. Send us the bill when you have it. And sorry again." I have to force the last sentence out. I turn to leave.

"But, Amy?"

"What?"

"Why do you think he did it?" *What the fuck is it of her business?*

"I don't know—little boys kick things sometimes."

"Do you think he could be struggling with social issues?" Seriously? Has she not met her own daughter—ever?

"Billy!" I call over. He looks up. "Lizzie wants to know if you're struggling with any social issues. Are you?" My face goes cold. I'm starting to lose my thin grip on civility.

"I don't know," says Billy. "What are social issues?" Lizzie's staring at me. She doesn't say a word. She doesn't need to. *I am a terrible mother.*

"I'll let you know when we have the bill, then," she says.

"Fine," I reply.

"You've got glue on your glasses."

"I know."

Sensing the atmosphere, both kids get in their car seats without a peep. Maybe this is why Peter sometimes exudes an air of grumpiness for days on end—he's learned it's a wonderful tool for controlling the children.

And do I broach the subject of theft and wanton vandalism with my son? No. Why not? Because I have no idea how to handle it.

The golden silence lasts about thirty seconds. My sleep-deprived brain spaces out on the first part of the argument, but by the time I tune back in, it seems to have reached some kind of crescendo.

"I need you to STOP touching my body!" That's Violet. "Mommy! Billy is touching my body!"

"Billy, stop touching your sister's body."

Okay, so that sounds *pretty* terrible out of context. Billy's preschool is "progressive." This is a fact that I normally happily forget until the teachers start talking to me about child development. It's like they've got their own private language. One of their faves is that they don't refer to the children as "you" when they want them to do something. They solely refer to their "bodies" as doing things. As in: "I need your body to take a nap" and "I need you to move your body away from Jason's body." It seems a little weird, doesn't it? Peter asked them about it and turns out that asking a child to do something with their body, as opposed to just doing something, is more likely to yield a compliant response. Allegedly someone somewhere did an awful amount of research on the topic.

Billy asked me to stop "touching his body" once, when I was trying to buckle him into his car seat midtantrum. Violet saw the instant and alarmed reaction the words had on me, and she took them on as her own. She knows she's going to get some immediate attention when she starts talking about people messing with her body. The attention is mostly based around trying to get her to shut the hell up in public. "Daddy, stop touching my body" has had us leaving restaurants before the food even arrives. The other well-used variant is "I don't like it when you touch my body." That's had us cross at least one local park off the list.

"I'm not touching your stinky body. I'm not doing anything," says Billy. He's as tired of the whole thing as the rest of us. Violet lets out a killer scream. This close to her "body," it's so shrill it's like someone just plunged a scalpel into my ear. I turn around in my seat and catch Billy red-handed squeezing Violet's arm.

"STOP TOUCHING HER BODY!" I yell at both my children in cold fury.

Can't we even drive the six blocks to school peacefully without emergency intervention? Some reptilian sense in the back of my brain tingles. I swing around to face front just in time to slam on the breaks for the stop sign as a car whizzes past us on the road ahead. If I'd allowed myself to be distracted by my children for just another half a second, that would have been a head-on collision. It's then that I really lose my cool. I don't remember what I say. I think I do refer to the fact that their arguing nearly caused the death of all of us and maybe that might not be such a bad thing. Billy stares back at me red-faced, crying. Violet just gets that glazed-over look she has whenever she's being told off.

I'm a monster.

We drive the last two blocks in the silence that I've been craving. By the time we get to school, both children seem to have recovered completely from my outburst. We pull up in the front. We're ever so slightly early, so the lot is deserted. If I can quickly run in and out again, I should be able to safely leave Violet in the car without anyone calling social services. The buckle on her car seat is so frickin' stiff, I nearly puncture my skin with my thumb bone every time I try to undo it. I'm already feeling weaker than normal because of my bout of insomnia last night. It's no more than sixty-nine degrees outside. She can stay in the car.

"Billy, out of the car. Violet, I'll be back in two minutes." She's singing herself a made-up song about a pair of fabulous red shoes worn by a happy pony, and it's so all-consuming she doesn't even notice when I close the car door. Billy and I head through the gates.

"Mommy, if you live in Chinatown, can you still speak Spanish?"

"Yes, of course."

"But why?"

"Why what?"

"Why would you speak Spanish if you lived in Chinatown?"

"Maybe because you were from Spain."

"But then why would you be living in Chinatown?"

"I don't know, Billy."

"Can you speak Spanish, Mommy?"

"Yes, sweetie."

"Have you been to Chinatown?"

"I have."

"Have you been to Spain?"

"I have not."

"Why not?"

Oh my God. And it goes on. Round and round in circles. Maybe he'll be a prosecutor when he grows up. He'll get people on the stand to fold purely because they'd rather take the jail time than keep trying to answer his endless, pointless questions. Questions. I thought that was going to be one of the best things about parenting: telling my kids about the world we live in, from my own wise point of view. Didn't work out that way. Maybe I'd be more into it if the questions made any sense or had actual answers. For example: "Where does rain come from?" or "Can you tell us about the carbon cycle, Mommy?" I'd be all over that. Instead, it's all: "What does five minutes look like?" and "If it's sunny in heaven, will I have to wear sunscreen?"

The minute I walk into Billy's school room, I remember. It's Flag Day. All the kids are supposed to dress in colors of the flag that represents their heritage *and* I was supposed to bring in, like, twenty-four party favors. Billy was meant to dress in blue and yellow to represent my Swedish background, but he's wearing a dirty fluorescent-orange Nike T-shirt and a pair of denim shorts. Quick as a whip I pull out my phone and Google "blue and orange flag color."

"Hey, Billy. Hey, Mrs. O'Hara," says his teacher. Damn, I can't remember her name. There are two of them working in Billy's classroom and they *both* have red hair, for goodness' sake.

"Hey," Billy says.

"So, those are the colors of the Swedish flag?" she asks, getting out her phone to take his picture for the wall. She must have figured out how to print photos from her phone. I haven't held a physical photo that I've snapped myself this century. There's a huge chart on the wall with all the kids' names on it, alongside the nationality they've chosen to represent for the day. By "Billy O'Hara," it says "Sweden."

"Actually, we checked with my father and Billy's great-grandfather was Armenian!" I say chirpily. I'm always surprised by how easily I am able to tell a lie. I deserve to be haunted by the entire clan of Janssons for at least the next six months of my life for denying my Nordic roots in the name of convenience.

"Your ancestry is Armenian?" she says, flicking a meaningful look over my and Billy's white-blond hair.

"Yup. Armenian," I say, and gaze over to her chart. She grudgingly picks up a thick marker and runs a big black line through "Sweden" and writes "Armenia" in its place. The chart is ruined.

From out in the corridor comes the urgent slam and scrape of a busy woman wearing heels. I turn around to see another Cheerful Cheetah mom in full office garb blazing through the front door. She looks exhausted, a little tense, perfectly groomed. Her daughter is wearing a beautiful patchwork dress of green, red, and white.

"Nice dress," I say before I can stop myself. I generally try to limit my interactions with the other moms. It always just ends with me finding out information that I really didn't want to know, like there's a special orange folder that Billy's supposed to take home every day that's stuffed with homework that hasn't been done for three weeks, or that we're zoned for an elementary school so low in the ratings that we're either going to have to go private or move.

"Thanks. Regina's grandma made it for her. The colors are for the flag of Italy." She smiles, and some of the tension leaves her face. She's pretty when you remove the first layer of stress. She's carrying a cloth bag brimming over with what I can see are party favors. Damn it. The party favors. Why is it that I can instantly recall which roasting recipes work best for eighty different types of bean at any waking moment but can't remember something as simple as bringing twenty-four national-ity-themed party favors to preschool?

"So I forgot the party favors I was supposed to bring," I say in the general direction of Billy's teacher. I really wish I could remember her name. "I can run to Target now and drop them off in about an hour if that's okay?" Billy looks up at me from where he's constructing some kind of epic tower from Lego. It's a look that's both embarrassed and scornful. If I wasn't already feeling like the C-minus adult in the room, I surely do now.

"No need," says Regina's mom. "I always bring extra 'cause some-one always forgets." She flashes me a genuine smile to show me she's not being Judgment Mom. "We're all so busy, aren't we?"

Finally. Someone who gets it. I'm just starting to think about a nonstalkerish way of asking her if she'd be down for our kids having a playdate sometime when there's the sound of a smashing Lego tower. We all turn around to see Regina and Billy on the floor fighting. Regina stands up and starts punching Billy hard on the arm; Billy's still down, but he's kicking out at her legs with everything he's got. We all swoop in, but before we get there Billy lands the ultimate one: he bites her, right on the fleshy part of her hand. I go for Billy and pull him out from under Regina. Regina immediately stops fighting and runs to her mother. Billy continues to lash out and smacks me square in the face.

One second later, the teacher with no name somehow grabs Billy from behind and manages to fold his arms square across his chest, hold-ing his wrists in both of her hands. She has the willful facial expression of someone who's done this plenty of times before.

"Billy. I am holding you because I will not let you hurt your body or your mother's body. I will let you go when you calm down."

Billy doesn't calm down. He's wiggling like a fish tangled in a net.

"Mommy, no! Make her stop—she's hurting me!" he screams, bucking up against her restraint. *What do I do? What do I do?*

"It's probably best if you just go," says his teacher.

"Really?" I ask.

"It's just easier. He'll calm down quicker. We've been through this with Billy before." I didn't know that. "Just go for now."

Stay or go? My natural instinct is to tell this woman to get her hands the hell off my son—but then what? Watch him as he goes on a rampage around the classroom? Let him wage a full-on war against Regina?

"Billy, I need you to listen to your teacher and try to calm down. Mommy will see you later," I manage to choke out. I then duck my head down and leave the room, fast. I haven't even got the balls to give an apologetic look to my almost-friend.

I step back outside into the sun and push down the sob that is threatening. It's not even nine, and this is shaping up to be one of the worst days of my life ever. And that's a title not won easily.

As I approach the parking lot, I see a gaggle of mothers surrounding my vehicle. That's why no one's in class yet. And then I remember: Violet. My instinct is to run to the car, but a flash of insight tells me that if I do that, I'll look guilty. I've technically done nothing wrong. Well, maybe technically I have. But really I haven't. My mother used to leave me in the car for an hour at a time when she ran errands. Mind you, that was in the eighties. She also used to drive around town with me in a Moses basket just slung on the backseat when I was baby. I doubt that would fly these days.

"Hey," I say to the group. The nervous comes out as hostile.

"Is this your car?" asks one of the gaggle.

"Yes," I reply.

"Your daughter is trapped inside!" she says, gesturing to the back where Violet's running *Titanic* hands down the window and yelling, "Let me out!"

"I just dropped off Billy. I was gone for two minutes." In the background I hear someone say, "That's *Billy's* mother." Apparently this is somehow significant as there's suddenly a ripple of comprehension through the crowd. I hear another voice speaking into a phone: "It's okay, the mother has returned to her vehicle."

My God. Someone actually called the cops! A heavyset woman wearing nothing but Birkenstocks and a paisley shirtdress pushes through the crowd; she has a fire extinguisher over one shoulder.

"Stand back!" she yells, and starts at a run for the back window.

"STOP RIGHT NOW!" I yell. She catches herself just before she throws the fire extinguisher through the window. "What are you doing?" I ask. It seems a pretty sensible question. It's not hot out. My daughter is in no danger. Or at least she was in no danger until people started threatening to throw fire extinguishers in her face. These women have gone insane.

"I was going to save your daughter!" she puffs, dropping the fire extinguisher to the ground.

"By showering her in glass?" This gives them all pause for the moment. The mothers at the edge of the circle start to step away, maybe perturbed by the realization that shattered glass in the back of a car might actually pose more of a realistic hazard to a kid than being left alone for a few moments. "I was gone ten minutes."

"It's against the law," says one of the mothers. I bite back an urge to say, "Blow me." Instead I open the car door, get in the driver's seat, and slam it closed again. I start up the engine, which quickly disperses the last of the crowd. Maybe they think I'm such a rogue outlaw that I'll mow 'em down on the way out of here. I sure would like to.

It doesn't take me the full six blocks home to 'fess up to the reality of what's happening here: I have no idea how to handle being a parent. This is not the kind of situation where you can learn on the job. These kids are too old. I never experienced the slow learning curve where you grow as a parent alongside your child. I've missed too much. They're too messed up. They need their father back. I have to escape this hourly realization that I've no idea what I'm doing. I have to get away from the knowledge that I'm a ridiculous stranger in the eyes of my children. Again, it's looking like I have no choice: I have failed at being a mother.

I have to get back to work.

CHAPTER 8

From: Libby_Jansson@hotmail.com
To: coffeegirl2000@earthlink.net

Hi darling! Hope you are all doing well. Send some piccies of the kiddies when you can—I know you don't have time for the Facebook but it would be nice to see their new long legs! I'd love to come and see them for myself at some point, but I've no clue when I'm next going to be able to visit—I'd be worried about leaving your father, to be honest. He's still managing to walk into Farsley and back right now, but it seems to get a bit harder each week. Plus, I'm sure you've seen the price of flights at the moment—good God! How do they justify it?

Anyway—love to all. Let's Skype when you're next not working.

Love, Mom

I hit the "Home" button on my phone—the quickest route to making the e-mail go away. We can't Skype. The first thing Billy and Violet would do is spill the beans about my job and then I'd be in trouble for not telling my parents, on top of getting them all riled up. Sigh. Oh, to have been one of those women who found a job, met a guy, and started a family in the same town as her parents, grandparents, and great-grandparents. I don't really remember ever making a conscious decision not to do that. Circumstance just decided to shred my chance at having that life the minute I hit double digits. It's too late to try and claw any semblance of it back now. Too many holes in the fabric.

After talking to Billy's teacher at pickup, I found out the reason for his almighty fallout with Regina, and it wasn't anything to do with her pushing over his epic Lego tower. It was, in fact, because of his nails. Or, as Regina called them, his "princess nails." Since I've been at home, Peter has given up on every single aspect of childcare, including the washing of the children and also, it would seem, the cutting of their sharp little nails. I gave Billy's nails a quick glance upon hearing what had caused all the drama, and I have to say, Regina had a point. They were like a row of shovels on the ends of his fingers. Along with the heads-up to cut my kid's nails, Billy's teacher also directed me toward a book she wants me to read on parenting highly emotional children. This is the first time there's been an advantage to attending this hippie-dippie preschool: Billy's been labeled an "emotional child" rather than a "problem child." I'll take it. I'll take anything that implies that I haven't raised my son to be an asshole but rather merely failed in the handling of his extreme emotions. I've downloaded the book to my phone. It hasn't happened yet, but at some point soon I will make the time to read it. Maybe it will give me some pointers for handling Peter too.

Speaking of Peter, Violet and I have come out to HushMush today to surprise him. He doesn't generally like surprises, but we're doing it anyway. From outside I'm looking right at his laptop screen. Straight through the window, over his shoulder, and what do I see? Cars. He's checking out Lexuses, or should that be Lexi? I don't know why he's checking out Lexuses—he's got zero hope of trading in his Honda mini-van anytime soon. Perhaps it's research related. I knock on the window. He turns around to see Violet and me, noses pressed up against the glass, and hurriedly closes his laptop. Not research related, then.

As Violet and I enter the café, the smell of refined sugar spirals up my nostrils. I can't even make out the scent of what coffee they might be serving; my senses can't get through the wall of sucrose. As we approach, Peter opens up the laptop again and starts rapidly typing on his keyboard. *Oh, don't try and fake it now.*

"Hey." I smile.

"Hey, guys! Want some coffee?" I give him a look. He knows I wouldn't drink this coffee. It's bad enough that I'm *in* HushMush. What if someone saw me? Does he not remember what I do for a living?

"Daddy!" Violet gives Peter a hug. He pulls her onto his lap and covers the top of her head in kisses. They both look so beautiful with their matching dark curls and night-blue eyes. I feel like the ugly impostor.

"I've missed my beautiful girl," says Peter, beaming and holding Violet aloft under the armpits like she's an animated rag doll.

"Thanks. I've missed you too," I reply. Yeah, I know he wasn't talking about me.

"Come here," he says, and pulls me in to him. He nudges the top of my head back and gives me a soft kiss right in the center of my neck. Jeez, that makes the tops of my ears go cold. Is this why I put up with what I put up with?

"What are you doing here?" asks Peter.

"We have to talk."

"And what does the love of my life want to talk about?"

"I'm thinking of looking for another job."

"Amy! Why? I told you, I've got this covered. This is your time with the kids. Enjoy it."

"Well . . ." I can't confess to my husband that I'm a lousy parent and have to get back to work to escape my children *in front* of my child. Can I? "How are you feeling about the screenplay?"

"Feeling?"

"Do you feel like Matt's definitely going to buy it? Do you feel like you could bear to see it go into production having someone else make changes to it?" Matt finally got back to set up our compulsory meeting. It's next week. It's been very hard work not to constantly think about it.

"Changes?"

"Any Lexuses in your screenplay?"

"No, why?"

"Never mind. I'm just trying to get a handle on how realistic a cash cow this thing really is."

"I don't know if I'd exactly call it a cash cow."

"So essentially you can guarantee nothing."

"I have a strong feeling that, at some point, this screenplay will sell and make us some money. I don't know what to tell you outside of that."

"Well, in that case, I'm going to Bean à la Bean to talk to Roth Ellis."

"About what?"

"What do you think? A job." Of course, you understand I was *already* intending to go and talk to Roth Ellis about a job today, but now that I've successfully squeezed a confession out of Peter that he realistically doesn't know when this screenplay of his is going to make any money, I have *justification*. And now my job search is no longer about the fact that I have to get away from my children; it can be about the fact that yet again my husband can't commit to bringing home the bacon—or even so much as a slice of toast to go with the bacon—and my salary is needed to save the day. Much better.

"Mommy, I don't want you to get a job and go away again."

Great. Peter looks up at me. It's a look dripping with the suggestion that I'm the actual most uncaring parent of all time. I don't feel like an uncaring parent; I don't feel like a parent at all. More like a biologically related reluctant babysitter. I am not going to be made to feel guilty because I have to bring his Internet-surfing career to an early close. He just doesn't want me to go back to work so he doesn't have to deal with the kids by himself again. I absolutely do not blame him. I just wish he would be honest about it instead of running off to HushMush to pretend to work on his screenplay and giving me a mommy guilt trip.

"Mommy isn't going away—we're just going to go and talk to one of my friends."

"That's nice. Lie to the girl."

"Mommy, are you lying?" Why am I the constant villain in my own life? There is no right choice here. It's not *new* news that there never is a right choice in my life these days.

"Mommy's not lying. Daddy's just making a funny joke."

"I don't think it's funny." She pouts. Such a pretty pout.

"Me neither. Daddy isn't very good at jokes." I pick up Violet in anticipation of a tantrum. "We'll see you later. Enjoy the Lexus perving while you still can."

"Amy? Can't we talk about this?"

"Nope." And with that I make my exit as huffily as I can while carrying a long-legged three-year-old on my hip. Yup, I can be pretty inflexible. Peter can certainly spin out from time to time, but I'm not far behind him as far as crappy communication skills go. We're a match made in heaven—maybe the rough inner-city part of heaven.

Surprisingly, I have my archnemesis, Dexter, to thank for my job interview today. While I sit, my sit bones digging into the hardest bench in the Eastside, waiting for Roth, I pull out my phone to read through Dexter's grovely e-mail one more time. I get a little bit happy every time I read it.

From: dexterwarnock@gmail.com
To: coffeegirl2000@earthlink.net

Amy,

Your recent reply of "You can shove your
kind concern up your ugly, hairy rectum"
to my text asking how you are leads me to
think that a phone call may not be the most
effective form of communication right now.
Hence this e-mail.

I know you are angry. I know you are wondering what on earth happened to our company and our mission to source and develop
the best coffee in the world. I also know
you're steaming mad that I didn't share the
buyout money with you.

I know it's a hard thing to hear, Amy, but two
million dollars isn't really a lot of cash. I don't
get all of it. There are taxes to be paid, cred-
itors. I'll be lucky to walk away with a few
hundred thousand. And, yes, that sounds like
a lot, but really, it's not that much for everything I've done. I'll barely be able to pay off
my mortgage. And then what? I know you
worked hard for this company too, but I was
the one who put my financial balls on the line
to get it started.

Having said that, you are right that I have let down our farmers and their families, and that's what I'm e-mailing you about today.

A friend of mine, Roth Ellis, owns Bean à la Bean—I'm sure you know of it. If you want, I can set up an introduction for you. Once he tastes the Yayu he'll be interested, seriously interested. Who wouldn't be? He's about the only guy in the game who has the financial resources right now. If he takes you up on the Yayu, maybe you can persuade him to bring on some of our other farmers too.

As I say—I can set it up, if you like. The rest is up to you.

Dex
P.S. Really, still with the EarthLink address?

Ultimately I'd have liked to have seen a little bit more guilt-ridden hand wringing. However, the overriding tone of supreme self-justification leads me to think that rather than taking pleasure in sitting around all day in his newly paid-off house, he's actually mentally torturing himself about all of this.

I look at my reply again:

From: coffeegirl2000@earthlink.net
To: dexterwarnock@gmail.com

Fuck you very much. I will take that intro.

He knows he's somewhat on the way to being forgiven. If I'd wanted to push the knife in deeper, I'd have been icy polite with him. He'll be sleeping easier in his eco-certified platform bed tonight.

Now Roth Ellis is very fucking cool. Quite a bit too cool if you want my opinion—which nobody seems to at the moment. Back in the nineties when I started working in coffee, coffee was definitely not a magnet for hipster nerds. At best it was probably slightly interesting to a few seriously noncool people. However, these days, to know your Kurimi from your Yirgacheffe makes you the hippest kind of hipster. Everyone in Bean à la Bean is dressed in a cutting-edge Silver Lake uniform of porkpie hat and skinny jeans, with big old holes in the earlobes. None of them have any real heartfelt knowledge of what actually had to happen in order for them to have their trendsetting beverage experience. When did all this hoopla come about? Can't it just be about the coffee anymore?

And then in the middle of this mecca for hipsters there's me, wearing cargo pants purchased in 2001 and a sensible Old Navy tank top. My ears were once pierced, but the tiny holes have since resealed through lack of penetration. And yes, there's another analogy in there, but let's not get off topic.

My lack of cool is clearly a problem for Roth when he finally turns up. He's on the opposite end of the style spectrum from me and seems to be going for the surfing-CEO look, wearing a tailored jacket over a pair of pin-striped board shorts. His hair is fascinating. It's shaved and dark at the sides but long and ash-blond on the top, with gas-flame-blue roots. Either he's part elf or he's been getting some serious assistance from someone at Supercuts. It all seems a little involved for a guy in his late forties. I can read the internal conflict scrawled across his face as I tell him about my new rust-resistant wonder bean: *This bean could be the answer to all of my pricing issues. Wait . . . are those cargo pants she's wearing? I've got to get her to cup those beans for me. Where is that clingy kid's nanny? Is that glue across her glasses?*

"So you can see why I need to get back out there as soon as I can. Getu trusts me. He wants to work with me, but he can't sit on this forever."

"And you have the beans now?"

"I have the beans. They're something special. They've got such a syrupy softness, Roth. It's like drinking just-cut sugarcane."

"How do you know it's rust resistant?"

"That's just Getu's observation. He had rust come through recently right before the rain and it's still over everything. But this varietal's completely clean. There's a lab nearby in Jimma—I can test it there." Violet monkeys up onto my lap and starts twisting my hair around her fingers. I can see Roth's interested, super interested. I'm just about to start talking terms, when someone behind me catches his eye and a smile bursts across his face like sunshine from heaven.

I turn around to see a supermodelesque woman and a little boy dressed like a miniature hipster approaching. This must be his family. His pupils almost double in size; he must be completely smitten with his wife—and no wonder, she's foxy. All swish-swash bouncy hair and almond-shaped eyes that take up half her face.

"Daddy!" The kid runs across the store and barrels into his dad. He may be dressed like a minifashionista, but under that flat cap and all that label, he's kinda dorky.

"Hey." Roth looks pleased and annoyed all at the same time. "Amy, this is Hendrix." Hendrix? As in Jimi? *Puh-lease.*

"Hey, Ji . . . Hendrix. This is Violet." Violet flashes her big eyes his way and then nuzzles into my neck. She's gone into full static-cling mode. Wait—could it be nap time? "And you must be Roth's wife?" I go to shake hands with the green-eyed goddess. She looks shocked.

"Oh. I'm Hendrix's nanny. Mirabelle." Nanny? Unless my husband was legally blind, I would not be happy with my nanny looking like that. I'm pretty sure disapproval flashes in neon lettering across my face, and we're all three suddenly thrown into the middle of a spontaneous conversational shutdown. My mistake about Mirabelle is only awkward because Roth's obviously in love with her. Hendrix, sensing the weirdness, breaks out into song.

"Winkle winkle wittle star." He's loud, high-pitched, with a certain grating quality, and the polar opposite of cool.

"You still free for lunch, Roth?" asks Mirabelle through the singing. I wonder if his wife knows about these lunch plans.

"Sure," he says, like the idea only just now occurred to him. "Go on over to Forage and order for us. I'll be there in a sec." He doesn't have to tell her what he wants to eat. She already knows. Obviously. *Creep.* "See you in a minute, li'l dude," he says, and yanks Hendrix's cap down over his eyes. Mirabelle leads the still-singing Hendrix out of the store. The hipsters are craning their skinny necks around to stare. They do not approve. Hendrix was obviously not named for his singing skills. I can sense Roth's attention wandering off out the door after Mirabelle.

"So . . . if this varietal does turn out to be rust-free, Ethiopia will be the only place it's going to be growing," I say.

"Still no export of seeds, then?"

"Right," I confirm.

"And plants?"

"The same. They've got it locked down. If someone else gets to this bean first, that's pretty much the end of getting this affordably."

"Mommy, I'm tired." Violet sighs.

"Looks like someone needs a nap." He smiles.

"Right." He's stalling.

"This sounds really interesting, Amy. So are you sourcing right now?" Damn it. He doesn't want to offer me a job. He just wants to pay a one-off finder's fee for the Arabica scoop of the century. That doesn't help me or my situation.

"Actually, I'm only interested in buying permanently for one roaster."

"Really? You still up for all that travel—even now?" He gestures to Violet, who's passed-out sleeping on my chest.

"Especially now." Oops. Fortunately, under the veneer of hip there's something of a sense of humor in there and Roth laughs.

"Well, I'd love to taste what you have. I'm going away tomorrow for a couple of weeks, but come by the lab at the end of the month, okay?"

"Sure."

Roth saunters off for his illicit lunch, and I carry Violet back toward the car. I know he wants those beans. Thing is, if he's going to employ me, he's going to have to ditch his other buyer. Bean à la Bean is doing well, but not well enough to employ two, especially not with coffee prices going through the roof. Employing me on the basis of this bean would be pure risk. If he ditches his other buyer (who I'm sure is super trendy), employs me, and the beans turn out *not* to be rust resistant or *not* to taste as amazing as promised en masse, he just looks disloyal and is stuck with a buyer whose wardrobe was put together when the Spice Girls ruled the charts. If he keeps with his old buyer and can't get me to consult, he could miss out on getting the next A-list celebrity bean at anywhere near an obtainable price.

And where do I stand if Roth decides *not* to offer me a buying job? Nowhere anyone likes to be stood. Financially, we are limping by right now. My unemployment checks don't even cover our mortgage payment, and we're galloping through our rainy-day savings at a terrifying speed. I'm still trawling the Net for buying jobs whenever I get a chance. And there's still next to nothing. If I could just start working for Bean à la Bean, everything would be back to status quo. Problems solved. Money in the bank, Peter back in the parental driving seat, and freedom would once more be mine.

CHAPTER 9

Violet's been talking about this for a week solid. I've been avoiding it for about two. However, today, in a brave attempt to try and get in touch with my inner parent, we are attending "Time for Twos" at the local library. Violet's actually three years old, but I'm sure no one's going to ask to see a birth certificate. Mind you, the Time for Twos' leader—Wendy, an ex-Yahoo employee turned career mother—is a little anal-retentive, so I wouldn't completely rule it out. Wendy, in fact, is the reason I've spent minimal time at the local library for about two years now. For there's no convert as zealous as a recent convert, and when I first made Wendy's acquaintance, she'd just quit Yahoo in order to stay home with her two kids. She looked at me that day with shining eyes and declared it the best and most fulfilling decision she'd ever made. I told her that she and her session-musician husband were headed for the poorhouse and pointed out that her son's diaper had just leaked and her arm was covered in solid-food poop. Since then I've attended Time for Twos twice, and both times she's studiously ignored me.

But today, Violet and I are the center of her dazzling attention. Word has got out that I'm staying home with the kids so Peter (a Time for Twos aficionado) can sell a screenplay. Word doesn't seem to have spread that I actually got fired, we might not make the mortgage next month, I'm scrambling to get a new job, and I'm meeting with an ex-boyfriend today for completely aboveboard reasons that somehow feel highly illicit.

Wendy starts to gently corral us into the "friendship circle," but Violet's having none of it and is off in the middle of the room, spinning round and round. I sit cross-legged in my designated spot, cautiously optimistic that at some point she'll give up and come sit on my lap like she's supposed to.

"Violet," I half call. She ignores me and grabs hold of a younger toddler, who's not that steady on her feet, and starts pulling her round too fast in a "Ring around the Rosy" frenzy. Oh God. Should I stop her? Is that being too helicopter-momish? Not sure what to do, as usual, I'm busy pretending I don't see any of it when Violet yanks too hard and the toddler takes a nose dive. Violet doesn't let go, and the little kid starts getting spun around on the side of her face. Fuck. I jump up, pretty certain that I'm supposed to intervene at this point. At the same time, massively pregnant Amber—who's been looking straight through me since I got here—lurches to her feet and slowly lumbers toward the situation.

"I'm so sorry," I gasp, not sure if I should pick her kid up off the floor before she gets there or leave her. Amber's always made me feel kind of nervous and I'm not sure why. Probably something to do with her being one of those moms who always know exactly the right thing to do, versus my being so constantly clueless.

"It's fine," she says, hauling her bewildered daughter to her feet. To her credit, she's not crying. Plucky little thing.

"Violet, can you say sorry to . . ." What's this kid's name again? It's something really random. Paucity? Chastity? Liberty? Variety? Piety? Sobriety? "Verity?"

"It's Rarity," says Amber. *Rarity.* That's it. I'd be so happy if she turned up at kindergarten on the first day and found another kid in her class with the same name.

"Such a big girl now! How old is she?" I ask. This is the kind of thing moms ask each other—right?

"She'll be sixteen months next week."

"Oh," I say, and start subtly pulling Violet out toward the edge of the circle. Months of age? If you're still marking the experience in months after their first birthday, you're taking it all too seriously. How can I be expected to find a kindred mom amongst these slim pickings? I give up.

"What happened to your glasses?" asks Lizzie, who's sat herself in my circle spot. Really, what is she doing here? Odessa's starting kindergarten next year, and she's so big she's sprawled across her mother's lap. Odessa's on a part-time schedule at preschool because Lizzie claims she can't bear to be parted from her a full five mornings a week. Can she really not think of anywhere more dynamic to take her daughter on her days off? Violet and I squeeze in next to them both. So—the glasses. The other lens popped out on the walk here and I'm one-eyed once more.

"The lens came out." Kind of obvious. But she asked.

"I mean, are they *old*?" she asks incredulously as if she can't imagine that a lens would ever spontaneously fall out of a pair of frames. In her world they probably never do.

"No. Not that old." Lies. I got these back in college.

"Maybe the sealant just got degraded with all the tropical travel you do. You know. In the heat."

"Hmm. Maybe." So now my career is to be blamed for my deficient glasses as well as my deficient children? I'd say if one of us looks the more bizarre right now, it's actually her. She's wearing a bright-blue pointy-shouldered jacket with gold buttons, as well as six-inch pin heels—to playgroup! I was under the impression that shoulder pads finished around the time they stopped shooting *Dynasty*. And with good reason. Point being: I don't mention her eighties wardrobe fetish, so likewise she should leave my faulty eyewear alone.

And then the singing starts. Surprisingly, this group of women can really carry a tune; however, none of that is of any comfort to Violet, who by the end of "The Wheels on the Bus" has reverted to limpet mode and is now clamped around the front of my body. It was something about the line "The doors on the bus go open and shut" that triggered it. Maybe there was a traumatic incident where she got slammed in some closing doors at some point and Peter forgot to tell me. Or I just forgot.

"Violet. You want to turn around and listen to the story?" asks Wendy. All eyes in the group fixate on my daughter. There's nonchalance, sympathy, and even a little envy from one mom whose son refuses to sit still for a second. Amber's still looking through us both as if we're made of water. Nothing out of the ordinary. Then I catch the eye of the woman sitting next to Amber in the circle. She looks straight at me for a microsecond. Whoa. The look's over so quickly that perhaps its message is just a figment of my paranoid imagination, but I think she might have just given me the stink eye.

"That's Jasmine." This is Annie, sitting to my left. She used to have a crazy traveling work schedule too. Divisional regional manager for some god-awful makeup brand. She gets it. But, of course, in the end she yielded to the pressure and quit her job. Her husband's an oncologist, so she got to choose. I suspect it didn't make her any less conflicted about her choice, though.

"Right," I say. Unsure whether Annie just saw that microsecond of disdain too. "How long's she been coming?"

"A while now. Don't worry about her. She's a bit on the intense side, but she's mostly nice. When Time for Twos nearly got bumped to make way for Elder Eagles, she fought the committee and got us reinstated. And when Erin first got diagnosed with leukemia, she organized us all to deliver meals to her doorstep. Jasmine's all right. She can just be a bit . . ."

"What?"

"Judgy."

"Judgy?"

"Yeah. Peter was complaining one time about you traveling so much for your job, and she got kind of worked up about the whole thing. She thinks it's super weird that you spend so much time away from your kids."

"Really," I say, catching Jasmine's eye and giving her my own microsecond of stink eye right on back. "And something tells me she's not obliged to work the nine-to-nine to single-handedly keep her family above the poverty line."

"Er. No. Her husband has his own business, and I think she comes from family money. So, no, she's never done the nine-to-nine, though she did once mention some volunteer work that allegedly took place in Borneo."

Well, no one likes to be judged on their life choices, we can all agree on that. Especially when you're not completely happy about the way it's all gone down. And, of course, it makes things extra icky when the person judging you has never actually been forced into that same corner and told to survive.

As Wendy continues to put us all through "Goldilocks and the Three Bears," I occasionally feel Jasmine's eyes flicking over Violet and me. It feels like she's doing a Concerned Parent Audit to assess whether all this time away from my kids makes me a bad mother when I'm actually home. Given the events of the last few weeks, she may actually be onto something, but even so—that's a hell of an assumption for her to make. I hug Violet closer and pretend I don't know that she's watching.

Story time eventually drags itself to a close, and everyone is relieved of the burden of trying to keep their kids interested in Wendy's feeble attempts at a variety of bear voices. The kids move on to "free play."

This seems to consist of them rifling through a bunch of musical toys and chiffon scarves that Wendy's dumped onto the floor from a hemp bag. On seeing the instruments, Violet releases her torso clamp, runs over to the pile, and happily starts going at it with a tambourine and a shaker. She's delighted. I make a mental note to stock up on a bevy of musical instruments to whip out and distract her with if I end up leaving to catch a plane again anytime soon.

Wendy seems to have procured coffee from somewhere. Eco-friendly disposable cups filled with black liquid that smells much like my emotional state these days: fatigued and borderline bitter. She places a cup in my hands. I feel obliged to accept it. I take a sip, just because it seems as if that's required. God. Awful. Wendy moves on and I allow my face to contort in disgust. I notice Jasmine next to me. She politely refuses the coffee—Wendy doesn't press the issue. Jasmine catches my eye again. This time it's conspiratorial. She crosses her eyes and mimes a minivomit. All the other mothers are gulping down the caffeine without complaint. If Jasmine gets coffee, then she can't be *all* bad. Maybe Peter gave her some warped view of my situation and that's why she was mouthing off about it.

I see Annie making for the bathroom, her son Harry under one arm, midtantrum. She sees me and makes her way back over.

"Before I forget." She places Harry down, still thrashing, and pincers him between her skinny legs. I'm impressed. She hands me a business card. "If you get fed up of the at-home thing, Sylvia's Angels are always looking for consultants. I think you'd be good!" She's got to be kidding. I don't think I've applied a mascara wand to my eyelashes since we arrived in the new century. She notices that I look less than convinced. "I'm serious! Everyone starts as a consultant, but if you make good sales, there's room to move up pretty quickly. You could have my old job in a few months! Lots of travel involved, as you know. But you're an old hand at that." I can physically feel a force field of disapproval emitting from Jasmine behind me. "Come on now. You don't need to look *that* scandalized," says Annie to Jasmine with a passive-aggressive smile. And then she lifts Harry up onto her hip and makes her exit.

So that was ultra awkward. I turn around to look at Jasmine. Her dark red curls get even darker and redder as her face turns alabaster. I can tell she is not used to Being Told. I suddenly sense that this is not going to end well for me. Half a second later Jasmine breaks out of it and gives me an ear-to-ear smile. My God. She's intimidatingly beautiful when she smiles.

"So, your husband told me you used to travel all over for work," says Jasmine. The smile seems like it's wedged in place with a coat hanger. This woman's expression is making my heart beat faster. I bet this is the same smile she gave to the librarians just before she kicked their butts over canceling Time for Twos. "That must have been fun for you."

"I don't know about 'fun' so much. Travel was a substantial part of my job."

"But how was it leaving your children behind?" She's looking at me as if I'd abandoned them to fend for themselves in war-torn Syria instead of leaving them at home with their father in a very comfortable LA suburb.

"It wasn't ideal. But I didn't really have a choice," I say, my tone hardening to a crisp.

"I could never . . ." She doesn't finish her sentence. She doesn't need to. It's all there, hanging in the air between us. She could never make whatever unfortunate and second-rate decisions I made that placed my family in such a precarious situation. She could never not be there to stroke her kids' heads till they dropped into their deepest sleep every night, and she could never miss out on their first kiss of the morning. She could never put her own ambition over being present for every new tooth and lost tooth, scabbed knee and birthday morning. She could never. She *would* never. But I did. Obviously.

There's such a nuclear bomb of emotion going off in my chest that at first I don't hear the screaming. And then I do. It's Violet. She's doing her high-pitched dramatic-wail thing. I run over. She's standing next to a boy who's also crying, though less dramatically. Jasmine rushes over and pulls the boy's cap off his head to reveal a healthy stream of blood flowing from his nose.

"What happened?" She gasps.

"Violet hit me with the tambourine." He seems to have calmed down instantaneously now that he has his mother's full attention. He wipes bright-red nose blood across his very expensive-looking T-shirt. This draws a gasp from the audience. I'm about to tell Violet to apologize and then swiftly remove us from the situation when Jasmine drops the accusation.

"Well, this is what happens," she says.

"What do you mean?" I ask softly. She could, for instance, mean "this is what happens when three-year-olds gather in a library alongside musical instruments" or "this is what happens when I leave the house on a Tuesday without a packet of Seventh Generation baby wipes handy." But I know that's not what she means at all. However, I want to hear her say the words. Out loud.

"Hmm?" she says. And then I see it. She's trying to backtrack! She knows what she really wants to say is totally un-PC. I've caught her on the hop. "Oh, I don't know. Sometimes kids get kind of antsy, you know."

"How so?" Let's hear it, then.

"I mean when one parent's a bit in and out of their lives. It just reminds me of some of the kids I volunteer with in Boyle Heights. When their dads are incarcerated, they can get sort of, you know—riled up."

I'm speechless for a moment.

"Are you comparing being a working mother to being a criminal?"

Jasmine laughs and turns the coat-hanger smile back on. "Oh no—not at all! I just mean that it's all the same to kids—whether you're in jail for two months or away on business—I'm just saying the effects are similar." I feel the entire group of women staring. Amber—who definitely seems able to see us now—included. None of them have the grace to look away or create a diversion. This is probably the most compelling drama they've witnessed at Time for Twos. And besides, what Jasmine's saying is validating every sacrifice they've ever made—validating their very day-to-day existence! God forbid they'd actually gone for that next rung up on the career ladder instead of jumping off the first chance they got—they might have ended up as vice president or CEO and become just as wretched a woman as I am.

I'm mad. I'm hurt. I feel the need to defend myself and every other working woman in the Western world. I see Annie return from the bathroom. Harry's recovered from his earlier meltdown. At least I know she's partially on my side.

"I don't think time away is just time away. My kids know I'm doing something worthwhile when I leave them. We talk about the people I've helped in Africa, the parents who otherwise might not have been able to send their kids to school or had enough for everyone to eat that year. My work's had a far-reaching impact on a lot of people. I don't know, I think we can all sometimes get so caught up in our own lives that we forget we all have the power to make positive changes for to the world around us."

"We" not meaning "me," of course. I give her my own coat-hanger smile. It is not returned.

"Well, I'd say I've definitely had a positive impact on some people. On a smaller scale, of course."

"Oh, of course," I say. And there I see it. The chink in her armor of self-confident righteousness. She's a little paranoid that she hasn't made big enough waves in the world because she never had a career. I realize this woman's as bitten up about her choices as I am. We're both mothers in the year 2016, two women confronted with nothing but impossible expectations and unsatisfying choices. Neither of us has taken the "correct" option. I've abandoned my children to spend the majority of their infancy overseas, playing the role of female Indiana Jones, and she's let the side down. She's embraced motherhood for all it is, because it's all she's got. It's all she's done. She didn't "achieve," which if you're living in the great plains of Wyoming is probably just fine, but here in LA she has on some level failed at least as much as I have.

We are two sides of the same objectified coin. Approaching exactly the same problem from two different vantage points. Under slightly tweaked circumstances we each could have made the other's choices. The choices we're attacking each other for right now. Realizing this, I should raise the white flag. Explain to her that we are just two star-crossed mothers. Make peace.

Do I?

I do not. Once my hackles have been raised, only the passage of time will lower them. Jasmine, meanwhile, has exposed the throbbing pulse of her vulnerability. I'm considering going in for the kill, perhaps asking her where she sees herself fifteen years from now. And then I hear it. And I can't imagine why I haven't put this together till now. Unlike Violet, who's clinging close, Jasmine's son is hanging off her arm without a care in the world. He's singing.

"Winkle winkle wittle star." The tone's instantly recognizable. Loud, high-pitched, with a certain grating quality . . . This is Roth Ellis's son. And Jasmine is Roth Ellis's wife.

"Actually, my husband and I own a coffee business, and we *do* do a lot of work with fair trade so . . ." She trails off. If this wasn't Roth Ellis's wife, I'd be giving her some pretty hard data on why equal trade in actual fact sucks, but I've spent the last week desperately hoping that her husband—who, incidentally, never mentioned that he "co-owns" his company with his wife—is going to be giving me a job pretty soon. Perhaps there's a way I can back out of this entanglement without her figuring out who I am and reporting the whole thing back to Roth.

"Wait," she says, tilting her head, "what did you say you did for a living again?"

As one of only three female green bean buyers in the entire United States, and certainly the only one with bright-blonde hair, I'm a pretty recognizable face in the coffee world. If she really does have any working knowledge of the coffee business, she should be putting two and two together any second now. I am screwed.

At my side Violet suddenly makes a deep upchucking sound and then deftly vomits all down herself. I silently thank God for the withdrawal method, without which this child would never have been conceived, and scoop her up, plastering myself in her puke. "Import, export. That kind of thing," I murmur. "Better run! See you guys next week," I say, and speed walk for the exit.

Like I'm going to return to that library ever again. Even if the zombie apocalypse was upon us and the library was the only fortified structure in town, I'd rather risk my entire family becoming zombie hamburgers than enter through those swinging doors ever again.

Time for Twos and I are done.

I've just about finished wiping the worst of the puke off Violet with an old baby onesie I found on the floor of my car when Annie comes out of the library.

"Oh my God, that was crazy!" she says. "I thought you were about to ask her how it feels to get to lie down instead of *Lean In*." I give a nervous bark of laughter. I'm still pretty keyed up by the whole thing.

One second later Jasmine walks past Annie, carrying Hendrix. She goes over to her car without acknowledging either one of us. Damn it! Did she hear us? Annie mouths, "Oh shit!" and ducks back inside. I make a big show of concentrating very hard on opening the car door and diligently buckling Violet into her seat. I pull my head out just as Jasmine drives past. I'm directly in her eyeline so I give her a quick wave, but she looks straight through me—Amber-style. It's like I'm not even standing there.

This is not good.

CHAPTER 10

I've just about enough time to get home and rinse us both clean from the remainder of the puke splattering before jumping back in the car, Peter's screenplay in the passenger seat, Violet buckled in the back. I'm supposed to be meeting Matt today at an impossibly hip restaurant in Silver Lake. I've got the feeling it's not exactly a family-friendly type of establishment, which is rather unfortunate seeing as I've got Violet in tow. She's asleep right now. Hopefully she'll stay napping and then I have a completely bona fide excuse not to come inside at all. We can do a quick round of niceties through the car window; I can hand over the script and get right out of there before any best-buried emotions are unhelpfully stirred up.

As I crawl around Silver Lake in stop-and-start traffic, I try not to obsess about the moment outside the library when I *think* Jasmine heard Annie and me laughing about her. She probably didn't actually hear the specifics—right? But then why didn't she return my wave when she was driving away? Should I try to track her down and make amends? Probably a bad idea. She still may not have realized who I am, and I don't want another flash of my fluorescent hair to trigger her memory. There's every chance she won't piece it together until after I've had my next meeting with Roth. And once he's tasted those magic beans, he's surely not going to let anything get between him and them. I wonder how deeply her co-ownership of the business goes. I don't recall hearing her name come up in connection with the company. Maybe she just feels like she co-owns the business by virtue of marriage?

Maybe I don't need to worry about any of this. Maybe Jasmine will find out about Roth and the nanny before my interview—they'll separate, only to communicate through their legal teams, and any supposed slights that happened at Time for Twos will just never come up. The best course of action in this situation is probably none at all. I pull up across the street from the fancy-pants restaurant and text Matt: *Parked opposite in blue Honda minivan. Little one sleeping in the car.* It's important to apply the same rules to this meeting with Matt: the best course of action is no action *at all.*

But even the mental declaration that Matt and I will not be having any action at all immediately takes my brain straight to where I don't want it to go. It is, of course, completely unfair to compare prekid sex with Matt to current-day postkid, nine-years-into-a-relationship sex with Peter. Or, should I say, nonsex. It's ironic that Violet—who herself was the result of a contraceptive faux pas—has actually become the most iron-clad form of contraception imaginable. Well, maybe that's not a technically perfect example of irony, but it's definitely somewhere on the irony spectrum. It's also very annoying. It's been weeks at least since Peter and I were alone long enough in the same room to even contemplate getting naked. And on the rare occasions that we do get time and space to ourselves, a nice nap and a snuggle seem so much more appealing. And don't blame it all on my denying Peter his husbandly dues and squashing his God-given manly sex drive—he's always the first to suggest we just snuggle instead.

Matt taps on the window, and the first thing that flashes through my mind is the sensation of my underwear pulling hard against my thighs as he ripped my panties off the last time we had sex. Actually tore them in two. To be fair, the pair in question was pretty old and also rather insubstantial. But even still . . . These are not helpful thoughts. Matt knocks on the window again. I lower it and unlock the door.

"Shh!" I hiss. "Violet's sleeping in the back." He opens the door and gets in the front seat. The awkwardness that should hang between two lovers who haven't spoken in almost a decade is nowhere to be seen. He pulls the screenplay out from underneath him.

"This it?" he asks, nonchalantly picking up Peter's brainchild.

"Yup," I answer.

"Have you read it?" he asks, leafing through.

"No, I haven't read it. I'm not allowed to in case I tell him it's a pile of old wank." He leans in and kisses me on the cheek. It lands a little too close to the lips to be as aboveboard as we're supposed to be being.

"A pile of old wank?"

"Not very good."

"You look beautiful."

"I don't. I look tired."

"Come inside. It's too hot in the car."

"I can't stop, Matt. I've got to go and pick Billy up from preschool."

"There's another one?"

"Yes. Two. You?"

"Two," he says. "And a wife that bores me solid."

"I'll pretend I didn't hear that."

Matt looks radically different than he did a decade ago. He used to be moderately cute in a tubby-round-the-middle, curly-haired kind of way. A bit like a grown-up cherub; the kind of unintimidating guy that girls are attracted to when they're not ovulating. He used to dress in a uniform of whatever jeans and a black T-shirt. We both did. I still do, more or less. Matt ten years on is a much, much hotter prospect. Disturbingly so, in fact. The tubby has completely melted away, and his hair's cropped so short I can't tell if it's curly or not. He's dressed in a pair of jeans that scream *money, money, money*, a short-sleeved checkered shirt, a light-gray tie, and Converse sneakers. It all looks rather expensive and very pulled together. I suddenly wonder if Kimberly's responsible for his wardrobe upgrade. Just as well he didn't stick with me or he'd probably still be dressed in Marshalls' finest. I hate to admit that all these external and superficial factors have an effect on how attractive I find him, but they do. He's no longer the guy you'd chat with in a bar because you were too intimidated to talk to his gorgeous model/actor friend (how we met). Somehow he's actually *metamorphosed into* the model/actor guy. Has this transition really come about solely through diet, exercise, and a new wardrobe? Is there perhaps a special Hollywood fairy that visits your house when you've had more than one box office hit and sprinkles magic glamour dust all over you, thus transforming you into Proper Hollywood? Whatever magic dust he's infused with now, he's glowing with it. I think it might be confidence. He's a different man from the one I knew. If this guy had asked me to leave that farm in Brazil in order to accompany him to premieres and oversee his macrobiotic diet regime, I probably would have got on the first plane out of Rio de Janeiro. No, that's not true. I'm not that shallow. At least, I wasn't ten years ago. It would probably be a good idea to wrap up this whole catch-up-in-the-car thing now before I discover how shallow I've actually become.

"I should get going," I say.

"So how have you been?" he asks, as if I hadn't just spoken at all. He's rubbing at his very neat goatee. He always used to rub his face when he got nervous. I'm kind of glad he's a little uncertain around me. I don't want him to think he has all the power in this situation just because he's gotten all coated in Hollywood glow.

"I'm good. Well, not that good. I just lost my job."

"Oh right. The fair trade stuff."

"Coffee buying, actually." Yup. This is why he and I don't work. He never listened with more than half an ear to what was important to me.

"That's it, the coffee. I heard something on NPR the other day about how the whole industry's going down the drain. Some kind of epidemic? So I guess you never found that rust-resistant bean you were always after?" Damn it. I guess he did listen a little bit then.

"Well, actually, I—"

"Amy, oh my God, it's so good to see you again," he says, running his hand firmly back and forth over the top of his head. For some reason I find that move disconcertingly sexy. So much cuter than the way he used to carefully tuck his curls back behind his ears for safekeeping. The air between us seems to get super still. I think he might be waiting for me to say that I'm happy to see him too. "I've always felt horrible about the way we ended things."

"The way *you* ended things," I say a little more hotly than I meant to. Okay, so I've probably still got a little bit of residual anger in there.

"I know. Twenty-eight-year-old me was a complete dick. I wasn't thinking straight about what was important. I want to apologize." Again the long, still pause. "Can you forgive me?"

"It was a long time ago, Matt. Don't worry about it."

"I want to make things right between us. It's important to me. You were important to me." He picks up Peter's screenplay again, flips it open to the first page, and gives me another quick, expectant look. He's not explicitly making the connection, but he *kind of* is: if you say you'll forgive me for my bizarre and unforgivable past behavior, I'll be more likely to look favorably on your husband's screenplay. Ew.

"I just wish we could have talked things over, that's all," I say. I also wish I could extract all the "huffy" from my tone. I obviously am more bothered about this than I thought.

"We can talk about it now, Amy."

"It's too late now. It's too long ago. None of it matters anymore."

"It matters to me. A lot."

"I've got to go; I'll be late to pick up Billy."

"So be late."

"I can't! If you show up late, they stick a sad-face sticker on his cubby. He's already gotten four sad faces since I've been home. If it gets to five, you need to have a meeting with Ms. Carmen and she's terrifying."

"Just say you forgive me. Even if you don't mean it."

"I forgive you." *And no, I don't mean it.*

"Do you ever think about how things could have worked out if we hadn't split up back then?" he asks. I ponder it from time to time. But there's no way I'm letting him know that.

"No. I moved on pretty quickly. Just like you did."

"Ah, yes." He rolls the screenplay into a telescope and looks down it at me. "The brilliant but litigious writer."

"And what about Kimberly? Is she brilliant?" I ask, knocking his telescope to the side.

"Brilliant? I wouldn't exactly call her that. You never did meet her, did you?" he asks with a secret smile.

"No."

"She's a sweet girl," he says. "She's what I thought I needed." Oh dear, this is getting way too close to the mark all around. So far we've uncovered that I'm clearly still emotional about getting dumped out of the blue, and he's confessing that his wife is perhaps not all that he thought she was. "I guess you're right. It's too late to ever make things completely okay between us," he continues.

Oh, man. Why does he have to get all chatty about this now? This would have been helpful nine years ago, but right now all this heart-to-heart stuff is just confusing. As he unhelpfully ruffles his hand over his cropped hair again, I'm suddenly hit with a welt of sadness over what I've missed out on. When Matt and I broke up, he said he needed someone to make him her full-time job. That sounded horrendous at the time, but after trekking around the world for years on end, and missing so much of my children's childhood that they're practically strangers to me, these days it sounds like a pretty sweet gig. I look Matt in the eyes for the first time since he got in the car and catch his gaze full on. It's transmitting pure regret at what could have been. For a moment I'm caught up in it too, imagining the life I could have had as his Hollywood wife—a life where everything came easily, where money was no issue, where I could spend as much time as I wanted or didn't want with my children. A life where I got to make choices. Sensing the shift, before I can move, Matt's lips are on mine. Just for a whisper of a second.

"Mommy!" I flash open my eyes to see Violet staring at me from her car seat—her face full of accusation.

"I want us to be friends again," says Matt. Friends? He just whisper-kissed me on the lips! Does he do that to everyone he picks up screenplays from?

"I'll call about the script, okay?" he says, getting out of the car and slamming the door behind him. I go to wipe away his barely there kiss. Even though he didn't make full-on contact, my lips seem to be buzzing from the near miss. I don't think Peter's ever given me buzzy lips.

As I merge back into traffic, I realize that it's a quarter to twelve. I'm supposed to make it all the way across town in fifteen minutes. It's not going to happen. Billy's going to get another frowny face. Right now, I'm wearing one too.

CHAPTER 11

I may finally have developed half a molecule of mommy instinct, because I'm making a pretty solid prediction right here and now that Billy's about to have a massive meltdown. Even though to any outsider he probably looks like a normal, if slightly flushed, preschooler enjoying a parade, I know the truth: this isn't going to end well for anyone who has the last name O'Hara.

It's hot. Hot even for Los Angeles in the fall and Billy's face is getting redder by the second. I can see him right at the back of the parade, shuffling forward slowly, waiting for his school's turn to do their routine. The grueling heat, the heavy energy of the crowd, the leaf costume, which I already know he considers to be highly scratchy, the boom and smash of the marching band, the two Cheerful Cheetahs squealing and pushing right next to him—how has he even made it this far? There's got to be two hundred people all jammed together in the space between me and my son. I'm not going to be able to get to him quickly. I make the choice and start moving anyhow. With any luck I'll get there just at the start of the breakdown. God knows what I'm actually going to do about calming him down.

I gently work my way through. Beer bellies, small and sweaty children, electric wheelchairs, bad dye jobs, flags waving everywhere I look. Billy's not the only one who hates crowds. At what point did I ever think that this would be a good idea? The sheet Billy brought home from school specifically said there would be "Fabulous Family Fun for Free," but it's pretty clear all that smug alliteration was just an ugly ploy to get us all to come out here. This isn't even our town that we're parading for. We're in Monrovia, ten miles east. All this fuss because they've been a town for a hundred and twenty-five years. When did this become something I needed to celebrate?

Blessedly, Violet doesn't seem to care at all. I've got her wrist gripped in my right hand, and I'm half dragging her behind me as I twist and squirm through the crowd. She's still singing a song about a clever fairy who loves brown cupcakes, which is my barometer for knowing that she's okay with all this pushing and knocking about. Not for the first time since I lost my job, I wish Peter were here to help me. He's still holed up at HushMush, writing. He hasn't stopped for one day since my trip was canceled. I was under the impression that after I handed off his screenplay to Matt he'd stop, at least for a moment. But no. Apparently, Peter has a backlog of ideas that he hasn't been able to get to over the past five years, and the writing fever is upon him. He said that if he stops even for one moment, the flow will evaporate and he'll hit another dry patch. He said he can't handle another dry patch. Well, I can't handle these children on my own anymore. Maybe he's actually got some secret agenda to get me up to speed by overexposing me to all of this so I can catch up to him in the parenting ranks. Wouldn't it just be easier for him to tell me all the information? Or write it all down?

Somehow I manage to fight my way through to the front of the crowd where I can see Billy again. I notice Regina's mother on the other side of the street. Regina is jostling against another girl in the formation, right next to Billy. They seem on the verge of a fight. A whistle whips through the crowd and I see Regina look straight toward her mother, who demonstrates a brief hand gesture. Regina stops immediately, stands dead still, and stares straight ahead. *What* is that woman's secret?

Billy's now got his hands over his ears and is shouting something, probably to try and block out the rest of the sound. I've got mere seconds here. I trot down the sidewalk, push through one last lump of humanity blocking a crosswalk, and then I'm directly across the street from him. We're all halfway up the street now and the Brighter Futures Preschool dance is about to begin. I get ready to dash across the front of the line, but suddenly there's a dry, heavy hand on my arm. I turn back around. It's Ms. Carmen. I feel completely chastised before she even says a word.

"No cutting across in front of the children, please. You'll be able to see just fine from this side of the street." This woman is consistently formal. I don't even know what her face looks like when she smiles. There ain't nothing progressive about that.

"I'm not cutting across to get a better view—I need to get to Billy."

"Why, what's the problem?"

"He's not doing well with all of this."

"This?" She actually tightens her grip. I'd have to wrench my arm out of her grasp to get away from her at this point.

"The crowd, the heat, the noise."

"Why don't you just wait and see what happens?" I look over to Billy. In addition to yelling with his hands clamped over his ears, he's also started stamping his feet rhythmically. Does she want to see him have a full-blown episode before she'll let me over there?

"I don't think that's a good idea," I say. I'm impressed with myself. This is the first time I've sort of stood up to Ms. Carmen. The few times we've met, she's always looked at me like I'm rather lacking the necessary qualifications to be a parent of an actual child. Up till now she's been mostly right about that.

"You have to let them fail sometimes," she says.

"Fail?"

"You can't always be there to catch them. Sometimes they have to fall so they can work out how to get up again. That's how they learn. Do you intend to follow him around his whole life bailing him out of uncomfortable situations before they arise?"

I'm not going to be busting into his apartment when he's thirty-five, asking him if he needs the air-conditioning turned up a couple of notches, if that's what she's asking. However, there's a difference between letting my kid get comfortable with being uncomfortable and leaving him to try to deactivate himself when he's a ticking time bomb of overstimulated five-year-old. Of course, I'm not brave enough to say any of this out loud, so she keeps on talking. "Billy needs opportunities to build up his tolerance for frustration. He's too sensitive."

"There's no shortage of opportunities for Billy to experience frustration. He's a five-year-old kid. He's pretty much frustrated all day long. This time around, I'm bailing him out." I turn away and start to twist my arm out of Ms. Carmen's hand. Just as she's about to give me a rope burn with the force of her grip, she remembers I'm not one of her preschoolers and lets go. Violet and I sprint across the front of the line of kids who are now just starting into their routine. Billy's not there. I'm too late. Where is he? Did he run off? Is he missing? My flaming-hot face flashes cold with terror . . . and then I see him. It doesn't look good. His teacher—whose name I've since found out and have now forgotten again—is crouched down in front of him, hands firmly on his shoulders. At least she doesn't have him in the straitjacket hold again. Violet and I make our way over.

"What happened?" I ask.

"Oh, hey! Billy was just taking a moment away from things. It all got a bit much."

"Yeah, I saw. We tried to get here faster, but we couldn't get through. Is he okay?"

"Almost," she says. "I should have taken him aside sooner."

I crouch down to Billy's level to look at him. His eyes seem weirdly glazed. His face is covered in sweat. Is this normal?

"Billy, are you okay, honey?" I ask. No response. "Can you hear me?" His teacher moves over to a cooler stashed against a wall and grabs a couple of ice cubes. She places one on Billy's wrist and one on the back of his neck. After a few seconds that seems to kick-start something and Billy sort of comes back.

"Mommy, I want to leave."

"We're leaving," I say. "What's going on?" I ask his teacher.

"Overstimulated. That's all," she says.

"I saw that he didn't look right from down the street. Ms. Carmen caught me on the way over. She said I should leave him to it so he could build up a 'tolerance for frustration.'"

"She doesn't know the right way to handle kids like Billy."

"Kids like Billy?" I ask. I want to know. Is there a sector of kids "like Billy"? Is Billy—as I'm starting to suspect—part of a tribe of children who aren't quite the same as all the others? His teacher gives a brief nod toward him. The nod says "he has ears and he can hear us." My mom used to forget all the time that I could hear what she was saying. I remember playing on the floor in plain sight of her, thinking, *I can hear you! I can hear you talking about Uncle Sam wanting Auntie Joanie to watch videos of other people doing it and her not wanting to and now they're going to have to get a divorce. Do you think I can't hear you?* And now I do the same thing all the time, presuming that because I'm talking to another adult, my kids suddenly don't understand a word I'm saying, when of course they're drinking in every single syllable.

"Did you read the book?"

"No."

"You should."

"Is that where you learned the ice-cube trick?"

"Among other things."

"Any other tips?"

"Always have a Band-Aid with you."

"Is that in the book?"

"No."

"What about hand gestures?"

"Like sign language?"

"I don't know. Regina's mom did this hand-gesture thing, and Regina calmed right down and immediately started behaving."

"That's the pinching sign," says Billy.

"The *pinching* sign?" says his teacher.

"When her mommy shows her the pinching sign, it means she'd better behave or she'll get pinched when she gets home."

"Does her mommy ever really pinch her?" I ask. Am I asking out of concern for Regina? Not entirely. I'm mostly hot on the trail of some evidence that there's a woman out there who's potentially a worse mother than I am.

"Yeah. Sometimes she shows me the black bits under her arm where her mommy did it." Black bits under her arm? This does not sound good. By the time they've reached five years of age, you can be pretty sure that your kids are going to start remembering all the messed-up stuff you do to them. What's Regina's mom playing at? If she still wants her kids to speak to her when they're in their twenties, any pinching punishments should have ceased way before her kids hit four. I'm sorry, Regina. Sometimes childhood really sucks. Sometimes the adults in charge understand the world even less than you do.

"I'd better get Billy home."

"Good idea. Get him out of this heat. And Mrs. O'Hara?"

"Yes?"

She's going to congratulate me on developing my mommy ESP skills, perhaps give me a verbal pat on the back for knowing my own parental mind and defying the wildebeest that is Ms. Carmen, or maybe give me a shout-out for *not* pinching the hell out of my kids when others have clearly been driven to it . . .

"Read the book."

CHAPTER 12

For coffee nerds, cupping beans is an unusual mix of science experiment and communion with the Almighty. Throw Roth Ellis and his clinical yet somehow incredibly stylish cupping lab into the mix and the whole thing also becomes the essence of hip. Today's cupping, however, is made measurably less hip by me leaning up against the stainless steel countertops—probably the only person ever to have entered this room wearing jeans purchased at Target.

Still, Roth seems to be willing to look past all that today. And Violet's spending the day with her dad for once, so at least he's seeing me out of mom mode. I've just ground the beans and so far he likes what he smells, very much so. He's got his flowing locks tied up in a silly little topknot right at the peak of his head. Seemingly to keep his mane from falling into the coffee when he plunges in for his first sniff. I'm sure he does enough cuppings a week that he'd be better off cutting it short. But I suppose if a man's particular enough about his hair to dye it, he's particular enough to go to the extra bother of tying it back umpteen times a week. Point being, in this moment, style is not the uppermost concern on everyone's minds.

I've brought my own equipment with me. This is not the time to be fiddling around trying to figure out how to convert someone else's scales back to grams. This process needs to be seamless. I've measured exactly twenty-three grams of ground coffee into three glass cups, which I've spaced out at even intervals on the counter. Roth works his way along, giving the grounds in all three cups a series of hearty and wholesome sniffs. When the thermometer on my kettle hits two hundred and eight degrees, I remove it from the flame and rush it over to the counter, where I reverently wet the grounds in my three cups. Everyone has their set of tics and habits when performing a cupping, and I'm as particular as the rest. I start a timer the moment the water hits the first cup and watch as the coffee granules bloom upward. Roth immediately dives in for another firm sniff of all three. I've never cupped for him before, but even still, we're like two courtiers performing a well-known dance, instantly familiar with each other's movements. After precisely three and a half minutes, I give him the signal, and he deftly breaks the crust of grounds on all three cups and takes yet another deep sniff. I dive in and spoon away the remaining grounds from the cups, and this is the moment when Roth takes a spoonful of liquid to his mouth for an especially aggressive slurp.

It catches him by surprise. I can see his initial reaction as the upfront lemon zest quickly pulls back to reveal the velvety soft texture underneath. And then I watch his eyes widen at the surprise of the caramel buttery essence following just behind it. He tries to hide his expression, but it's too late. He knows it. I know it. He's just felt the light of angels. He's just had a sensory experience that can only have come from the divine. Roth's already red-rimmed eyes turn a little bit redder. If I weren't in the room, he'd probably go ahead and cry.

"Shall we talk?" I say. He carefully nods. I am about to broker the deal of the century. I can feel it. I'll be back in Ethiopia before you can say "twenty-two-hour flight." The status quo I've been struggling to get back to is about to be restored. I'm going to be able to sidestep any future confrontations with Matt, escape the realization that I'm not cut out to be a parent, and we'll be able to pay the mortgage next month after all. I'm not going to lose my home. Did I mention that I love my house with all my heart? It's just a modest three-bedroom Craftsman cottage, but it would just about cut me in two if I lost it.

When I'm away and it's the kids' bedtime, I can close my eyes and re-create every detail of their rooms. I can visualize the way the light of the streetlamp breaks through the blinds and falls across Violet's bed, making soft lines on her Strawberry Shortcake bedspread. I know the way Billy will listen to the old groaning pipes from Peter's "the kids are finally in bed" shower and it will comfort him to sleep. The hazy view of "my" mountains from the living room window, the way the jasmine smells at the start of spring, and the smoky scent of the inevitable forest fires before summer drags to a close. The house is the one thing I can look at, even though it's just a physical structure, and say, "Yes. Behold. It's all been worth it. I have *achieved*." It's home.

"Hey, you," says Roth, quickly looking up at someone who's just come in behind me. He sounds guilty. What's going on? I swing around to see who it is.

It's my flame-haired nemesis, Jasmine.

"What are you doing here?" he says, sounding more nervous by the second.

"Just popping by. You know. As I do," she says. The way she says it makes it pretty clear to me that she actually *doesn't*. "Amy," she says. "What a surprise to see you again. Why are you here? What's all this?" she says, looking pointedly at the tasting cups.

"Amy's a friend of mine; she was in the area so she just came in to say hi," he tells her. "She had some interesting Ethiopian beans with her, so we did a quick cupping." *Why is he lying?*

"I didn't know you worked in coffee, Amy," says Jasmine. The coat hanger is firmly back in position. "I thought you worked in imports and exports?"

"Imports of coffee, I suppose you could call it. I'm a buyer," I say, and I watch her face freeze as it all clicks into place.

"Why don't you taste it, Jaz?" says Roth a bit too quickly. Honestly, the guy is freaking out. It's like she walked in on us making out or something. "Amy, did you bring enough to do another tasting?"

"Sure."

Turns out Jasmine's not as familiar with the ceremony as Roth is. She skips the scent test, and it's Roth who ends up pulling the grounds away from one of the cups for her so she can have a taste.

"Hmm. It's nice," she says. She's having about ten percent of the reaction Roth had. "I wouldn't say it's any better than our Kurimi, though." Roth looks at her like she just said one plus one equals six.

"Did you taste the caramel at the end?" he asks.

"Not really," she says. He takes a quick sip to confirm it's still there. Sometimes beans can be pretty inconsistent. *It's still there.* "My beautiful wife doesn't have the most developed palate ever. There's a large spectrum of coffee that all falls under the label of 'nice' for her," says Roth by way of explanation. I'm surprised he said that. So is Jasmine by the look on her face.

"Are you sourcing right now, Amy?" she asks.

"No. As I told your husband, I'm looking to buy for one company." Jasmine looks confused by my answer.

"I'm not sure we can help you out in that case. We already have a buyer." She catches Roth looking at her, half intense alpha male, half pleading puppy. "What?"

"This could be a great bean for us, Jazzy."

"I'm sure it's not so great that we'd consider ditching Darren so we can get hold of it. Why would we take a risk on a buyer we don't know anything about? No offense, Amy."

"None taken." Plenty taken. If she doesn't know about me, she should. I'm like the Nicole Kidman of the coffee world. Okay, maybe more like the Naomi Watts—but still. It doesn't mean she has to employ me, but if she co-owns a coffee roastery, she should at least know of me.

"Darren's been with us from the start." She's beginning to heat up a bit.

"I know that. Why don't we talk about it later?"

"There's nothing to talk about. She's not sourcing, and we're not getting rid of Darren for a bean that doesn't taste any better than anything we've already got."

"But it *does* taste better," says Roth, imploringly.

"Not to normal people."

"It's rust resistant," I say.

Jasmine's large, mouth jumps into a tiny O, all thoughts of employee-employer loyalty tossed firmly out the window.

"How do you know?" she asks.

I tell her about Getu's farm, how the rust epidemic wiped out everything he had except for the Yayu.

"So you only have his say-so."

"I've been working with Getu for a long time. We're pretty straight with each other and he knows his stuff. There's a lab nearby where I can do some further testing, but I trust Getu completely. If he says this varietal's clean, it's clean."

"Is it resistant to *all* strains?" she asks.

"There's no possible way to know that without studying samples. As I said, there's a lab nearby so—"

"So basically you're asking us to fund your research trip."

"I—"

"Where exactly is he located?"

"I . . . can't tell you that." That's like asking someone to give you their ATM PIN. There's no way I'd ever reveal that information to her. It's completely awkward of her to even ask me.

"Can you at least tell me the size of the farm we're talking about?"

"It's midscale. About five hectares." That's pretty tiny for a farm in most places, but actually on the slightly larger size for the region.

"Five hectares? Amy, one tiny farm isn't going to prop up our entire business." She says it almost with relief. "We don't have the capital to make a long-scale investment like that."

"And what if Darren leaves, Jasmine? Then we've passed this up for nothing."

"Darren isn't going anywhere," she says pretty decisively. Roth and I both immediately go to the same place, wondering *how* she knows that Darren isn't going anywhere. Perhaps she's actually closer to Darren than Roth might be comfortable with.

"My wife's a little more sentimental than I am," says Roth with a smile that's never going to bridge the chasm of awkwardness here.

"I'm certainly not sentimental when it comes to money. The benefits of this don't outweigh the risks for a business our size. We're going to have to shift to using more Robusta until prices start evening out again. We've talked *and talked* about this, Roth. That's what everyone's doing right now, and if we want to survive, we'll do the same."

Roth's disgusted. And he's disgusted with her for even saying it out loud.

"You could run it alongside your other coffee as a single-origin artisan item," I offer.

"I'm sorry, Amy. It's just too difficult in the current climate. I'm sure you'll find someone else who'll be very interested," says Jasmine.

"We'll discuss it and let you know," says Roth.

I won't hold my breath.

"Thanks so much for meeting with me anyhow," I say, quickly packing my stuff. I just want to get away from here. The tension between Roth and Jasmine is toxic. Roth mournfully watches as I put my magic beans back in my burlap satchel. Under normal circumstances, I'd leave the whole bag with him. After his wife's hijacking, that's not happening.

"We'll be in touch!" says Roth optimistically as I walk out the door.

"Great. Can't wait!" I reply in an equally upbeat tone. This is tragic. The door doesn't swing closed all the way, and before I can walk back down the corridor, I hear them start yelling at each other.

"Are you crazy?" asks Roth.

"Are *you* crazy? What on earth do you think you're doing interviewing a new buyer behind my back?"

"I don't know—trying to radically improve our product?"

"We don't need to radically improve our product; we need to stay above water. It's not enough just to break even anymore. We do actually have to start making money at some point, you know."

"How can you *not* taste how special those beans are? Do you even like coffee at all?"

"Of course I like coffee. That's an ugly thing to say."

"I just don't get it. You don't show a flicker of interest in anything going on here for weeks on end, and then you saunter in like you own the place—"

"I *do* own the place," hisses Jasmine.

A woman wearing an apron and a headscarf suddenly turns the corner.

"Can I help you with anything?" she says, a little too loudly for me to be sure that Roth and Jasmine didn't hear.

"Nope, I'm good," I say, mentally scavenging around for some reason why I'm standing in the middle of this corridor listening to someone else's highly private conversation. "My shirt got caught on the door, but I pulled it free so . . ." We both look at the smooth metallic swing door for a moment. "I'm going to go now."

"Okay."

I haven't even made it back to my car before I get the call.

"You do realize this is a seriously amazing opportunity you're passing up. This could be the next Geisha—and you know it," I tell Roth. There's really no reason for me to rub salt into his wounds; however, I can't quite help myself.

"Believe me, I'm not happy about it. It kills me to say it, but why don't you take this over to Urban Monocle?"

"Yeah, I'll probably try that," I say. But I have tried Urban Monocle, and several other roasteries, and it hasn't worked. Third-wave coffee roasters seem to be going through some kind of financial implosion right now. The Arabica bean shortage has tipped their precarious business model right over the side of the cliff, and whereas before owners would have been throwing all the money they could find at me, these days I haven't been able to get face-to-face with anyone but Roth. The third wavers are simply running out of capital.

"Let me know how you get on with it. I'd be interested to know. I wish things were different on my end, but Jasmine and I are on rough financial ground right now."

"But think about it, Roth. This bean is good enough. It could carry your whole enterprise."

"It couldn't, not until there's more of it. Jasmine doesn't want to take the risk. Her dad's been propping us up forever, and he's been getting antsy about it since the downturn. We have to tread carefully. Your timing sucks, O'Hara."

"I know."

"I'll keep working on her, but I doubt I'll get anywhere—we're moving away from quality right now, not toward it. Just like everyone else."

"How do you sleep at night?" I'm only half joking.

"I often don't." He's completely serious.

"Well, you have my number if you want to reconsider," I say.

"It won't be anytime soon," he says. "It's off the table for now. Good-bye, Amy."

"Bye."

Good-bye, Roth Ellis—and good-bye, financial security. Hello, potential destitution.

CHAPTER 13

And so it's come to this. I'm here in this auditorium surrounded by all my worst fears. And all because of the promise of money. I glance from side to side, trying not to move my head too much and attract attention. If the apocalypse happened while we were all sequestered away in this seminar and the world had to repopulate itself from this group of women and the parking attendants outside, the human race would not last very long. The gene pool would get all gunked up with an irrational love of "crimson blaze" highlights and the need to "get right" with baby Jesus, and before too long the human race would come to an end simply because its IQ was too low to continue.

Religion, makeup, sales: all things that make my whole body shudder like I've been chewing on bone-dry cotton wool. And I'm sitting right in the center of a reptile's pit of it, with no obvious means of escape. If I could only somehow creep out of here without bringing any attention to myself . . .

So I realized this setup was not for me the moment Sylvia made her entrance. Rising up from out of the stage, clouded in a puff of dry ice, she benevolently looked down on us all from up on high, backlit by nothing but a pink crucifix.

"My angels," she said. "Welcome." It all seemed a bit calvaryesque to me. Who does she think she is, Russell Brand? As Sylvia started talking about the divine mission of us, her "angels," I glanced around to see if anyone else was wearing the same quizzical expression that I was. Not the case. They were all lapping it up like a group of stray cats given their first taste of pink-tinged cream.

"Welcome to your future," said Sylvia. "Welcome to a world where every woman can be beautiful. Where beauty can be every woman. Where woman and woman work together to build a better world. A beautiful world. A world for all women."

And on it went. Before long the woman next to me, wearing very shiny panty hose and a blue skirt suit at least one size too small, sang out "Amen!" in agreement. And, well, I couldn't help it. I snorted. And . . . it was probably a little loud. I tried to snuffle it back down, turning around my head in derision, offering up a gesture that hopefully relayed: "What fallen woman made that noise? Is there a *Democrat* in here somewhere?"

But it was too late. Sylvia had seen me.

Of course, this was all Annie's idea. After Jasmine ruined my deal of the century with Roth Ellis, I called Annie up in desperation, remembering her vague offer of her old sales job when I last saw her at Time for Twos. We were one minute away from not making the mortgage. The listing for the buyer's job with Stumptown had been taken down. Driven by the need to feed and house my children, I applied for the job at the Penny Bean, but didn't hear a whisper back. The more Annie talked about Sylvia's Angels, the worse it sounded, but it did seem like I might be able to make some decent money fairly quickly. She was talking about thousands of dollars a month, and this was not a "maybe" or a "could be"—Annie had the second home in Big Bear to prove it. "The house that Sylvia's Angels bought" she called it. She had made it sound like the money was already there, just waiting to sashay its way over into my checking account. All I had to do was attend a training seminar, purchase some inventory, hit my "territory" hard, and all would be fine. In order to quickly earn the kind of money I needed, Annie said I was probably headed for either sales or a stripper pole. And as I'd likely have to *pay* people to look at my gangly body rather than the reverse, I took her suggestion and opted for sales. Thinking on it now, though, we might actually have some luck with Peter working as a Chippendales dancer . . . Okay, that's never going to happen, but it's an idea to keep in the back pocket in case things get truly bad. The man has to start paying his way at some point.

And now I've been rooted out: identified as a nonbeliever. I don't believe that JC died to save us all from our sins, I don't believe that blue-tinted mascara is ever the answer, and suddenly I don't believe that Annie bought that second home in Big Bear by selling makeup. The entire seminar has drawn to a halt. Unable to avoid the inevitable any longer, I look up. Sylvia locks me in her pale-green stare (she apparently does believe in the virtue of tinted mascara) and I feel it: she has the heart of a snake.

"Come on up, honey," she says. There's no getting out of it. She's talking directly to me. I'm honest to God as scared as the time our guide accidentally took us through the middle of drug-dealer turf in the coffee hills of Huila and I came face-to-face with Victor Toro, the local drug lord, who promptly shoved an AK-47 in my face. He had snake-green eyes too. The longer I pause, the longer I draw the room's scrutiny. My face is numb with humiliation. My chest seems to have turned to iron, and I don't seem to be breathing. I have less than two seconds to make my choice. I can either bolt for the doors and hope to God they aren't tricky to open or I can pretend I'm in the game as much as anyone else, get through this temporary embarrassment, and leave this whole operation as soon as I can make a graceful exit.

I decide to opt for the temporary embarrassment.

I rise and make my way up to the stage to a backdrop of applause. I'm immediately bathed in pink light. In the outstretched gloom of the auditorium I see rows upon rows of women sitting in a crop-circle formation, all waiting for Sylvia to make their financial dreams come true.

"What's your name, sweetheart?"

"Amy." *And I'm not your sweetheart.*

"And what brings you here today, Amy?" *A moment of appalling lack of judgment.* I realize I can either tell it to her straight and try to defend my position on the resurrection and tinted mascara in front of a room full of believers . . . or I can play along.

"I'd like to make some money," I say.

"I'm sorry, I didn't hear that, sweetheart. You'll have to say it a little louder."

Of course she heard it, the silly cow. This is the actual most cringe-worthy incident of my life. Even worse than the time I was wearing khaki pants to Billy's winter concert, and Violet peed on my lap and it looked like I'd wet myself. Violet herself was wearing black leggings so no one ever suspected the real culprit.

"I said I'd like to make some money." I say it right into her microphone, along with a tight smile and folded arms. I know she wants me to add some enthusiasm to this statement, but I'm not sure I can. Even in the name of not being embarrassed. In fact, I think I've almost reached my limit. Much more of this and I'll just take my chances with the fire escape. Sylvia smiles her teeth-whitened, lipstick-framed smile and beckons a group of women over from the wings of the stage.

"Well, we need to make you look pretty first, don't we?" she sings. And I realize this is all part of the act. Part of the show. Pluck some innocent woman from the audience, the less groomed the better, and overhaul her in the name of beauty. Show off the "wonder products" for the tools of miracle that they are.

I'm placed on a sticky folding chair, draped in a white sheet, and two women armed with big fat makeup brushes have at it.

* * *

An hour and a half later, I know more about the application of mineral eye shadow and emulsion-based, matte-down, shimmer-up products than any green bean coffee buyer has since the beginning of makeup, or coffee. Whichever came first. It all sounds very similar to painting a room. They even have a primer that they gloss over my face before they start troweling on the other stuff. I can't even begin to imagine what I look like. The closest I have to a makeup kit at home is one blunt eyeliner and an expired nude lip gloss. And those are ancient castoffs from my mother. I don't wear makeup. There's no point in the tropics, and I certainly don't have time at home. I'm sure this whole process must take at least fifteen minutes, even if you pare it right down. Who has the time? I will say that having my face massaged with products and my skin stroked with a variety of soft brushes is quite relaxing. Maybe on the other side of all this awfulness, when life gets back to normal, I'll treat myself to some facials. That's what Goddess Amy would do anyway. Real-Life Amy will probably just panic about how on earth to pay off all the credit card debt that's racked up in the meantime and cook up schemes to persuade her husband to try out for the Chippendales.

"Amy?" Ole Snake Eyes is calling me back. "Do you want to see how you look?"

"Sure." I yawn. I start to do a mental calculation of exactly how long it will take for all these chemicals to find their way into my bloodstream. I hope I'm not going to have some kind of toxic-overload reaction. The white drape is pulled away. I'm allowed to separate myself from the sticky chair, and a full-length mirror is brought forth. I feel as if some kind of emotional reaction is going to be expected. She's picked the wrong girl for that, I'm afraid. There's a TV camera up close to my face, and I realize the whole incident is being broadcast on a huge screen behind me. *Awesome.*

I look in the mirror.

I've disappeared. And in my place is a woman who's wearing my old clothes, but she's . . . well . . . pretty. No, beautiful. My bright-blonde hair is no longer the most striking thing about me. I've got a face underneath it that bears noticing for the first time ever. I've got succulent, plump lips. I had no idea it was possible for me to have lips like that without surgical intervention. My eyes are sparkling, my cheekbones are haughtily curved, and my nose—which was always my face's most strident feature—has taken its rightful place in the background. I look like Violet's mother. I'm no longer the ugly impostor in my own family. What happened? I can see that my eyes—which are now huge and, yes, framed with green-tinted mascara—are filling up a little with tears. I find myself doing that very girly shaky-hand motion in front of my nose—the one that's supposed to stop you from crying, or supposed to express that you *want* to stop crying. This is a nightmare. What have they done with the Amy who single-handedly took on the corrupt CafeGro cooperative regime and got them to give the money back to all the coffee farmers they'd weaseled it away from? Where's the Amy who chased an escapee spare tire down the side of a ravine, pulled it out of a muddy riverbed, hauled it back up to the pothole-ridden road, and then successfully affixed it to a four-thousand-pound Jeep?

The audience is going crazy. From the corner of my blurry vision I can see Sylvia taking a bow and smiling like she's just fed the fucking five thousand. This is not how it was supposed to play out. One of the beauticians brings forth a crown and sash and reverently places them on my body. The sash reads "Sylvia saved me 2016." My mortification is complete.

Or so I think.

"See now, isn't it great to look pretty, Amy? Don't you feel good about yourself?" says Sylvia with a sigh. Oh, here it comes. I think I'm about to get the hard sell.

"I guess I'm just surprised that I look so different," I say.

"Surprised. Is that all it is?" She doesn't let me reply. "Wouldn't you like to look like this every day? Don't you think you deserve to look like this every day?" She's got a point. I'm sure Goddess Amy would barricade the bathroom door every morning and put in the requisite fifteen minutes in order to emerge looking like the deity she actually is. But still. It's not me. These colored powders and triple-performing emulsions are not who I am. And again, like she can read the inside of my brain, Sylvia sees she's losing me. "Let me ask you this, Amy. Have you achieved balance in your life?"

"Balance?" I snort. "What's that?"

"It's being able to hold on to one thing without letting go of the other." She's talking about having it all. About making enough money to survive and still being able to read my kids a bedtime story every night. She sees my infinitesimal reaction and pounces like a feral feline. "My Angels come from all walks of life. Corporations, schools, hospitals. They come because I can offer the thing they most crave, the thing that so few employers realize all women want: balance. A way to earn a living and still spend time with your children. To stop missing the moments that matter and start becoming a mother that matters. Because all too soon, Amy, playtime will be over and your children will have grown and gone." *Oh God.* I'm starting to do that hand-shaky thing again. "I think we have our first Angel of the day!" she says.

Wait—what? My waterworks quickly dry up as a clipboard with some kind of legal-looking form is handed to me.

"What's this?" I ask.

"It's your new beginning. It's your new you. It's your time to shine, Amy, and your time to sign."

"My time to what?"

"Sign! Sign! Sign! Sign!" Sylvia starts up a chant and beckons for the audience to join her. They do, and in a matter of seconds I've got an auditorium full of Walmart shoppers screeching at me to sign a document that I'm suddenly certain is going to commit me to investing irreclaimable dollars and days to the benefit of this cosmetic behemoth.

I find a cold silver-plated pen placed in my hand. I notice it's embellished with a pink bejeweled crucifix. The crowd has reached a frenzy point. If I don't sign now, there's every chance the chant might change to "Crucify her." I am the woman who went head-to-head with SEED's entire board to get them to raise their social premium from ten cents per pound of coffee to fifteen and won! And here I am, cowed into signing my life away by a crowd of women in shiny panty hose.

And do I sign? Well, as they say, there's no pressure like peer pressure. And with a few strokes of a mascara brush, it seems that Sylvia's Angels have just become my peers.

And so I do. I sign. And the crowd roars.

CHAPTER 14

"Not to worry, my snippet, because I have a magnificent announcement," says my husband.

Snippet is what Peter used to call me, back before life got twisted up into a paper ball of complexities. He must be feeling happy. Maybe taking a break from writing and spending the morning with Violet did the trick. Or maybe the smear of makeup over my face has induced these fond feelings toward me. His ancient great-grandmother had once called me a "snip of a girl." We *think* she meant a "slip of a girl," but "snip" seemed much more accurate and I became Peter's snippet. That was almost a decade ago. Somehow seems longer. Actually, it counts as about half a century when you factor in parenting years. Parenting years, of course, being like dog years: you just age faster.

"Well, what is it?"

I've just given Peter the bare-bones outline of this morning's Sylvia's Angels debacle. Turns out what I signed up for was the purchase of six hundred dollars' worth of inventory, with just under two months to shift it. Any stock not sold after the two-month deadline is, of course, unreturnable. I already tried to return it, of course, but it also turns out I'll only get fifty percent of my money back if I return it within the first eight weeks. So I've got to try and sell at least some of this stuff. A couple of months ago, six hundred dollars down the drain would have been a mere annoyance. Right now, it's a major catastrophe. It's my old party trick: by trying to incrementally improve the situation, I've actually managed to make it much worse. I'm really hoping that Peter's magnificent announcement is that he's found a fabulous job doing something that's going to pay the bills—even a job at Trader Joe's at this point would be wonderful.

"I have an idea for *another* screenplay." He pauses, waiting for my jubilant reaction. It's not forthcoming. "And I've already started it! It's just pouring forth, Amy! I'm just so excited about this chance with Colburn Entertainment that everything's flooding out like someone turned on the faucet." *Husband, darling, I'm about to turn the water off at the source.* The truth is, Peter's never going to get another screenplay out to the wider world. His old contacts are blown, and I doubt Matt's going to do a thing for him. I'm sure he only met up with me the other day out of curiosity. Peter's got no way back in. If he's ever going to sell a screenplay, he's going to have to start all over again at the very bottom, alongside all the twenty-two-year-olds who just moved here from Denver. But he doesn't know that yet, because he doesn't know the Matt thing is going nowhere.

"Amy, what's wrong?" asks Peter.

Do I tell him? How much do I tell him?

"What's wrong is that we need money now."

"What about the makeup?"

"Not going to work."

"Why not? You seemed so sure after you talked to Annie about it."

"I buy coffee. I don't sell stuff. Especially not makeup to middle-aged women. Why do I always have to be the one doing ridiculous things in order for us to survive?"

"No one asked you to."

"No one formally asked me to pay the electric bill this month either, but it was kind of expected that it would happen." And we're back to this old argument again. The one where I want him to be the man in the relationship so I don't have to be. Because I will tell you this: being the man sucks. Perhaps it's more fun if you have an actual penis.

"Peter, we're broke. We can't pay the mortgage. We're living off credit cards. One of us needs to get a job. I'm trying. But you have to try too."

"The money's coming. I can feel it. Just hang on for a few more weeks."

When is this man going to wake up? What will it take for him to realize how screwed we are? He's got the financial astuteness of a nineteen-fifties housewife. Is he expecting me to pat his hand and say, "Now you run along, dear, and don't you fret that fine-lookin' head about this whole money thing. I've got it all figured out," before retreating into my study to sip whiskey and pore over our bond investments? Not happening.

"Peter." I pause. How do I convince him that it's time to put this dream away and get a job? I'm going to have to go in for the hard hit and take him out at his ultimate weak spot: his ego. "Listen. I read the screenplay." I did read it secretly a few days ago. I wanted to see if it's really as wonderful as he thought it was. Admittedly, it's pretty good. By the end of it I was crying my heart out. Peter caught me sobbing over his laptop, and I had to say it was because my favorite character had just been killed off in the season-three finale of *Downton Abbey* . . . And he *believed* me. Does this man even *know* me?

"Oh. I see." He's annoyed. As I've mentioned, Peter doesn't like people reading his work in case they tell him it's a lump of twat, which I'm about to do.

"Peter. It wasn't very good." Damn it. That didn't sound convincing at all.

"You're lying to me."

"Sorry to say it, Peter, but I'm not."

"You are. I can always tell when you're lying."

"Peter, honestly, I'm not lying. It's just not very good."

"I know you weren't crying the other night because some dude got cut from a show you don't even like. You were crying because the Loyalists shot Ronan for trying to save Cara's father, and now they'll never get to elope and start up their Castlegregory bed-and-breakfast paradise. You were crying because you knew he was screwed either way. If he hadn't saved her father, she'd never have forgiven him. So he saved him, even knowing they'd kill him too for being a traitor, because he'd rather die than lose her love. *Oh, why can't people just get along?* you thought to yourself as you wiped your eyes with my last desk Kleenex. It's Ireland's answer to *Romeo and Juliet* and you know it." *Damn it.* "The money's coming. And when it comes, there's going to be tons of it. Hollywood money."

"Okay, so I lied. I *was* crying because Ronan would rather die than lose Cara's love, but Peter, no matter how heartrending its plot twists are, *Draker's Dark* isn't going to pay for us to eat this month. You *have* to get a job."

"Doing what? I'm not qualified to do anything else. What would you have me do, flip burgers?"

"Yes!"

"I don't flip burgers. I write."

"You don't have to do one or the other completely exclusively."

"Amy. It's never going to happen." I suddenly realize that even if I threw myself down at his feet at this point and screamed, "We are all going to be living in the gutter!" he'd just step over me so he could get to his laptop and keep on typing. I suddenly know that Peter's never going to make so much as a gesture toward trying to be gainfully employed. That's it. It's all on me. I may as well have married a painter for all the financial contribution I'm going to get out of this man. At least we'd have had something pretty to hang on the walls all these years.

"So it's just my responsibility, is it? I'm the one who's always got to keep us from starving, 'cause you're just too magnificent a scribe to care about crap like that?" At this stage of the argument Peter would normally be gearing up. He hates being accused of not pulling his financial weight. Probably because it's so thoroughly true. But today he's oddly mellow. I can't imagine the level of mental implosion that's going to happen when he gets the word that Matt isn't going to buy his screenplay.

"Of course I care about things like that. But we've got money for another few weeks, right?"

"It's not our money. It belongs to JPMorgan Chase's credit card services. And they are charging us plenty for the privilege of borrowing it." The doorbell rings. Maybe that's Mr. J. P. Morgan himself, risen from the grave purely to tell us he's seen the lay of the land and he's changed his mind.

"Let them charge away. I have a good feeling about our situation, Amy. It's all changing for us. I don't want you to worry a minute more about it. I have it handled." Great. I wanted him to be the man and here he is, acting all manly and telling me not to worry my pretty little head about our dire circumstances, but somehow my head is not reassured. He turns to leave.

"Where are you going?" I ask.

"The garage."

"How long?" Now that we can no longer afford even HushMush, Peter has placed a chair and desk in the garage and spends as much as twenty-four hours at a time pecking away on his keyboard out there. I'm not even sure when he uses the bathroom. Maybe he saves it all up for when he knows the rest of us are sleeping. Maybe he's got some kind of bucket system in there. I'm too scared to go in and look.

"Don't know," he replies and wanders out the back door.

My skin is starting to feel a bit tight underneath this makeup. It feels oddly heated, like it's got a smoldering energy force layered on top of it. I haven't got any prior experience to compare it to, but I have a feeling that this is not normal. I hear Violet open the front door.

"Have you come to kiss my mommy again?" she asks.

"Certainly! If she's available," says Matt.

"My mommy's too old to be kissing boys like you." Old? She thinks I'm *old* and that Matt's a *boy* in comparison?

"Mommy's not old; she's middle-aged," says Billy, who's come to join his sister at the door. Somehow "middle-aged" hits even harder than "old." Probably because it's closer to the truth. After briefly wondering if I'm small enough to hide inside the fridge (probably—but how would I close the door once I got in there?), I take a large breath and walk out onto the front porch behind the kids.

"Hello," I say. "It's me. The middle-aged crone."

"Ah, yes. Just the crone I was looking for," says Matt.

"Actually, this isn't a great time, Matt." I improvise. I'm using my most formal tone yet. I sound weird even to myself.

"It won't take a minute."

"Okay. Two minutes. But I'm late. For something very important. So you'll have to be quick."

"You don't have anything important to do today, Mommy. You don't even have a job anymore," says Billy.

"Why don't you take your sister and go and play on the iPad for ten minutes?"

"But I've already used two hours today. What about my brain getting eaten?"

"I'll set the force field for another ten minutes." I take my phone out and pretend to tap on it. "You'd better go quick. The timer's ticking." He doesn't need to be told twice. Billy runs inside with Violet thudding after him. I turn back to Matt.

"Force field?" he asks.

"What are you doing here?"

"I came by to say hi," he says.

"Okay. Perhaps in the future you might call first. We live in LA. Not Kentucky."

"And to offer Peter a job," he says.

"Really?"

"Your face looks different."

"I've got makeup on," I say.

"I like it. You look pretty." Merely pretty today, huh? What happened to *beautiful* from the last time we met? Not that I've been replaying the entire scene in my mind again and again and again, or anything.

"Were you saying something about a job?"

"Yeah. I'm starting a new project."

"Another reality show?"

"No. Reality TV's almost over. This one's scripted. It's not that good, but that doesn't seem to matter to anyone these days. As long as it's got 'Colburn Entertainment' stamped on it, they'll all tune in."

"Er. Okay." I recognize this sideways attempt to evoke my reassurance from our dating days; however, I haven't got time to indulge a "pity me and my underserved success" party today. I have to get this man off my porch before he starts whisper-kissing me again and someone sees him. My lips start buzzing at the thought of it.

"I want Peter to come and work on the new show. I read his script. It's really good. *He's* really good. Probably even good enough to look past the drama that goes with him."

"You mean with us?" Matt looks up and we lock our startled eyes for a full moment. I can tell he's shocked that I've broached the subject. I'm a little shocked myself. I've actually implied out loud that there is an "us." And now we're both wondering if I mean past "us" or if I've taken the whisper-kiss to mean there's a current "us." I'm about to clarify that I mean past "us," but then I don't. He's the one who started the whole thing with his demands to see me and his whisper-kisses. He should be the one to clarify what's going on.

"I mean the drama with Peter's litigious tendencies."

A real writing job for Peter. This would solve all the problems. Long-term. Short-term. Mr. J. P. Morgan's overpriced assistance would no longer be needed. This *needs* to happen.

"Why don't you come in and talk to Peter about it?"

"He's here now?" Matt looks surprised and weirdly disappointed. Where did Matt think he'd be? A teahouse in Japan? "It's okay, I can't stop now. Just tell him to come by my office when he can. If he's interested."

"He'll be interested." He'd goddamn better be.

"It's good to see you again, Amy."

"You too." I say it with an "I'm finishing the conversation" tone and then step back a little from the door, taking an "I'm about to close the door" position.

But he just stands there.

Would it be weird/rude just to continue with closing the door? I suppose I should keep things polite, seeing as he's going to be my husband's new boss. Trouble is, I really, *really* don't want him to start up another attempt at a deep dive into why our relationship should never have ended. I actually haven't given much thought to Matt over the past few years. I was a little rankled at the breakup, I'll admit, but it's not as if our reuniting has ever been some kind of secret fantasy of mine. However, since our car encounter I *have* let my mind wander there, just a couple of times. Okay, seven, *tops*. I think me being so reluctantly unemployed and Peter being so enthusiastically unemployed has created the perfect storm in my brain, and the upshot is that I've actually started to daydream about what could have been. I'm worried that if Matt doesn't get off my porch pretty soon, he'll be able to see what's been going on in my head for the last few days. And that would be just plain embarrassing.

"Why don't we go out sometime? Just the two of us?" Horror and scandal and shock must be emanating from my facial expression as he quickly adds, "No, no, no. Nothing weird!"

"Matt. Honestly? I think it would be a bit weird."

"I completely get it. I don't know, it's just now that Peter and I are going to be possibly working together, I want to make things normal again between you and me. I still feel like there's a bit of tension here."

He's pulling the "new boss" card.

"It's Peter you'll be seeing every day. Not me."

"I know. But it can really throw the creative flow off if someone on the team has an issue with someone else. Peter might feel that you weren't comfortable with the situation. And then he'd bring that to work. And then the whole team would feel it."

What are they, a bunch of empaths?

"Matt, I'm completely comfortable." My tone at this point does not sound very comfortable.

"I just want us to be friends again, Amy. You used to be my best friend."

"Okay, sure, let's be friends." What the hell. We need the money. I'm sure if I do some advanced Googling, I'll eventually find a message board where everyone agrees that it's totally possible for men and women to be just friends.

"Friends," Matt says very grandly, and extends his hand. We shake on it. I hope he doesn't notice that my palm is a little more moist than his.

"So I'll see ya soon? We'll hang out!" he says, and starts back toward his car.

Now that he's got what he wants, he's all business again. He's so immersed in his phone, he doesn't even wave good-bye as he gets in the driver's seat. I'm left standing on the porch, feeling like a clueless seventeen-year-old. *Are* we going to hang out? When? What will we do? If I say no, will he fire Peter?

But worse than all these questions ricocheting around my head is the realization that I actually kind of do want to go out with Matt, just the two of us. And I know I'll give it much more thought than I should, until the day it happens.

CHAPTER 15

So everything was going just fine until the three-day mark. Days one and two, Peter came home from the new job late, but happy. However, it's now day three and he's home early. Not so early that the kids are still up, but way too early in the evening for a network writer to be coming home. Too early for it to be anything other than a bad sign. He's been sitting on the couch now for about ten minutes looking seriously tense. We've exchanged guarded hellos, but that's it. I know better than to try and coax out whatever's troubling him. Firstly, because with Peter, it's definitely better off *in* than *out*, and secondly, I already know what the trouble is. It's the trouble that's been inevitable from the beginning of this new job: Peter's not a team player. In fact, if we can get to two weeks in and claim just one paycheck, I'll be happy—and rather surprised too.

As if he's just been stung on the butt by a wasp, Peter jumps off the couch and charges out the front door. I sneak a look out the window. He's making a phone call. The front yard is his private call place. I don't know why he thinks it's any more private than sitting beside me in the living room. I can hear every word he says through the windows. Somehow, the glass that was used in the twenties, when this house was built, has survived in those same frames for almost a century. It lets in the cold, the heat, and also Peter's phone calls much more generously than modern-day windowpanes would. It's pretty clear from the first few sentences that Peter's talking to Matt. It's also clear that Peter's doing everything he can to control his temper and that Matt seems to be doing everything he can to provoke him.

"It's just that this seems directly oppositional to everything you said before . . . Yes, I do understand the new direction, but I still don't think that . . . Uh-huh . . . I think you're wrong about that . . . Yes, I know what executive producer means . . . I just don't see why you have to tear me a new one in front of the whole room . . . *fine.*"

The phone call comes to an abrupt end. I wonder if Peter's already blown it just three days in. Why can't he just play nicely, for God's sake? I leave him sulking on the porch, and knowing what I'm going to do even before I've granted myself permission to do it, I make my way to the back of the house for a private phone call of my own.

So, after pressing me to pledge my eternal friendship the other day, Matt has yet to contact me about us "hanging out." And frankly, I'm annoyed about it. It's like he's dumped me all over again. It's like he's too busy for me *all over again.* If I were a wiser sort of person, I'd surely be focusing my attention on the other areas of my life that need serious help right now—for example, my lack of employment, my terrible parenting skills, my sticky marriage—but like a scab that demands to be picked, I keep coming back to Matt and wondering why he hasn't called me for this hangout. It's ridiculous! This is one of the reasons you get married: so you never have to worry about this kind of crap ever again. And it's not that I even want to hang out. I just *want him* to want to hang out so that I can say "no thanks" and then put the phone down, shaking my head at what a sad loser he is to be so desperately obsessed with his ex. However, this little fantasy of mine has been ruined by the fact that he's clearly demonstrated that he's got more on his mind than calling me. But now, after overhearing Peter's phone call, I have what I've been waiting for: a bona fide reason to call *him.* And while

I'm doing my wifely duty of asking Matt to take it easy on Peter, he'll suddenly remember what an idiot he is for losing me, urgently ask to see me, and I'll say no. Mission accomplished. It really is disgraceful the lengths I will go to satisfy my ego.

I tap out Matt's number. It rings. It rings for way too long. I use the time to try to convince myself that ego has nothing to do with why I'm calling; I'm just trying to help out my husband here. Right as I'm about to hang up, he answers.

"Amy. I've been meaning to call you."

"Really? Well, what happened? All the skin on your index finger fall off?" is what I want to say. Instead, I give a noncommittal "Oh?" and move straight on. "I just wanted to talk to you about Peter. See how he's getting on. He seems a bit . . . tense."

"Let's meet."

"Meet?" I ask the question as though the thought never crossed my mind. If they gave out Oscars to normal people for Excellent Acting in a Real-World Situation, I would be awarded one purely on the strength of my "Meet?"

"Can you get out now?"

"No, Matt. I don't want to meet." There. I've said it. For some reason my ego is not doing the happy dance.

"Why not? Is it because you still have feelings for me?"

"What? No!" *Yes.* Damn it. This is not how I saw this conversation panning out. Why does he have to be so *sincere* about everything? It's like he's taken a course in sincere conversations since I last knew him. It makes everything so much harder to talk about with no wall of humor to hide behind.

"Okay, I just wanted to check. You didn't seem completely comfortable around me the last time we met."

And what's with his heightened concern for my comfort these days? Maybe he spends so many hours walking around passing out emotional cushioning to writers that it's just become a habit. "Are you comfortable? Does this make you uncomfortable? I'm just concerned that you might not be completely comfortable." Such an insipid word. If comfortable was a color, it would be beige. Rental-unit-carpet beige.

"I'm fine."

"Great. Then I do think we should meet quickly to talk about Peter. I have some concerns."

Sigh. Now it's all got twisted around, and if I continue to resist our meeting, he won't think it's because I'm so over him, he'll think it's because I *never got* over him.

"Fine. Where?"

"McKlusky's. Half an hour."

Forty minutes later I'm sitting on a very wobbly stool at the bar, by myself, looking like a weirdo. I'm waiting for Matt. He's late. He's always late. That's one thing that hasn't changed, I suppose. I'm kind of surprised that Matt picked McKlusky's for our late-night meet-up. I thought he would be way beyond the dive bar thing by now. Especially as McKlusky's isn't one of those ironically cool Los Feliz–type dive bars. It's just a chintzy Scottish bar that's a complete dive. We used to hang out here all the time when we were together. In fact, it's where we first met.

Ten minutes and another Coors Light later, Matt finally makes his entrance.

"Can I get a Glenlivet?" he asks the bartender. "Amy, hi." He kisses me on the cheek. It bugs me that he ordered his drink before he said hello to me—the person who's been waiting on a wobbly barstool for him for twenty minutes.

"We don't have Glenlivet."

"What single malts do you have?"

"We don't have single malts. We have Jack Daniel's."

Matt's acting like he's never been to this bar before in his life.

"I'll just have a water, then. Thanks. No ice."

"Why did you ask to meet here if you were going to ask for single-malt whiskeys?"

"Sorry. I forgot. I just wanted to go somewhere where you'd be, you know . . ." He glances at my torn-up are-they-slippers-are-they-snow-boots. There's at least one button missing on each one.

"Comfortable?" I ask.

"Yes," he says. "I'm concerned . . ." He takes a sip of his water and then makes a face. "Do you have anything bottled?" he asks.

"Bottled? No." The bartender half laughs before walking off. I'm glad McKlusky's is dark enough that no one can see me turn two shades pinker. I'll never be able to come to this bar ever again. Not that Peter and I get to go barhopping much. Or at all. "I'm concerned for you," he says.

"Why?"

"Because you're married to Peter. And he's an ass."

Looks like we're diving straight in, then.

"What do you mean by *ass*, exactly?" My tone comes out edgy and I do nothing to soften it. I'm allowed to criticize my husband all I like, but that doesn't mean I like it when other people jump on the band-wagon. In fact, I feel obliged to shove them off.

"*Rewrite* is a dirty word to that man. It's ridiculous. He insists his vision for every scene is completely perfect, and he takes any suggested changes as an affront to his entire character. He's impossible."

"I know he can be difficult." Matt raises one eyebrow. Goodness, he's really perfected that move. "Okay, he can be a complete asshole. He just gets triggered by criticism. His parents were super critical when he was a kid, and it's like his capacity for hearing it just got all filled up by the time he was eighteen. And now he can't handle it. I know you have to suggest changes and stuff, but maybe you could try not to do it in front of other people. Send him an e-mail or something."

"It doesn't work that way."

"Just go a little easy on him. For me. Just while he's finding his feet. Give him the benefit of the doubt for a couple of weeks at least."

"And why should I do that?"

"Because he's had a rough time up till now."

"Not really my problem."

"You made it your problem when you gave him a job." Matt stares down into his glass. I wonder if he feels silly that there's only water in there. Who comes to a Scottish dive bar and drinks water? "You knew he was hard to work with. Everyone knows that. But he's good, right? That's why you decided to take the risk."

"He's not good enough to put up with that bullshit. No one could be that good. But you're right: I knew what I was getting into. And I did it for you." Now, friends do friends big favors all the time. However, Matt is not looking at me like he's a friend who just did a bud a solid right now. He's looking at me like I'm breaking his heart. "I still care about you, Amy. Really care. Maybe I shouldn't say that."

He reads the confused expression on my face and knocks one of my knees playfully in between his. We always used to knee wrestle on these barstools. I always won. One time we broke a stool and got banned for an entire week. We smile at the unspoken memory and without another word said, I get it. I know what we're doing here. Our story isn't done. It's like a book you got tired of that keeps flipping open to the same page where you left off, demanding to be read all the way to the end. We never finished our story properly. So maybe this is our chance to figure it out the right way this time. And, of course, the right way is to be nice grown-up friends and has nothing to do with thinking about leaning forward on our wobbly barstools and kissing in the middle of a Scottish dive bar. But then before I can stop it, like a fat bluebottle that's impossible to swat, that notion of My Rightful Life is buzzing around my head again. Only this time, the idea is wondering if I could still have it. If maybe all I have to do is be brave or selfish enough to claim it. It suddenly occurs to me that if I were living a life of luxury with Matt and sharing custody with Peter, I'd actually get to see my kids more than if Peter and I were together and I was working as a buyer. I compel myself to squash that thought. A family is a family. And besides, I love Peter. That's the reason I'm here—to try and help him out. Right?

"I'll keep Peter on a little longer. See if he can settle into things," says Matt.

"Thank you," I say. "And do me a favor: don't mention that we talked, okay?"

"I won't. And I guess I won't mention either that we went to our old bar and I beat you flat out at a game of knee wrestle." Before I can answer him, he's got two knees around mine and my barstool's tipped almost ninety degrees. I grab the bar, hook my trapped leg around the back of his, and deftly send him flying toward the floor, the stool clattering down behind him. He falls hard on his hip.

"Shit! Are you okay?" I ask, suppressing my laughter. I have a socially unacceptable tendency to laugh extremely hard whenever somebody falls over. If they hurt themselves, I find it even funnier. I read somewhere once that it's actually a neurological condition.

"I'm fine," he says. He doesn't seem fine. He seems really hurt. My chest is shaking with the effort of holding the laughter in. "I don't remember it hurting this badly before."

"That's because you were a decade younger and usually very drunk." I help him up off the floor. "You forgot about my ultimate leg-hook move."

"I did," he says. "I forgot a lot of things about you, but I'm gradually remembering."

"Good," I say. We're standing pretty close to each other. From here he could easily grab the top of my jeans just like he always used to and pull me in toward him. I bend down to pick up the barstool before either one of us gets any ideas about moving closer.

"You've bruised me," he says.

"You bruised yourself," I reply. "Can you walk?" He shuffles forward a little. He's fine. He sits himself back on his barstool.

"Another drink?" he asks. "A proper one this time."

"I can't," I say. "I told Peter I was popping out for wood glue."

"Wood glue?"

"For Billy's homework."

"You love being a mom."

"You sound surprised."

"I am. I guess despite what you always said, I didn't think you'd ever really want kids at all. Just didn't seem like it would be realistic." I must look pretty annoyed, because he adds, "I just mean with all the other stuff you do."

"Work stuff?"

"Yeah, work stuff."

"Women do both these days, you know. It's not normally a one-or-the-other type of situation."

"I know that. I just thought it might be hard for you. Anyway—looks like you have it all figured out."

"Yup, I do. It's all figured out."

"Good for you."

"Great for me. I've got to go." I give him a brief kiss on the cheek. He even smells expensive. And then I take a step away. I walk out of the bar. And I leave.

Matt and I will not be meeting up as friends again. That was too close. *We're* still too close. I'm shutting this down now, before either one of us gets any more bruised.

CHAPTER 16

In the spirit of shutting things down before they even begin, I diligently ignore Matt's texts over the course of the next week. There's been a *Hi*, a *How are things?*, and then a few days after that a *???*. I gave a bland response about being fine/busy to the multiple question marks—just to keep him happy (he is my husband's boss, after all). And after that there came a text about meeting, which I didn't respond to. After another set of indignant *???*, I was busy formulating a suitably beige response about not being comfortable with us meeting up again when he took control of the situation, and now I'm sitting in the reception area of Colburn Entertainment. Waiting. For Matt. And Peter too as it turns out. And all of the other writers' significant others. Matt's arranged some kind of social event. And my presence is, apparently, necessary.

I made a valiant effort to get out of it. Of course I did. But Peter really wanted me to come. And the more I made excuses, the more suspicious I could see him getting. My last hope was that we'd never find a babysitter (we haven't needed one up till now), but unfortunately Lizzie gave us numbers for the four college students she uses on continuous rotation. So my last legitimate excuse went out the window, and here I am.

Best-case scenario, it's going to be super awkward. Worst-case scenario, we all get drunk, Matt and I hog the karaoke machine, start singing "Reunited," and end up making out in front of everyone. Less than ideal.

I'm on time—which is my first mistake, as this actually translates as horrifyingly early. Matt's receptionist (whose lips really are as sultry and pouty as I'd imagined) made that clear when I first announced my presence.

"Ummm, they won't be done for a while yet," she said. I believe the way she drew out the "umm" for about thirty seconds was specifically in order for me to realize how ridiculous I was for showing up so "early." It looks like the other spouses know how this works as I'm the only one who's showed up so far, even though we were supposed to have met twenty minutes ago. My second mistake is what I'm wearing. Trying to get into the spirit of Going Out And Having Fun, I put on a pretty tight pair of jeans, my only high heels (which are made from some kind of scary material that squeaks loudly whenever the shoes touch one other), and a white top covered in tassels. I was going for bohemian chic, but after looking at Pouty (who's dressed in leggings and a T-shirt but somehow looks two hundred percent more ready to party than I do), I can see that I just look old.

I'm sipping an extremely bland cup of coffee that she's prepared for me from the ten-thousand-dollar espresso machine in the corner. Maybe that could be a good idea for a business: go around teaching Hollywood's assistants how to make a drinkable cup of coffee using nothing more than a drip cup and some decent beans. I know for a fact that Matt makes people lug that ridiculous machine on set when he's filming. I read about it in some stupid *Forbes* profile I came across during my most recent "Matt Colburn" Googlefest. If the machine was some bizarre way of trying to impress me, it's backfired horribly for him.

I just start tapping out a text to Peter to tell him I'm leaving when the door opens and another wife shows up. At least I presume she's a wife. She looks too casual for an executive, and the very few female writers I've met usually reveal much less skin. I'm sure they'd be worried about distracting the rest of the all-male writing room.

"Kendra! OMG, it's been for-ev-er!" the wife says to Pouty. She actually says the letters *O-M-G*. I didn't know you could do that.

"Oh, hi! How are you?" replies Pouty, who suddenly pulls her eyes fully away from her phone for the first time since I got here and stands to attention. "They're still working. Shall I go in?"

"No, don't worry. I've got nowhere to be. So how have you been? Did things ever work out with that guy you were seeing?"

"Which one?"

"The photographer from Match?"

It seems that things did not work out with the photographer from Match, and the wife stays rapt for Kendra's whole monologue. As I look at her, I wonder what she does for a living. PR maybe? I don't think she's an actress. She's pretty, but average. She only looks good because of the manufactured polish; she's got no natural sparkle. Her hair is styled in big bouncy waves, and every time she shakes her head in disbelief at Kendra's story, the entire structure shakes as one. The hair is quite mesmerizing, but eventually as the story unfolds, and it turns out the photographer *still* wouldn't agree to be exclusive, it's not enough to hold my interest. I try to stand up and make an exit as discreetly as I can. It's not discreet enough. The wife turns around when I'm just three paces from the door.

"Oh my gosh, I didn't see you! Have you been there all that time?" she gasps. It's my biggest conversational peeve—people asking questions they already know the answer to. I know, I know, that's just how nice people make nice conversation, but to me it just seems to advertise dumbness. I hold back on replying that in fact I just arrived in the room four seconds ago via an intergalactic wormhole and give her a lukewarm nod.

"Are you coming out tonight?" she asks.

Not if I can help it. "I was thinking of skipping it, actually. They seem like they're taking a long time and—"

"No, don't do that! I don't want to be the only girl at this thing! So embarrassing! Let me just text Matt and see what's going on. I'm Kimberly, by the way."

Wait! This nothing-really-special woman is *Kimberly*? The woman Matt opted to marry in my place? Hoping I'm not looking too stunned, I extend my hand to shake, like a robot.

"I'm Am . . ." I say, my name dying on my lips as I wonder what Matt's told her about me. Which would be worse—that she's never heard of me or that she has a meltdown at the surprise visit from the Ghost of Girlfriends Past?

"I give hugs, girl!" she says, and pulls me into a firm one. I'm not ready for it. I don't move my head in time and my face is suddenly awkwardly slammed up super close to hers. At least, I find it awkward. I don't think she minds at all. Just as she's releasing me from our face bump, the door behind us opens and a creature who looks half man, half hobbit announces himself with something of a cough/grunt.

"Matt says: Do you want to come in? We're almost done."

"Into the writing room?" Kimberly asks. She seems disturbed. This offer has clearly never been extended before.

"It's okay," I say. "We'll stay out here and wait for the others."

"There are no others," says hobbit man, addressing the comment to Kimberly's cleavage. If the rest of the writers are as charming as he is, I can see why.

Matt sticks his head around the door.

"Come on in!" he says, beckoning. "We're nearly done. Just a few more minutes."

Kimberly and I cautiously step into the room. If I were a writer, I'd definitely have a hard time being creative in here. Everything is white, it's freezing cold, the shutters are closed, and the lighting is borderline neon. Eight men who look like they've had their souls recently sucked out of them sit around the table. In the center of the table lies a mound of pizza like a holy shrine. I see Peter at the back. He sees me come in and gives me a quick wink. He's the only one not wearing a baseball cap. Maybe they all wear those to protect themselves from the glare of the overhead lighting. I think I'd last about twenty minutes in here without getting a serious headache.

"This is perfect," says Matt. "We were just discussing a scene that could definitely use some female perspective. Please, come on in. Sit down."

"You could always hire some female writers," I say. It's as if no one heard me. "You know, maybe just a token one," I say a little louder. One writer awkwardly adjusts the screen on his laptop. That's the extent of the room's reaction. Fine.

"They don't normally hire women on the show," Kimberly whispers into my ear. "Not unless it's a must-hire."

"What's a must-hire?"

"Somebody that they must hire," she says, looking at me like I'm the dumb one. "You know, like someone's niece or something. I wonder if that's why they got us down here today, for the 'female perspective.' He never normally does anything social. I've never even met these writers before. The whole thing is totally weird."

As Kimberly and I uneasily sit down at the table, I wonder if it's possible Matt set all this up in order to see me. Is he so desperate to be in my presence that he'll even arrange a meeting in front of our respective spouses and his entire writing team? I realize that Kimberly is still whispering in my ear. She never stopped. I tune back in and find she's midway through a lament about how she had to have one of the guesthouse bathrooms taken out and put back in a total of three times this year. It seems that the problem lies in the planning permit. From the way she's talking about it, it's obvious that this is the biggest challenge she's had to overcome this decade. This woman is totally average in every way possible. She's vaguely nice and seems to know the right people to call to get a bathroom ripped out and reinstalled again, but apart from that . . . there's nothing much else there. How could this woman have bridged the gap that I left behind? How could she? All she's done to earn this fabulous life that she's living is just turn up at the right time, be available, and be more or less pleasant. How does that happen?

I'm distracted from Kimberly's bathroom diatribe by the change in Peter's voice. It's growing louder, harder; his sentences are getting shorter.

"It just doesn't ring true of the character. At all." This is Peter. "Delores is passionate, but she's also smart. She's a lawyer, not a superhero. She knows she can't get in there on her own. She'd try to find help."

"So, ladies." Matt turns to us. Conversational pet peeve No. 2: being referred to as a *lady*. "Ladies," for whatever reason, is even worse. "This is where we need your help. We've got a woman outside a burning building; she knows her kids are inside. As Peter mentioned, she's a smart, logic-based attorney. However, not so smart that she managed to install a phone charger in her car; her phone is dead. Does she run and find someone to call the fire department to help her extract her children? Or would she run straight in and try to save them herself?" He pauses for our response. There isn't one. "I'm pretty sure she'd run in. What mother wouldn't, right? It's the feminine instinct. But Peter here vehemently disagrees."

The other writers look toward Kimberly and me, dead-eyed. I've a feeling this dueling has been going on all day.

"Kimberly?" he asks. It's obvious he expects her to sum up, in a few quick sentences, what every person in possession of a vagina would do in this particular instance. Right now. In front of this room full of people. To her credit, she doesn't seem unnerved at all.

"Um. Well. How many children does she have?"

"Three," says Matt, containing his exasperation admirably. It's pretty clear that Kimberly's not going to offer an illuminating perspective on the feminine psyche when cast in the role of heroine.

"And they're all in the building?"

"They are all in the building," says Matt.

Kimberly pauses. The room waits. After a few seconds it becomes apparent that the pause is actually a stop. We've reached the extent of Kimberly's natural response on the topic.

"Kimberly—would you try to save our children from a burning building?" Matt rephrases for her. Another pause from Kimberly. I can tell that this is not what he was hoping for.

"I mean, I think I'd run in. But then I don't know. It might be pretty hot. So then maybe I wouldn't run in. But then my kids would be in there, so I can't say for sure." She sees Matt's frustration starting to seep through his expression and switches into trying-to-please mode. "I guess, yes, I would probably go in. I'd do my best, anyway." She seems reluctant to make any firmer commitment on the topic in case, perhaps, she's going to be asked to prove what she's just said. And thus Kimberly's theorem comes to its stunning close.

"Amy?" he asks me next.

Of course I'd run straight in and drag my kids out. I've done it before from a farmhouse in Colombia and that wasn't even for *my* kids. It's just the way mothers are wired. And Kimberly doesn't know it, but God forbid it actually happened, she'd do the same thing too. When you're with your kids, logic rarely comes into anything, least of all a situation like that. *However* . . . my husband is saying the opposite. And the last thing I want to do right now is provoke him any further. Especially if it's going to come back at me in the form of accusations of my taking Matt's side over his.

"I think most women would probably stay outside," I say, avoiding eye contact with everyone and squinting up into the harsh lighting. This situation is extremely *uncomfortable*. "Even the most desperate person would know that they wouldn't be able to walk into a fire without some kind of equipment. I've been near a structure fire before and that heat will have you backing right off, no matter what your heart is telling you to do. She'd go for help. For sure."

Peter looks up at me. I expect him to be pleased. He's not. My mention of once being near a structure fire has reminded him that in fact *I did* once run into a burning building to try and save some children. And *that's* what mothers do. And he knows I'm lying to agree with him, and he also now knows that he's wrong. He hates being wrong and he hates people lying. I've succeeded in doing the opposite of appeasing him.

"But you're not one of those girly girls anyway, Amy," says Matt. "I still think that most normal women would run in. Let's just go with that."

Really? Because I've never owned a set of false eyelashes, I'm not interested in protecting my children from death? I'm about as offended as I've ever been. But I sit on it. This will all be done soon. I just have to get through this, drink a couple of martinis, keep Peter calm, and get home.

Peter suddenly stands up. It's instantly clear that he's not going to sit on it. In any sense.

"You know what?" he says. I mentally cower under the chair. "You're a *complete* asshole." Matt turns to face Peter. I can tell he's shocked. Peter has obviously not hit this level of insubordination before. Peter's face is pale. "You won't listen to anyone else's ideas. This isn't a writing room, it's a dictatorship. I don't know why you even employ us. Why do you need us at all? Just write the whole thing yourself—that's what you obviously want to do." He throws his writing pad across the table toward Matt. Perhaps that was supposed to accentuate his point. "You ask my wife's opinion and then call her *abnormal* because she doesn't agree with you and your ideals of what a woman should be." He picks up one of the pens and scribbles "ASSHOLE" on the board and underlines it three times. "That's you. There." He bangs the pen on the board. "An *asshole.*"

"We're done here. Get out."

"I *am* out." Peter gives the whiteboard a shove, and it skids across the room and bashes into the wall. If that didn't leave a divot, I know it at least left a massive mark. Peter barrels out of the room like he can't leave fast enough. I mouth, "Nice to meet you," to Kimberly so she doesn't think that I'm as insane as my spouse and then follow him out the door.

I can't help but glance at Matt as I leave, but he's not looking at me, he's looking at Kimberly. Maybe I'm reading way too much into the look a man is giving his wife, but I think seeing Kimberly and me in side-by-side action just then sort of sped up the inevitable. He just realized he married the wrong one.

CHAPTER 17

And so Peter blew it for us again. He managed to rack up a grand total of one paycheck. One. The first since our children have been born, and now he is unemployed once more. Just sitting at home all day in the garage, cranking more unsellable screenplays out of his laptop. We are doomed.

Now that we are back in the poorhouse, in a valiant attempt to recoup my wasted six hundred Sylvia's Angels dollars, I decided to visit my "territory" today and try to sell something. And did I manage to sell one lousy lipstick? Nothing. Not. One. Sale. And, of course, I had to take Violet with me.

Violet's pretty quiet on the drive home and as soon as I pull up to the front door, switch off the engine, and turn around to see if she's asleep, I see why. She's covered in makeup. My makeup kit is lying open next to her, and she seems to have daubed on every available color to every single part of her face. She looks like she's been dunked in a murky rainbow.

"Violet!" I have to get this stuff off her skin before anyone sees her. I open the glove compartment and pull out a pack of baby wipes. They're completely dried out. If Miss Havisham had owned a packet of baby wipes, these would have been them. If I crunched the top one, I'm sure it would crumble in my palm and blow away in the wind like apocalyptic wipe dust.

"Hey, Amy!" comes a muffled voice through the window. Oh, of course. It's Lizzie. It's like she's got some kind of "crappy mommy" radar. The second I approach any kind of parental fail, her sensor starts a-beepin' and she's over here as fast as her Bikram-toned legs can transport her. She looks super annoyed. I wonder what the drama is this time. I fleetingly remember that I haven't cleaned off the boogers I caught Billy wiping on her mailbox last week. But still—she couldn't *know* those were his? She hasn't got a booger DNA lab in her basement. And then I remember her video surveillance app . . . I lower the window.

"Hey, Lizzie."

"They're waiting!"

"Who?"

"All my friends. In my living room. Right now. They've already gone through all the Chardonnay and now they've started on the Pinot!"

I stare at her. She stares back. It seems like she really wants me to do something.

"You're extremely late!" She more or less squeals, going pinker by the nanosecond.

"For what?"

"Your party!"

Oh no. Now I remember. Earlier this week I practically forced my way through Lizzie's front door under the guise of "catching up." Nine minutes in, I changed tack and somehow talked her into hosting a Sylvia's Angels party. I played the "hoping to be able to make this a success so I can stay at home with my kids" card, so how could she refuse? And now there's a horde of Pasadena princesses in her living room, their children deposited with their nannies, waiting to be sold a bunch of toxin-laden makeup from a fifty-year-old brand that has never been popular. Not even in the eighties, when everything was popular. I wonder how on earth Lizzie got them to come.

"I'm so sorry, Lizzie. I've had a bit of a weird morning and I totally forgot. I'll just take Violet inside and wash her face, and we'll be by in a minute."

"Just come now. Everyone's waiting," she says, already helping Violet out of her car seat. "Good Lord. You look like a psychedelic Oompa-Loompa." She grimaces and puts Violet on her hip, starting out for her house, knowing that I'll have to follow along. I've always been extremely jealous of women who can carry kids on their hip and walk at the same time. I'm so lacking in hip that whenever I try it, the poor child has to cling to the side of my body like an abandoned monkey and eventually ends up just falling to the floor. There's a *ding* from my phone. It's a text from Matt. *Call me.* Not going to happen. If he's so desperate to chat, he can make the call, not text me a directive to do it.

As soon as we walk into Lizzie's living room, I realize this is a mistake. A big mistake. The room is filled with some of the most beautifully and artfully manicured women I've ever seen. There's not a thing I could say about makeup or the application of it that they don't already know. There's not a single item in my fourth-rate makeup inventory that they would want to buy. These women probably pay at least seventy-five dollars for a lipstick. And buy four at a time.

"Oh, look. You put the makeup on your baby," says one particularly perfect blonde. Three instant reasons to dislike this woman: she's practically perfect in every way possible, she thinks I'd purposefully splodge makeup on my child, and she's calling my three-year-old a *baby*. Last week, in another failed attempt to be a normal mother, I took Billy and Violet to the park. While they were off scampering around, some woman on the bench started desperately searching through her bag.

"Damn it! I've forgotten the milk for the baby," she said.

"Oh no," said I, wondering how she bore the pressure of being the only nonbreastfeeder at the park. And then I noticed her "baby" was absent. "Wait! Where is your baby?" Had the baby been snatched while she was searching for milk?

"There," she said. "On the swings. And she is going to be pissed." And stomach-down on the swing was one long-legged four-year-old wearing knee-high boots and spinning with her legs stuck out as far as possible in an attempt to hit the kid standing behind her waiting for a turn. Baby? Babies stop being babies the minute they can walk and talk, let alone don heeled boots and try to dominate the swing set. Violet hasn't been a baby for a long time. In fact, I don't think I have any actual memories of her being a baby. There was just the birth, and then now. The in-between is kind of just not there. It's documented by a series of photos taken by the snap-happy Peter. But that's the only real evidence it ever happened. For me, anyway.

"Actually, she put it on when I wasn't looking," I say to Perfect. "If you all can bear to wait just a couple more minutes, I'm going to quickly wash it off."

"It's hard to watch them every moment," says Perfect with a smile. She's looking at us like she's the Duchess of Cambridge and Violet and I don't own any shoes. And what does she know about "watching them every moment"? I expect she's got two nannies on alternating twelve-hour shifts for every perfect child she's ever popped out of her perfect vagina.

Before Lizzie can put Violet back up on her hip again, I grab my daughter's hand and make for the bathroom. The first one's almost out of soap—and I'm going to need a lot—so we end up in a room at the back of the kitchen. It's filled with laundry, various soaps, and two huge sinks. It seems to be a room created purely for the washing of things. Perfect. I fill a sink with tepid water and get to work.

Just as I'm starting to make some progress, I hear a clitter-clatter of heels as someone enters the kitchen. Seriously. Who wears heels during the day? Unless you work in an office or host a daytime television show, there's really no call for six-inch heels before the sun goes down.

"Did you look inside that terrifying box? It's like the Twinkies of makeup in there," says a voice that's vaguely familiar.

"Stop it," says Lizzie, not sounding like she wants her to stop it at all. I hear another bottle of wine being opened. These women are going to be plastered by the time they leave. Maybe I'll just call 911 on the way out with a list of license plates. Perhaps they'll all lose their licenses, and their husbands will make them choose between a driver *or* a nanny and *then* they'll start to see exactly how "hard" it is to watch the children every moment. I put my finger over my lips to signal to Violet to be quiet. That sign has never worked up till now, but there's always hope. Maybe she'll see the look of terrified embarrassment in my eyes and decide to comply.

"Why on earth did you get us all over here? The whole thing is ludicrous."

"I feel bad for her, okay?" says Lizzie. "Just buy something for goodness' sake. You don't have to use it."

"You're right I won't use it."

"Think of it as a fund-raiser if that makes it any easier. Your nonprofit venture for the week," says Lizzie.

"Mommy," says Violet, as loud and insistent as a car horn, "what's a nonprofit venture?"

Busted. From the other side of the wall I hear a delighted yet stifled gasp, a suppressed snort of laughter, and then they're gone. Should I just sneak out the side door now and escape the whole thing? If Lizzie weren't my next-door neighbor, or if we could afford to move, that would totally be my plan. But seeing as I'm stuck with this woman in my life, at least until we have to move to Riverside, I'd better go out there and put on the dog-and-pony show she's after. Maybe I'll send Violet around at the end of the demo with an emptied-out makeup bag for them to toss pennies into. That's obviously the kind of thing they're after here.

* * *

I step into the room to face a pack of red-faced late-thirty-year-olds. Red-faced because they've been mixing Chardonnay and Pinot or because they've been delighting in the news that I overheard someone bitching in the kitchen—I'll never know which.

The most face-saving thing would just be to request that they all take a good long look at themselves and then leave the premises. But, as Lizzie mentioned, this is supposed to be something of a fund-raiser. I may as well make some cash out of this hellacious situation.

"First of all, thank you so much to Lizzie for opening up her home to host this party today," I start. This settles some of them down a bit. "I know this brand of makeup probably isn't a natural choice for any of you, so I also appreciate the generosity you've all shown by choosing to be here today, to support my new *venture*." Okay. That shut the last of the snickerers up. I've set the tone. We all know what's going on here, so let's just get to it and pull the checkbooks out, shall we?

"I need a volunteer." Silence. I'm not surprised. Why would any of them want to remove their beautifully applied luxury-brand makeup to expose their skin to this cheap crap? I'm considering whether I might have to use Violet as a model, when from the back of the crowd comes a voice I recognize from my moment of exquisite humiliation in the laundry room.

"I'll do it," she says. I see a lavishly long arm raise itself into the air like a giraffe going for a leaf at the top of the tree. And then its owner stands up and I see her, surrounded by a haystack of endless red hair: it's Jasmine. Why the frick did Lizzie invite her? She witnessed the throw-down at Time for Twos. Was she hoping for a rematch? Of course, what Lizzie doesn't know is that Jasmine also just cost me my one and only likely opportunity to be gainfully employed in the foreseeable future.

Jasmine unfolds the rest of her body and pulls herself up to her full height. She's exactly double the length of Lizzie, who's standing right next to her. It's like looking at a small, puffy white rabbit positioned next to the tallest, leanest giraffe on the horizon of the African savanna.

"I came straight from the gym so I've got no face on," she says by way of explaining her act of martyrdom. In contrast to the rest of the group, Jasmine's decked out in designer yoga gear. Her T-shirt says "Bodhi Beautiful." I suddenly recall a news clip I saw once where one of the directors of the company blamed some alleged pilling on the seams of the pants on the women who were wearing them, saying they had thighs that rubbed together where they shouldn't. I imagine Jasmine's pant seams are absolutely pill-free. Her thigh gap is so large the whole Bodhi Beautiful board of directors could hold a meeting in the space there and be quite comfortable.

My face has set to a thin, hard brittle. I don't like to be a hater, but it must be said that I intensely dislike this woman.

"Jasmine. What a surprise to see you again," I say, without the enthusiasm necessary to convince anyone that the surprise is a happy one. The red-faced gigglers have started up again. Everyone knows I overheard Jasmine in the kitchen. I'd rather be anywhere on earth than here right now. Even in the depths of Africa covered in mosquito bites and ankle-deep in organic fertilizer. The truth is, I'd love to be in Africa right now grading people's coffee-pulp-and-chicken-shit fertilizer—but I'm not. I'm here, trying to flog the "Twinkies of makeup" and whose fault is that? Jasmine the Giraffe's.

After a moment of shuffling, a suitable seat is procured and Jasmine is faceup, ready for me to inflict my worst. I decide to start with the lips. I can't remember the order this stuff goes in, but the mouth is surely as good a place to start as any.

"Now if your lips are a little on the skinny side like Jasmine's"— death glares abound. What? She's got skinny thighs, so it's only biologically fair that she got the skinny lips too. I'm merely pointing out what we can all see—"you can use this beautiful lip plumper right under your lipstick." This time last month I had no idea that society had made a place for a product to plumpen the lips. I pull the spongy brush out of the bottle. It's covered in something that looks vaguely like semen. And on it goes. "Doesn't that feel great?" I ask Jasmine.

"Actually, no," she replies. What was I expecting? A sugarcoated, glowing review? "It feels like my lips are burning."

"That's the plumping sensation," I reply. Or, I don't know, she could be having a reaction to the niacin . . .

"It's more like a burning sensation."

"It's a tingling sensation that soothes while it plumps." Or that's what Sylvia said anyway.

"It feels like somebody just punched me in the mouth." Whoa. That stuff works fast. Jasmine's lips have gone from reedy to Angelina Jolie on a pouty day in just a few seconds. And it doesn't look like she'll be needing the lipstick either as her lips have turned a blistering red. *Hmm.* I think this might not be the intended effect. "I've got to get this stuff off!" She jumps from the chair. "Have you got a wipe?"

"Nope," I answer, thinking about the dried-out pack back in the car.

"Here," says Perfect, and hands Jasmine a pack from somewhere. "Use these."

Too late I realize they are in fact the Miss Havisham wipes that somehow got stashed in the makeup kit. Jasmine pulls the first one from the pack and puts it straight on her mouth. The mummified wipe instantly bonds with the semen plumper, and Jasmine now has a coating of wipe dust over everything. She looks like she's been making out with a snowman. She runs straight out of the room. Everyone else is frozen to the spot in horrified delight. A second later a howl comes from the bathroom.

"Fuck's sake, no soap!" A couple of the gigglers start up again. "It's not funny!" Jasmine reenters the living room. "I'm going to have to go to the ER." Lizzie has had the presence of mind to find a damp cloth and some ice and nervously offers them up to Jasmine, who furiously wipes at her lips and then presses the ice pack to her mouth. I can see that the lower half of her face is flushed red. Goodness. Perhaps she *should* go to the ER. From the corner of my eye I see Violet pulling out the sponge tip from the plumper, about to eat it.

"No, Violet." I rush forward and grab it out of her hands. "Don't touch that stuff." Jasmine removes the ice pack from her mouth. The right half of her upper lip is fantastically swollen. If I didn't know better, I'd presume she'd been in a brawl. "You seem to have had a bit of an adverse reaction to the lip plumper," I observe unhelpfully. Though looking at her now, her entire face and neck are actually turning a little pink. But that may just be because she's super angry.

"That stuff is toxic," she says. "It should be kept away from the public." She probably has a point. "How much did you pay for all that junk?"

"Six hundred dollars." Come to think of it, that does seem an awful lot now for a relatively small amount of crappy product.

"Why?" asks Jasmine. Honest to God, it looks like she's done a round in the ring.

"Why what?" I ask.

"Why are you intent on selling these awful products to innocent people?"

"I wouldn't have to if you hadn't destroyed my only other employment opportunity."

"You were going to work for Bean à la Bean?" asks Lizzie.

"*Was* going to. Until Jasmine shut the whole thing down. Now I'm trying to do *this*. I need to feed my children." I point toward Violet, who's chewing on the corner of the makeup case as if to demonstrate she's so starved she's been reduced to chomping on faux leather for daily sustenance.

"I'll write you a check right now"—Jasmine scrambles through her purse and pulls out a checkbook—"for one thousand dollars if you promise never to inflict these products on anyone in this room ever again." The red-faced titterers have become stony silent. Jasmine's crossed the line from entertainingly rude to embarrassingly hostile, and the whole room is feeling icky. She rips the check off the stub. "Here, take it." She presses it into my chest and then snatches the makeup case away from Violet.

"Hey!" says Violet. "I was eating that."

Jasmine flings open the front door with an unnecessary flourish and stomps to the curb, where the garbage bins are perfectly lined up. She throws open the lid of the first one—again with an unnecessary essence of heightened drama, in my opinion—and proceeds to empty the entire contents of the case into the trash.

"Wow," says Lizzie. Wow, indeed.

"I feel like at least some of that stuff should have gone in the recycling bin," I say.

"In the future, don't take your problems out on us," Jasmine says, throwing the emptied case in after the makeup. "I appreciate that you and your husband are having financial issues, but that doesn't give you license to poison half the women in your neighborhood."

"We may be 'having financial issues,' but at least Peter isn't banging the nanny," I murmur. Lizzie looks at me sharply. Oops. I think she might have heard that.

"What was that?" asks Jasmine, gripping the rim of the garbage bin. Jeez, she must be really rattled by all of this. She'd never consider putting her hands anywhere near there otherwise.

"Nothing," I say.

I'd dearly love to tell her that her husband's infatuated with the woman she's employed to watch her child. Especially as Jasmine's cost me a much-needed job and just completely embarrassed me in front of a bunch of women I'm going to have to hope and pray I never run into ever again. However—I'm not the kind to bring a gun to a knife fight. Her marital mayhem is not my mess to sort out. It's partly her own fault anyway for employing a nanny with an inhuman hip-to-waist ratio.

"Come on, Violet." I retrieve Jasmine's check from the floor where I let it fall earlier. Embarrassed to the point of nausea, I fold it in two and try to subtly tuck it into my pocket—but I'm clearly fooling no one. This has done nothing for my generalized inferiority complex.

"I want to stay. This party's fun!"

"We're going," I say, grabbing her hand.

The distance from Lizzie's porch to mine has never seemed so long. The second we're home, I draw all the blinds on the east side of the house and blast Journey as loud as I can so I don't have to hear the drunken laughter as they pack themselves into their SUV hybrids and swerve on home. I'm not sure how I'm supposed to carry on being Lizzie's insufficient-but-more-or-less-okay neighbor after this. She knows I've seen her catty side. I know she knows we're broke. The delicate ecosystem of our relationship has been more or less ruined. The O'Haras might be moving to Riverside much sooner than anticipated.

CHAPTER 18

"Twenty minutes, Peter! *Twenty minutes!* It's nine in the morning—I'm not going to hear back from any college student within twenty minutes!"

"Why not?"

"Because they'll have been up all night partying and drinking and doing all the things we're always too tired to do since we turned thirty, and now they'll be *sleeping*."

"Not necessarily," says Peter. And just to annoyingly accentuate his point, my phone makes a lethargic *ding* right at that moment. It's a text message from the girl who watched the kids the night of our failed attempt at drinks with the writing room. It shows my level of desperation that I'm more relieved than annoyed at Peter being proved right. My relief evaporates in a hearty puff upward the minute I read the text: *Sorre cant help u got econ this am.*

"Damn it. Arielle can't do it." I show Peter the text. Well, at least that proves my point about her being up all night drinking. Or maybe she's always that shitty at spelling and grammar. I am currently anticipating text messages from three more potentially sleeping college students. Peter and I have a problem right now. Or, actually, it seems to be metamorphosing into *my* problem, as it looks like Peter is putting on his shoes.

"Wait! Are you going? You can't just *go!*"

"Amy. You've got no fewer than three babysitters about to text you back. One of them will certainly be able to come over and watch the kids."

"Not to get here within twenty minutes. And what if they're psychos?"

"They will be fine. It will be fine. We don't live at the end of the earth. People have cars. People can get from one place to another place within twenty minutes. I have to go."

"You can't!" He can't!

"Amy, I've got to." And with that, he holds up his hand in what is probably supposed to be an apologetic gesture, and before I can physically stop him from doing so, he heads out the door and he's gone. What. The. Fuck.

So, as you may have gathered, Peter and I have a scheduling conflict this morning. It's all about as messed up as it can be. I got a call yesterday asking me to come in for an interview this morning for an agronomist position I applied for a couple of days ago. And then first thing this morning, Peter gets an e-mail summoning him to a meeting—apparently, some fool he e-mailed *Draker's Dark* to is interested in producing it. Peter's so eager to get to his meeting with these people that he won't dare ask them to postpone. I've called FMC Trading to ask about rescheduling my interview, and the soonest they can get me in after today is three weeks from now. I know someone else will have that job three weeks from now, so I told them I'd keep today's meeting.

About seven thirty, in an act of Herculean pride swallowing, I knocked on Lizzie's door and asked if she could watch the kids for a couple of hours. Billy's school is closed for "teacher training"—don't they know what they're doing by now?—so he's lumped into the whole equation too. Things were a little cool between us, kind of understandable given what happened last week, and she said she was too busy to watch the kids this morning. Doing what, she didn't say, but she did pointedly remind me that she recently gave me the numbers of four babysitters to be used exactly in situations such as these, so here I am. Waiting for texts. Like a desperate teenager.

How could Peter just walk out the door like that? Is that the new ruling? Whoever gets their shoes on last is lumbered with the childcare crisis? Is that a male thing or a Peter thing? I would *never* pull a stunt like that. And is that an Amy thing or am I just hardwired to please? Gender equality, my b-hole. It's all good and fine until some dude pulls the asshole move. It's times like this when I wish, *dream*, that we had family living closer. Even some e-smoking, alcoholic great-aunt who force-fed the children Cheetos—any viable humanoid to help us out in situations like these.

Two more *ding*s, one right after the other . . . Neither one of them can do it. Allegedly, they also have economics this morning. Are they all in the same class? Wasn't that rather shortsighted of Lizzie? Though I suppose she only needs a sitter for date night, so it doesn't much matter to her what they do during the day. One sitter left. There's no reason to think she'll actually te—*ding*.

And there it is. Sitter number four. And she can't make it either. I feel my face go ice-cold with panic. What am I going to do? Am I really going to miss this job interview? Is that really going to happen? I am about to Google "Is it okay to leave five-year-old looking after three-year-old?" when I remember a fragment of a news story I recently heard about the government logging everyone's web searches. They'll have social services round before I'm halfway down the street. What do people *do* when shit like this comes up? I surely can't be the only woman ever to have been faced with this situation. I turn to the Google oracle once more. And within forty seconds I have my plan. If it's good enough for Michelle Obama, it's certainly good enough for me.

* * *

The head office for FMC Trading is downtown—oh joy—so, of course, the GPS and I both got completely lost on the way there. I spent the last ten minutes following Waze around in an optimistic loop-the-loop, until I gave up and pulled out my outdated Thomas Guide, which didn't do a lot to illuminate the situation. Honestly, give me a map with some actual land contours and I'm fine, but trying to navigate this rabbit warren of a city without some kind of insider's knowledge is too much to ask of anyone. However, I'm pulling into the FMC lot now, amazingly with ten minutes to spare before the interview.

"Did we eat any breakfast?" asks Billy from the back. Damn it. No, we didn't.

"Mommy, I'm still in my jammies," adds Violet. I turn back to look at her, and indeed she is still in her jammies. At least it's jammies and not a nightgown. The particular jammies in question might just pass as very casual leisure wear if you don't look too closely. They're Billy's old ones—dark blue, with a bear on the front declaring that he's "Not Sleepy Yet," which can surely only help my case.

"I'm hungry. I'm so hungry I'm going to die right now, in the car." This is Billy. Okay. I've got ten minutes to spare and I saw a McDonald's one block back. I'm totally going to pull the slacker mom move. Completely justified given the circumstances.

Fifteen minutes later, we're back in the parking lot. Billy wolfed down his entire breakfast sandwich in about twenty seconds, but Violet's still working on hers. Showing up to an interview with kids in tow is bad enough, but I *just can't* show up with one of them wearing jammies *ana* munching on fast food.

"Violet, I need you to finish that in the next twenty seconds or you'll have to leave it behind." Her brother consumed a whole muffin in that time. She only has to eat half of one. Completely doable if she sets her mind to it. "Agreed?"

She doesn't answer. I start to count down from twenty, quickly. She manages to take two bites, but she's still not done by the time I get to zero. I'm already five minutes late; I can't wait out the time it's going to take her to eat this thing. Violet is a notoriously slow eater.

"Okay, put the muffin down. We have to go."

"Nooooooooooooo! No! No! Nooooooooooooo!" she screams, straining against her harness and thrashing all of her legs and arms at the same time. I note that she manages to keep hold of the muffin. I have no time for this McDrama; we're going to have to take the muffin in. If I stink out the reception area with McDonald's reek, then so be it. I'm guessing it didn't go down like this for Michelle.

As soon as we push through the glass doors into reception, I realize that FMC Trading is a bigger deal than I thought. I suppose I shouldn't be this surprised at the swankiness of their head office. FMC's the second-largest coffee trader in the world and provides the beans for the big guys: HushMush, the Penny Bean, et cetera. Before now, I've always purposefully sprinted in the opposite direction whenever there's been an opportunity to work for a big conglomerate. However, as we all know, I can no longer afford to be the Picky Patricia of my past. If I have to work for an evil corporation in order to feed my children, then that is what will happen.

We head for the front desk.

"Thelma?"

"Amy?"

"How did you guess?" I ask with a smile. I called ahead before I rolled up with my two monsters. I'm not a complete numbskull.

"You two must be Billy and Violet," Thelma says.

"I'm wearing my jammies," says Violet.

"So you are. I wish I was wearing mine too. Then we'd be matching."

"Do you like ponies?"

"I *love* ponies."

"Even pink ones?"

"Pink ones are the best ones of all." And they're off. Thelma's at that stage. I remember it so well myself. Engaged to be engaged to her boyfriend and already spending a lot of time daydreaming about the beautiful biracial children that they'd make. She informed me of all this on the phone when I called her on the way in. She said she'd be delighted to watch both kids for me while I had my interview, and I implied that if I got the job, I'd put in a good word for her with upper management. Sorted.

"They're running late," Thelma tells me. "The candidate before you only just went in."

"Thanks."

Oh, well. At least the sweat will have a chance to dry off my upper lip before I see them. That was quite the ordeal to get here. Violet and Thelma are absorbed in a pony game, and Billy is in holy communion with his iPad. I have nothing to do. I spent most of yesterday cramming every factoid about FMC available on the Internet into my head. If I prep any more for this interview, it's just going to make me nervous. I flick open iBooks on my phone. I need a distraction. I'm going to start that emotional-child book Billy's nameless teacher keeps talking about. I still haven't had four minutes straight in a row to start reading it. This is as good a chance as I'm likely to get.

And so I read. And then I read. And then I read some more. And I keep on reading till I'm so overwhelmed with guilt and sorrow that I can't read another word. I've been doing it all wrong. And not just wrong in an "I put the wrong factor sunscreen on my kids" kind of way. I've been talking to, dealing with, and parenting Billy in a way that's completely incompatible with his nervous system. It's like he's a brand-new Mac and I've been trying to run ancient Office software on him this whole time and then yelling at him for not working. All the things I've thought he was being a drama queen about: the freak-out over scratchy labels, the time he threw his electric toothbrush out the window because it was too "buzzy" and I was insisting he use it, the meltdown over any and all changes to his routine, the inability to cope with the slightest physical pain, his constantly accusing his sister of smelling of "horses," the zero tolerance for crowds, noise, shouting of any kind—it's all because his central nervous system is basically on twenty-four-hour high alert. He's a bit different. Not worse or inferior. Just a little different. And there's been no consideration made for that whatsoever. By anyone. It's like I've been yelling at my dyslexic son for not being able to spell. I am a fraud.

"Amy O'Hara?" I quickly flick away a spilled tear and jump up. "I'm Lexi, Bob McLeod's PA. Please come through." I toss my phone into my purse. I'll be going straight back to that later.

Bob's office is a huge glass box, a hop and a skip away from reception. I take a seat opposite his empty desk. I'm going to be sitting with my back to the door—good—less chance of getting distracted by any potential mayhem going on behind me. "Bob will be with you in a moment," she says.

As soon as she leaves, I jump up and try to figure out how to close the blinds so no one will be able to see any of the craziness that's sure to erupt any moment in reception. I get them about halfway closed before two guys walk in.

"Amy? Nice to meet you. I'm Bob McLeod, head of North American operations. And this is Jay Jones, our chief sustainability adviser."

I give both of their hands a firm shake. I see Bob flexing his hand a little after. I tend to overcompensate on the handshake thing. If this is a man's world, then it must be said that coffee is a dude's universe. Agronomy's just as intense as buying, and I'll need to prove I've got the physical, emotional, and mental stamina to do the job before they even think to ask themselves if I have or if I haven't.

"So, Jay and Bob?" I ask, smiling. A couple of blank looks back. "Like Jay and Silent Bob?"

"The other guy mentioned something about that too. What does it mean?" asks Jay. Oh, dear. Corporate. Must think corporate.

"Just a film reference," I say, and hope they don't think to look it up later, especially as Jay Jones is tall and blond and Bob's a little on the dumpy side.

"Are these your children?" I ask, pointing at a picture of four extremely wholesome-looking kids on his desk.

"Yeah, my crazy crew," Bob says, glowing a little. Score. Common ground. "So we wanted to get you in today to see if you'd be a fit for our agronomy program that we're expanding to the African region."

Damn it. I missed my opportunity there. I guess discussing off-spring isn't the topic at hand. I've been doing business too long in South America. No one down there even thinks of talking shop till everyone's discussed their families for at least half an hour. Bob proceeds to give me a pretty thorough rundown of what FMC's been up to recently. It's kinda interesting. Looks like someone at the top of the food chain has decided it's time to support overseas farmers rather than grind them into the ground. I wonder what prompted this sea change. Last time I worked with a coffee conglomerate, it was all "gas everything with fungicides and fuck the farmer."

"We've had enormous success in South America, and now we're expanding the program to Africa. Ethiopia first. That's where you fit in," says Jay.

"So I'm curious, what's with the large-scale turnaround?" I ask. They pause for a second. Maybe I didn't phrase that quite right.

"Sustainable supply chains. It's more important than ever with the epidemic. We need to develop and enhance whatever we can," says Bob. "The program almost doubled the yield in most instances in South America. If we can help farmers boost the quality of their crops, they'll make more money. We all will. It's the economically viable thing to do."

"I can't argue with that logic," I say with a smile.

"We were interested in hearing if you'd had any experience helping farmers heighten production, specifically in Ethiopia," says Jay. *Have* I? I'm about to blow these two middle-aged men's socks off. I hope they're prepared to be super impressed because—

"Mommy?"

I freeze. The door has swung open behind me. I turn to see Billy and Violet standing next to a strung-out Thelma. Billy is completely white and has vomit all down the front of his shirt.

"He just threw up all over himself. I'm sorry, I didn't know what I should do," says Thelma. All trace of the woman who was happy to talk about pajamas and pink ponies has loooong gone. Good God, it's only been five minutes. Try five years of it, girlfriend, and *then* you've got the right to look that sour about it all.

"Hi! I'm Violet. These are my jammies." Violet does a funky little turn to show off said jammies. She's still brandishing that awful muffin. I grab it off her. "Hey!" I open it up. No cheese. She must have switched with Billy. *I know* I gave him the one without cheese in it.

"Good morning, FMC Trading," says Thelma. We all stare at her. No, she's not been driven to insanity; she's talking to someone on her headset. "Putting you straight through, one moment, please." Then she mouths, "I have to go," and starts speed walking back to her desk. I've got a feeling she's going to be renewing her NuvaRing after all.

"I'm sorry about this," I say to Jay and Bob, who are actually looking less horrified than I would have thought. "I had to bring them—my husband normally looks after the kids, but we had a last-minute conflict and none of our sitters could make it, so here we are."

"We do appreciate that we asked you in here on very short notice. It's not a problem at all," says Bob, smiling. He's *smiling*? Violet slides a stapler off the side of his desk and pulls it open to examine its inner workings.

"Violet, put that down!" Too late.

"Ow!" She drops the stapler to the ground. Jesus Christ, has she stapled herself? I rush over and grab her hand. It's fine. She just broke the skin. I pull her over to where I slung my purse over the back of my chair and unzip the back pocket. It's still there, my one solitary, teacher-recommended Band-Aid.

"Here's a free tip: always have a Band-Aid handy when there're kids around!" Do I look like Parent of the Year yet?

"Mommy, this is an Angry Birds Band-Aid. I want a normal one." I ignore her.

"I'm going to get my eldest cleaned up, then I'll be right back," I say. *Please don't end the interview. Please don't.*

"I think all moms deserve a medal," says Bob. This is promising. "I know my weekends are harder work than my weeks." Yes! He gets it.

"Yeah, Suzie's certainly got her work cut out with four all day!" says Jay.

"She sure does. We both do," says Bob. Okay, so he's probably over-estimating his portion of the "work" there, but I'll roll with it.

"The bathrooms are just down the hall on the right. We'll see you in a minute."

"Thanks."

"Violet, come on."

"I want to stay here."

"Oh, she's fine for the minute," says Bob. "I think I've got some crayons somewhere in here from when the kids last came in." I seriously love this man.

"Violet, be good. We'll be back in two minutes."

Violet slams her muffin down on the desk and crawls up onto the chair I just vacated.

"So what exactly happens in this office here?" she asks. Oh Lord. Maybe she'll have wrangled herself a job by the time I get back.

I spirit Billy down the corridor and usher him into the women's bathroom.

"What happened?" I ask him. "I gave you the muffin without cheese."

"Violet said it wasn't cheese. She said it was yellow melted plastic and she didn't want to eat it. I asked you if it was okay to switch, and you just said 'one-way system,' so I ate it. I was hungry." Okay. If this ever comes up again, note to self: order both muffins with no cheese. In fact, when I get home, I'm going on a dairy purge. No harm can come of it.

I gingerly work his unzipped hoodie off him so it remains clear of vomit. I pull his T-shirt off, bundle the vomit up into the center of it, and throw the whole thing in the trash. Some puke unavoidably gets smeared onto the front of his hair when his T-shirt comes off, but I manage to get the worst of it out with a handful of wipes. (I have fresh wipes in my bag!) I put the cleanish hoodie back on him and zip it up to the chin. In the section of my purse where I'd stashed the Band-Aid, I've got a brand-new pack of Lactaid Chewables. I hand him one.

"I need water."

"There's a tap. It's full of water." He can just about reach the sink, and he manages to gulp down a few mouthfuls while I rinse off his Crocs. Within four minutes he's more or less cleaned up. There's a faint scent of McDonald's-style puke about him, but you can't have everything. Okay, now to quickly divulge my plans for redeveloping the entire agricultural model for the East African region to Jay and Bob before the inevitable second act starts: diarrhea.

The moment I step back into Bob's glass office, I can tell that something's changed. Bob and Jay look up at me guiltily, almost as if they've been assessed and found wanting. Somehow Violet looks like she's just been handing their asses to them. I suddenly get a firm image of her thirty years from now laying it down in a meeting. It's a bit terrifying.

What on earth has gone down here? I pop my head out into reception. Thelma is nowhere to be seen.

"Do you know where Thelma got to?" I ask.

"Not sure. Maybe she's on a break," says Bob. A break? A break from what? Billy's already slunk over to the side of the room and has reattached himself to his iPad. I sit down and Violet clambers up onto my lap, her warm cheek pressed into my chest. Well, it appears we can just continue on like this, then. *See, Bob, I'm a modern working parent just like you. Nothing like you.* I'm about to jump right in and tell them all the things I've done in the past to get African farmers to sort out their soil, when Jay suddenly stands up.

"I've actually got to run." This is not good. Despite Bob leading most of the "interview" so far, Jay's the guy who's really going to know what I'm talking about.

"Oh, really?" I say. "Could I just quickly outline some of the agricultural processes I've helped farmers to put in place?"

"I'm sor—"

"Organic certification?"

"Another time." *Another time?* The interview is *now.* "Our CEO just got in a little early from Geneva, and he just called me up so . . ." He swoops forward to shake my hand. "It was great to meet you, Amy, and your family. Take care now." Something about that sounds very final somehow. I'm officially worried. As soon as he leaves, I turn back to face Bob. I wonder how interested he's going to be in hearing about my grading scale for fertilizer. I'm going to try it anyhow . . .

"How have you handled the work-life balance so far in your career? With all the travel involved?" he asks. *Your Honor, I object!* Would he be asking a man that question at this stage?

"My husband stays at home with the kids, so the travel's never been an issue for me."

"Even so, there's nothing quite like mommy at home, is there." Wha . . . ? Is there some kind of hotline number I can call to report this level of sexism?

"They all manage just fine without me when I go away. It's fine." I meant to give a slight warning edge to my tone, not a full-on snap. "Sorry."

"It's okay. I know these are the tough issues. I just wanted to see how your family was set up to handle the unusual circumstances. Looks like you've got it all worked out." Oh yes. I've got it all figured out, just perfectly. Damn you, Unsilent Bob. "I apologize, but I actually have to get going too." You've got to be kidding me! "We ran late with our other candidate, and I've got a conference call with Oxfam that we've been trying to get on the books for about six weeks now."

"I understand." I don't understand at all. This is just plain rude. I had to feed my kids *McDonald's* in order to do this interview.

"We'll get you in again. Perhaps just you next time! Though it was lovely to meet the family." Violet pops her head up to give him a scowl. Unhelpful.

On the way out I try to thank Thelma, but she's typing furiously away on the computer and gestures to her headset when I try to say something. I mouth, "Good-bye," she gives me a half smile, and that's the end of that.

It takes about four minutes in the car before the true reason behind my early ejection emerges: Violet.

"I didn't like those guys, Mommy."

"Why not, honey? Didn't he give you some crayons to do a drawing?"

"We never got to the crayons. We were too busy talking."

"About what?" My recently evolved mommy senses are turning the back of my neck icy cold. What did Violet say to Jay and Bob?

"I asked them if they were going to give you a job. They said that's what we were all there to talk about, and I told them why it was a bad idea."

"You what?" What was I thinking? This is *all my fault*. Of course she was going to sabotage the whole endeavor. She's been waiting for this opportunity since she's had conscious thought.

"I said life was awful with you being away all the time. I told him about how you missed my daisy cupcake tea party I had for my birthday this year. I cried for two whole days and nothing Daddy did could make it better. Not even Strawberry Shortcake ice cream. They said that sounded terrible and then I told them all the other things too, and after that they didn't say much at all. They just waited for you to come back."

"What other things?" I may as well know the worst of it. Pandora's box is well and truly opened now.

"That time Billy had the flu, and he had a temperature of one hundred and three point five. We thought because he was so sick, you'd be able to call your boss and say you had to stay home, and you did, but in the end you still had to get on the plane and go anyway." How can she remember that? Isn't everything that happens in the past supposed to be a blur when you're three years old? Trust me to get the kid with the superpowered retentive memory that she uses solely for the purposes of shaming me in job interviews. Ask her what her favorite thing to eat for dinner is or where she put her only pair of shoes that still fit and she's all, "I can't remember."

"I told them about the time Daddy was sad and didn't get out of bed for two days and all we ate that week was Lunchables." What? My God. Is Peter actually depressed as well as crazed? No wonder they called time on the interview. A sad Daddy who can't get out of bed and Lunchables for a week? I wouldn't have felt all roasty toasty inside about employing me either. Well, that's the end of that opportunity. And what am I supposed to do about Violet? Tell her off? It's not like she's done anything wrong. It would be like reprimanding the nine o'clock news for going on about the bad stuff in the Middle East all the time.

"We'll have another tea party for you tomorrow, honey."

"Really?" she asks, all remnants of sulky—brought on by her own reminders of her "tragic" past—instantly dissipated.

"A daisy cupcake tea party?"

"For sure."

"Thank you, Mommy!"

"You are welcome."

You'd better live up those cupcakes, sweetheart, as they'll be the last item of "fun" food you'll be getting for a while. I don't think they let you buy cupcakes with food stamps.

We pull into the driveway. Maybe this is all for the best. Maybe Peter just sold *Draker's Dark* for tons of money, I'll never need to work again, and I can focus the next decade on making up for everything I've ever missed. Peter has friends who make bundles of money from selling screenplays all the time. Okay, there was that one guy, that one time. Not too long ago, one of his old writing buddies sold a brand-new script for exactly one million dollars! Worst, or perhaps best, of all—the screenplay was from an idea that Peter had given him. If Peter has supplied million-dollar ideas to people who don't even have half his talent, surely it's not completely illogical to think that he could sell a script for at least the going rate of fifty grand? I'm not crazy to think that. In fact it's very possible that this could have just happened. I've almost convinced myself that this is what has come to pass by the time I open the door, that the last few months have all just been part of the universe's funny dance.

"What happened with the script?" I ask breathlessly as we pile through the door.

"Nothing much." Ambiguous. Maybe he's about to do one of those Hollywood reversals where he fakes disappointment in order to make the victory allegedly so much sweeter. For example: "Nothing much . . . apart from this check for one million dollars in my back pocket!" It's about the only thing that's not going to land him in an elephant shit-ton of trouble right now.

"Nothing much?"

"The guys hadn't gotten their funding together yet."

"Funding? Which studio was it?"

"It wasn't. It was independent. Turned out they were looking to crowdsource to get the money if you can believe it."

"Crowdsource? Where did you find out about these people?"

"Craigslist."

"What the fuck!"

Everyone looks at me, shocked. I normally swear only in my head and generally not in front of the children; it's all been confirmed long ago that Peter's the one with the temper. *Not today.*

"I basically just got kicked out of a job interview I should have nailed because Violet told them I missed her cupcake tea party this year, and they suddenly got all paranoid and patriarchal about employing a woman who would have to leave her children alone for weeks on end in order to get the job done."

"I'm sorry. I just . . . Snippet, *I know* that's not what you really want, to leave the kids. I know you don't want that."

"What I want is for us to be able to eat."

"Look, I just needed to put my career in first place this time."

"You career doesn't get to go in a *place* on a list because it doesn't exist!"

There's a silence. I've kind of crossed a line here. But can you blame me? This has been brewing for a while.

"It does exist. You have no patience."

"You're completely right. I'm all out of patience."

"Look," he says, standing up and pulling his ancient leather laptop case onto his shoulder. Oh, I used to think that laptop case was so cool. It was one of the things that first drew me to him. Younger me really needed to work on what makes a man a good catch. "I know you're upset. But I'm telling you this is all going to work out for the best. I picked up a few really great notes from the meeting. This thing's going to be razor-sharp before I send it out again."

Oh, I know what this smells like. He's already inching toward the door. He's heading off to write.

"Not so fast."

"What?"

"I haven't had a mother-beeping second to myself since I didn't get on that plane to Addis Ababa. You're going to watch the kids right now. I need a moment."

"We know when you say 'beeping' that you really mean 'fucking,'" says Billy.

"Okay, thanks, Billy." I pick up my purse. I already *have* my shoes on. "I'm going out, alone. And I probably won't be back in time for dinner."

And with that, I leave. No one is more shocked than I am.

Half an hour later I'm at The Solid Cup, my very favorite coffee shop. Not that you'd have any reason to think it was my favorite as I haven't been here in about a year. I'm three sips into a heaven-sent and also heaven-scented cup of exquisite Ljulu Lipati prepared by Ana, my favorite barista, who incidentally won the US Barista Championship last year. Girl knows how to make a brew. I open up my iBooks again and turn to where I left off. I pull a notepad out of my purse and rip off all the messy pages on the top. There's no room for scribble in here. I'm devoting this notebook to holding information on one subject only: how to be a mother.

CHAPTER 19

So after two weeks of silence from FMC Trading, I finally broke down and called them about coming in for another interview. After leaving a couple of messages that weren't returned, I managed to call just as Bob was walking into the office. Lexi forgot to mute her end of the conversation and it became pretty clear, pretty quickly that Bob did not want to speak to me then, or ever again. When she came back to the phone, she lied and told me I'd just missed him, and a few days after that I received a formal rejection letter.

This does not leave us in a good situation. At all. We're finally out of savings, and this month I'm going to have to skip the mortgage payment in order to buy food and keep the lights on. Billy's preschool tuition hasn't been paid since I lost my job. They've been pretty understanding about it up until this week, when I got a slightly salty reminder notice asking for payment. I intend to push their bohemian generosity to the limit, but at some point it's inevitable that I'm going to have to withdraw him.

Right now, Peter's sitting at the kitchen table wearing nothing but a towel, his wet dark curls stuck against his forehead. It must be said he looks quite appealing, and if my children weren't running the entirety of the house playing Viking warriors, I might be tempted to snatch that towel off him. And *why* is he not wearing any clothes? Because no one has done any laundry in recent memory, and once he'd peeled off his pajamas in order to have a shower this morning, he didn't have anything clean to change into. And why has the laundry not been done? Because I'm on strike. There are *two* unemployed adults living in this house now, and I don't see why I should always have to be the one to do the laundry when I actually fill way less than my allotted quarter of the hamper. Peter used to be quite the whiz at laundry before I lost my job, so I'm sure the empty drawers that were once filled with clean clothing will, at some point, cause him to remember how it's done. However, right now Peter seems completely uninterested in getting dressed anytime soon and is busy typing on his laptop.

"I thought you'd finished the rewrite?" I ask.

"I have," he says. "But the whole thing's shit, so I'm starting again."

Billy roars into the kitchen.

"Mom! Water!"

"Say please, Billy."

"Please Billy."

"Smarty-pants. Sit at the table." Billy sits at the table and gulps his water as fast as he can.

"This thing needs a major overhaul, and then I'm thinking of sending it to Nico."

"Is it really necessary to start all over again? Can't you just send it to him as it is and ask for some feedback?"

"No way. It's a complete mess. If someone sees it as it is, that'll be the end of my career. Forever."

"Don't be so dramatic," I snap as Billy helter-skelters out of the kitchen again.

Aside from the brief flicker of approval a moment ago upon seeing my husband in nothing more than a towel, I'm actually completely mad at him. I just got off the phone with Matt, who told me he's been leaving messages for Peter, basically offering him his job back. Has Peter returned his call? No. Has Peter said a word to me about it? No. All he has to do is this weeklong anger-detox course that Matt's found for him and then he's back in. Employed once more. Money going into the bank instead of out of it. It's the answer to all our problems. What on earth is he playing at?

"So Matt called me just now." Peter continues to tip-tap into his laptop. "I said Matt called. We talked." Still no response from Peter. I know he can hear me. And I know he *knows* he's in trouble.

"Called to catch up on old times, did he?"

"No!" I respond a little too quickly. "We talked about you. Will you stop typing into that thing for a minute?"

He slams down the lid of his laptop. I don't care if he throws a fit right now; we are going to have this out. If he does explode, it will only underline the point that he definitely should do an anger-management course.

"I heard his messages."

"So why haven't you called him back? Do you not realize how badly we need someone in this household to be employed right now?"

"He and I have a personality clash. A weeklong course isn't going to fix that."

"It might. And anyway, it doesn't matter if it doesn't cure you. He said if you do the course, he'll take you back."

"Why?"

"I don't know why. Does it matter?"

"There are hundreds of excellent writers out there looking for work. Why's he wasting his time running in circles setting up fancy courses for me to do?"

"He said HR told him he had to do it."

"HR? Colburn Entertainment doesn't have an HR department, Amy." Well, that is a little weird. "He's probably just trying to get me off the scene for a week so he can get his hands on you."

"What?" I say, a bit shrilly. I squash down the quick thrill of pleasure that this might be true.

"You know this course is an inpatient program, in Malibu?"

"I didn't know that."

"It's basically like rehab. You'd be on your own here with the kids for a week."

"That's no problem. I don't know why you're not jumping at the chance. I'd love to go and spend a week in Malibu. It'd be like a vacation!"

"I'd be locked up in a facility with a bunch of nutjobs, not surfing with Matthew McConaughey every morning. I'm not doing it."

"It's a week of therapy, which someone else is paying for, and after you've done that, you get your job back. You need the therapy. We need the money. There's no way you're not doing this."

"There's no way I *am* doing it."

"If you don't do it, I'll leave you." This is, of course, a completely idle threat that I've no intention of going through with. But still I'm surprised when I hear myself say it.

"Oh, please. And go where exactly?"

A nanosecond later Peter and I both jump to parental alert as an awful sound comes from the living room. It's a scream, and not one of Violet's high-pitched attention grabbers. It's Billy. And it's the scream that comes after that long opened-mouth silent scream and the ragged inhale of breath that comes after it. It's a heart-stopper.

Peter and I race into the living room. It's probably the pinnacling moment of my career as a bad mother that I notice Peter's lost his towel before I notice the bleeding gash at the corner of Billy's right eye.

"Look, I'm Tinkerbell!" says Violet, making the perilous leap from the ottoman to the recliner, trying to give everyone the instant replay of what just happened.

"Off the chair, Violet!" I yell, as Peter dives forward to scoop Billy up. He's the one who handles medical emergencies in our household.

"No, I want Mommy," says Billy through his tears.

Everyone freezes on the spot. Even Billy stops crying for half a second. This is unprecedented. However, this is my moment; I don't need to be asked twice. I've been waiting for him to show even a vague preference for me over his father—or over anyone at all, really—for five long years, and I'm not about to bow out just because we're suddenly going against the normal order of things.

I pick him up and almost buckle under his weight. What happened to the little toddler I used to be able to hold under one arm when he was throwing a tantrum? Staggering, I manage to somehow make it across the length of the house and dump him down next to the bathroom sink.

"Why did you carry me?" he asks in between snotty sniffs.

"The situation seemed to require it. Bear with me. I'm new to this handling-emergencies thing," I say softly.

"You're doing okay," he says. And gives me a tiny smile. He's got blood smeared down one side of his face and it still seems to be flowing. I start tearing the cabinets apart looking for Band-Aids, a bandage, ice pack—anything! There's nothing here. Where has Peter moved it all to? He has a habit of moving essential things and not telling me where they've gone that frustrates me to the point of frenzy. I've got my own medical kit I use for travel, but it's still buried right at the bottom of my backpack, which I've yet to unpack. I squash down a silly suspicion that this whole scenario's been engineered by Peter to expose me as a terrible mother. All I can find to stem the flow of blood is one rather old maxi pad. If maxi pads had expiration dates, this one would be well past it. Still, this is material designed to absorb flowing blood, technically speaking, so I carefully stick it over his eye and apply pressure. That will have to do till I can dig out my kit.

At that moment Peter walks in with a basketful of first aid items, an ice pack, and a damp washcloth.

"My son has a sanitary pad stuck to his head," he says.

"I couldn't find the first aid kit. It's stemming the blood loss," I reply.

He gives me a look that I immediately translate as: *So not only have you usurped my hard-earned place as the parent to run to after receiving an owie, the first thing you've done in your new role is to stick a product for menstruating women on my firstborn's face.*

My look back translates as: *Get over it. And in the future, keep the first aid kit in the bathroom like the rest of the world does.*

I notice with a little disappointment that he's now wearing a pair of jeans that he must have pulled out of the laundry pile.

"Shall I?" he says out loud, indicating that he's going to remove the maxi pad.

"I'll do it," I say. *You're not overthrowing me that quickly.* I give it a little tug.

"Ow," says Billy. The damn thing's stuck to his head.

"Let me try," Peter says.

"No, let Mommy do it," says Billy.

"Okay," says Peter, hands up in the air. "If you want me, I'll be doing laundry."

Double score! Now I have to figure out how to get this pad off. Genius strikes. I wet a sponge and gently squeeze it behind the pad, over Billy's eye, and after a moment it releases. I pull the pad away and try not to let my face show any reaction. There's blood everywhere. I consciously repress an urge to call Peter back and instead start dabbing at the cut. Billy's being remarkably brave about it. Especially for Billy. He and I have been cautiously moving toward a new understanding over the past few days since I read all of that parenting book and got some pointers on how to handle a child with an "overactive emotional system." It mostly boils down to this: when dealing with a crazed child, be as mellow as he is insane. I've been trying the extra-calm approach with Billy, and I keep getting flickers of signs that it might be working.

Finally, I manage to get the area clear, and after a short while the cut seems to stop bleeding.

"What happened?" I ask.

"Violet said I couldn't fly, so I was trying to show her that I could, but when I tried to go up, I just went down and hit my head on the bar."

"Right."

Does he really think he can fly or was he just trying to prove Violet wrong about something? She can be annoyingly pedantic sometimes. Now that the bleeding's stopped and I can get a proper look, I can tell that this could probably use a couple of stitches. I quickly pull the two sides of the wound apart and get a flash of red. Yeah, stitches needed. Even though Peter's the one we all go to in a medical emergency, from my years traveling around developing countries, I'm actually the parent with the most hands-on medical knowledge. The wound's long, from the top of his eye socket to out beyond his eyebrow. If Peter knew it was this bad, he would not be leaving me in charge. If Peter knew it was this bad, we'd be heading for urgent care right now. But he doesn't know. He also doesn't know that we have no medical insurance right now either, because I couldn't afford to pay the last COBRA bill. I'm going to have to stitch this myself before Peter discovers what I'm doing and shuts it down.

"Billy, I'm going to give you a couple of stitches, okay? Just so you don't get a scar."

"But scar's are cool, Mom."

"I know. But stitches are cooler. Trust me," I say. I sneak into the bedroom, heave out my backpack from under the bed, and dig through, looking for my medical kit. Can't find it. I upend the contents all over the bed. Still not there. Where is it? Oh yes, I packed it in the side pocket. I unzip the compartment and there it is. Being organized did not work in my favor today.

Back in the bathroom I clean the wound again, this time adding a little soap. One more item needed. Should still be under the sink.

Found it. Vaginal numbing spray. This is the stuff they gave me after I had stitches all the way up to my rectum after I gave birth to Billy. If Peter had moved that, I'd have *really* wanted to know why.

Considering I've only done this a couple of times before, I make pretty quick work of the whole thing. Billy seems more fascinated than squeamish, which is handy. I heat the needle, douse the wound in iodine, squeeze the gash together, and then go for it. The vaginal numbing spray must work better than I remember, because Billy doesn't make a peep, bless him.

"What a brave soldier," I say, looping the last stitch through and making a neat knot. Billy looks up at me with his kaleidoscope eyes, so like mine, and doesn't say a word. He doesn't need to. His look says it all: *I love you.*

After Billy's run back off to *Peter Pan*, the remake, I go in the bedroom to return my medical kit to the backpack with plans to ram the whole thing back under my bed again. Yes, I should probably get around to unpacking properly. But today is not going to be that day. I start picking up bundles of clothes and shoving them back in, unfolded, of course. As I pick up a pile of maps, a small envelope slides out from between them and falls to the floor. This will be my letter. Every time I go on a trip, Peter hides a letter somewhere in my stuff. He always uses the breadth and depth of his writerly skills, and its contents normally have me sobbing into a dirty T-shirt on some dusty continent miles away from him.

I open the envelope. This time there's no letter inside. Just a photo. It's *the* photo. The photo that's more or less the reason we got married so soon after meeting. The photo that's been Peter's "get out of jail free" card since the beginning. It's a picture of him and me. And we're both about seven years old. He's in the foreground next to his mother. I'm a little hazy, about four feet behind him, holding on to my father's hand and looking directly into the camera. We're all at the Lincoln Park Zoo in Chicago. Just to clarify, this picture was taken in 1984, more than two decades before Peter and I ever met.

This picture would be crazy coincidence enough if all the families involved had actually lived in Chicago all our lives, but none of us did. Peter's family was visiting his grandparents that week, and my family was taking the one and only "city break" we ever did. The first time I saw the picture was after things had started taking a serious-ish turn between Peter and me, and we went to visit Peter's family in Boston. His mother was doing the obligatory run-through of embarrassing childhood pics when she turned the page in the family album and all of a sudden, there I was. Seven years old, snapped in a shot alongside my future husband.

I took it as a sign. How could I not? Peter did too. A lack of imagination was never one of his weak points. Not long after we saw the picture, we were engaged and then married. And anytime I've ever been really seriously close to throwing in the towel on our relationship, I remember—or he reminds me—about the picture and we relive the moment all over again. For how can such synchronicity be random? How can it *not* be significant that two kids, living hundreds of miles apart, have a picture of themselves together at an out-of-town zoo, only to fall in love years later in a completely different part of the country? I met a statistician once who told me that the odds were high, but not impossible. Peter and I think the odds are way too high for it not to be meaningful. We're fated to be together. It's just too weird and wild to think about otherwise. He and I are meant to be.

As I look at the picture of us both as sweet seven-year-olds, with no clue that we're feet away from our future spouse/tormentor, I start to cry. Maybe that dinner-party statistician was right, and I've put too much meaning onto this coincidence. Maybe it's not written in the stars that Peter and I are supposed to be together. Maybe no one's up there writing anything at all. Perhaps the only writers are down here on earth and it's simply a snapshot taken at a zoo. Just a random occurrence out of the millions upon billions of occurrences that happen every day. We, the silly humans, are the ones who have attached significance to it when in reality there is none. It's just something that happened.

Peter's standing in the doorway, holding a basketful of laundry. When he sees I'm crying, he balances it on the bed, on top of the other mound of clothes, and comes to sit down next to me. He gives me a soft kiss on the cheek and strokes the hand that's holding the photo.

"You and me," he whispers. "Together before we were even together."

"I know," I say, and snuggle in to his neck. His beard's got so fulsome now I can almost disappear right behind it.

"I know I've been driving you crazy with this script," he says.

"Um, just a bit."

"It's the only way I know how to make our lives right again. Half measures aren't going to fix this. Whatever needs to happen to pull us out of this, it's got to be big." We pause. I think we're both contemplating the "bigness" of what we might have to do in order to make our lives even nearly livable. "It kills me that you haven't had the relationship with the kids that you've wanted, that I haven't been able to give you that. I love you so much. I just want to make you happy."

"If you do this course, you will make me completely happy. I promise. That's all I ask. Do the course. I'll be so happy, you won't even recognize me."

I come out from under his beard. He's looking down at the picture. It's always meant so much to him. Out of the two of us, I think he's the one that always put more meaning on it.

"It is my mission," he says, and kisses me hard on top of my head, "to make you happy. I'll do it. Just don't say that we'll split up ever again. Even if you don't mean it. Promise me that and I'll do the course."

"I promise," I say as he slips the picture out of my grasp.

"Good," he says.

"I love you," I say.

This makes him smile; he's normally the one who says it first. Is this love, or is this feeling of eternal attachment, of no boundaries between his brain and mine, because we've just been in this for so long? Maybe I love Peter just because he's become part of me? If I don't love him, that means I don't love myself either.

"I love you too. And I always will."

CHAPTER 20

I'm officially having a bad morning. I just got back from dropping Peter off in Malibu, and now I'm going through the cupboards in an attempt to comfort eat my way out of my emotional state, only to find there isn't one carbohydrate-based food substance in this house. I'm starving. Delivering Peter to the "nuthouse" (his words, not mine) was always going to be a little bit fraught. But the way things went down this morning, it ended up being downright traumatic.

We were heading down the Pacific Coast Highway and everything was going as well as could be expected when Peter got a call from Nico, his old agent. Apparently, somehow the script that Peter thought would be a career stopper if it made its way into circulation, made its way into circulation. And how did the beast get free? Nico got an e-mail from Peter's account with the script attached. He was calling Peter about it not because he thought the script was fabulous but because he was furious. No one likes to receive an unsolicited script—especially not from a writer who's known for his tendency to lawyer up at the drop of a hat. Right after Peter hung up from talking Nico down, he started laying in to me. He'd decided that I must have sent Nico the script in order to sabotage his writing career so he'd retrain as a dental hygienist

(I mentioned that *once*) and start earning a normal salary. I told him that I didn't send his stupid script out, but he refused to believe me, and within seconds the whole thing flared up into one of our hugest fights ever. I pulled over on the side of the PCH, told him to get his butt out of the car and walk the rest of the way to the nuthouse, and then I sped off. In my defense it's been a somewhat stressful time. Of course, I circled around to come and pick him up again, but it takes longer than you'd think to find somewhere you can do a U-turn on the PCH, and by the time I got back to him, he was *steaming*. At least when we finally arrived at the clinic, they got a good sample of the kind of behavioral problem they're supposed to be dealing with.

Despite the fact that we were both spitting mad at drop-off, when it was time for him to go, we clung to each other like we were being separated forever. We've had some good-byes steeped in drama before, but this one took the chocolate cake.

I shake the last of the pumpkin flax granola into the kids' cereal bowls. The doorbell rings and I hear Billy open the door. I search the bread bin. Empty. Looks like I'm skipping breakfast today. I need to get right on that food stamps thing.

"Mom," says Billy. "It's Lizzie—she wants to talk to you." Oh, great. Just what I need when my blood sugar is so low I can barely remember my name: a visit from the Organic Goddess herself. Maybe she's found it in her heart to bring us some of those minipancakes I could smell her microwaving this morning. And how did I know she microwaved them? My kitchen window looks into hers, and if I stand in the right spot, I can see directly to the place where the microwave is. For someone who has a produce basket attached to the front of her bicycle, she uses the microwave more than you would think. I get to the door and see it's not minipancakes she's come to offer us; she, in fact, is holding Banksy aloft for my inspection. Poor Banksy seems to have been what I can only describe as shorn—which might seem a strange word to describe a cat's haircut, but the only one I can think of to sum up the look accurately. But perhaps that's just because of the low blood sugar. His shearing doesn't seem to be completely uniform. In some places I can see the skin; some places the hair is still as long as it always was. This was not an expert job.

"What happened to your cat?" I ask.

"I thought you might be able to help me answer that," she says. I notice her outfit today isn't nearly as concocted as it normally is. Just a pair of jeans and an oversize T-shirt that reads "twerk." The jeans aren't even skinny jeans. No fashion parade plus premade breakfast? What's going on over there?

"How so?" I ask.

"Billy," she says to him, "I need you to be honest. Did you do this to Banksy?"

Billy does a great show of being completely surprised and also scandalized by the question.

"Of course not," he says. "Why would I do that to your cat?"

"Well, *someone* did it." She glares at us both.

"Why would it be Billy?" I ask. I'm about ninety-nine percent certain it most definitely *was* Billy, but in case we all forget, I've been making tentative steps into my eldest's good books recently, and I'm not about to give all that up in order to satisfy Lizzie the Pet Detective that her case is closed. She's going to need to produce hard evidence before I'll even entertain the notion.

"Oh, why indeed?" she asks.

"What happened to innocent until proven guilty?" I reply. The law is on my side here.

"Are these your kitchen scissors?" she asks, holding up a pair of scissors labeled "Amy's Kitchen Scissors" on one blade. Don't ask. Okay, one day a couple of years back Peter and I deviated from our usual "who has it harder" fight into a "who brought more furniture and household items to the marriage" argument. It resulted in him getting the labeling gun out to make a point. Peter's spoon. Peter's microwave. Peter's nasty vintage Plymouth mantel clock. Et cetera. The only things I could find that were definitively mine were the kitchen scissors and the coffee-making equipment. So I labeled them. It seemed like a sassy thing to do at the time, but now it looks like my sass has come back to haunt me. "They were found in my front yard. They had Banksy's hair on the blades," she says.

"Circumstantial evidence," I respond, grabbing the scissors out of her hands. "Have you checked your spy app?"

"Spy app?"

"Your cameras." I'd better backtrack a bit here. If she's got footage of Billy doing this, I'm going to have to apologize.

"It's surveillance. Not spying. And the cameras are down," she says. "The Internet's been cut off."

"Cut off?" I ask.

"I mean, it's not working," she says. She's lying. And I've no idea why. My phone starts ringing from the dock in the living room where I generally keep it these days so it can act as our alternative sound system. (We sold Peter's fancy audio equipment a while back.) I ignore it.

"Do you want the password to our Wi-Fi?" I ask. It's an olive branch.

"Sure," she says.

I'm using "our Wi-Fi" in a rather loose sense here. It's the Wi-Fi of the bed-and-breakfast across the street. We stopped paying our Time Warner bill weeks ago. Peter stayed the night over there once, back when we had money—wanting to drive home his point that it was He Who Has It Harder. It seemed a bit insane at the time—and a complete waste of money—but now I can see how he felt justified in sleeping away from home for one night after I'd had weeks and weeks away. The cost of his one-night rebellion has more than paid us back in Wi-Fi access over the last few weeks.

"Username: The Lemons. Password: Lemons," I say, my insides turning ice-cold as I suddenly realize that if by chance she or Daniel has ever stayed there, this situation could get very embarrassing very fast.

"Is that because of your lemon tree out front?" she asks. *Phew.*

"It's a lovely tree, isn't it?" I say. "Help yourself to lemons anytime." Lie technically avoided.

"Billy, I just need to know you won't do this again," says Lizzie.

Poor Banksy really does look a sight. I always gave him the benefit of the doubt and thought his big hair was why he looked so stocky, but with his fur mostly gone, you can see he's just a very portly animal. Quite the potbelly.

"I won't do it again," he says. I give Lizzie a weak smile. "Because I didn't do it in the first place!" He thunders back into the house. A moment later I hear his bedroom door slam. He's five! I didn't get into slamming bedroom doors until I was at least fourteen. The foundations of our house will be shaken to dust by the time he leaves home.

From the corner of the room, my phone starts up again. I go over and pick it up. It's Matt, calling for a second time. I hit "Decline" and stick it in my pocket. What does he want?

"Well, I'll catch you later," I say to Lizzie, closing the door. "Enjoy the Wi-Fi."

"What about my ca—" And the door is closed. I suppose it's a rude way to terminate the conversation, but I don't think there's much more room for negotiation today. My son gave her cat a terrible haircut, he denied it, and I gave her a Wi-Fi password to compensate. I'm not sure where else there is to go from here. Suddenly I get a flash of how wearisome life must be for a member of Congress.

I knock on Billy's door and then carefully open it. There's a boy-sized lump under the bedcovers.

"Billy," I whisper, and slowly pull back his comforter. "You can't slam doors like that. I know you feel angry, but please, think of the poor doorframes."

"Thanks for telling her I didn't do it," he says. He looks like he's been crying. This is terrible.

"Of course," I say. I seem to remember my role more as questioning his involvement than flat-out denying it—but I'm not about to point that out.

"You're an okay mom, you know," he says, and my heart flies through the sky like a liberated helium balloon. Maybe this is how it all starts. Twenty years from now I'll be on the stand at Los Angeles Superior Court: "I swear he didn't do it, Your Honor—he was in all night, virtual-hiking through the Schiaparelli crater."

"Do you think you're going to go away again soon?" he asks, but instead of looking expectant like he normally does when he asks that question, he looks worried.

"I don't think so, sweetheart," I reply. It's true. It's not looking likely. Violet has more or less given up her limpet act these days and stopped looking at me with suspicious eyes. Even she's sussed out that my employment prospects are more or less nil at this point. Even if I don't bring her to the interview.

"I didn't like it when you used to go. It made me feel sad. And angry too. Sometimes I'd slam the bedroom door after you left." I'm immediately depressed and overjoyed all at the same time. Peter never told me about any of this preschooler drama. "I was mad about the cat thing. That's why I slammed the door."

"Hmm."

"You know it wasn't me, Mommy?" I allow an infinitesimal pause before opening my mouth to reply and it's my undoing. He sees the doubt in my eyes. I don't need to say a word. "It wasn't me! I don't lie about things. Now go away!" He's back under his covers before you can say "fractured mother-son relationship." I've blown it.

My phone starts ringing, *again.* Damn it. It's still Matt. This is the third time he's called in the space of a few minutes. I'm about to hit "Decline" again and switch the thing off when I suddenly wonder if something's happened with Peter. I'm not sure if the rehab even has my number.

"I love you, Billy," I say to the covers, and leave him to it. Maybe we'll get a chance to talk again later. Or maybe that's it, I've lost him forever, and the next time we have a proper conversation will be on the long drive back from the police station after I've bailed him out on a joyriding charge.

"Matt? What's going on?"

"Oh, hi!"

"Is it Peter? Is he okay?"

"Peter?"

"You just called me three times in a row. I thought it was an emergency! With Peter?"

"I was just calling to say hi. Why weren't you picking up?"

"I was in the middle of something! Why don't you leave a message like a normal person? Calling three times in a row is the international sign for There's Trouble. You know that."

"Sorry. I'm just used to people picking up when I call them. I don't like voice mail."

"Nobody likes voice mail, or paying taxes, or eating broccoli, but we do it anyway."

"I like broccoli."

"What do you want?"

"I want to take you out for the night."

"No, thank you."

"When was the last time you went *out* out? When was the last time you had some fun? Just one night, we'll talk it all through, and then if you don't want to hang out anymore after that, that's fine."

"Peter says Colburn Entertainment doesn't have an HR department. He says you only sequestered him away to a clinic in Malibu so you could get your hands on me."

"I don't have a department, but I do have a consultant. Her name is Wendy Wong and she lives in Brentwood. Do you want her number?" Damn it.

"And what exactly is it that you feel you need to talk through?" Is he finally going to drag me through that blow-by-blow analysis of why we split up?

"I want to talk to you about where things stand with Peter."

"We were still married last time I looked."

"I mean with his career."

Awkward. "Right."

"Listen. I'm free tonight—I'll pick you up at seven."

"I can't tonight."

"What are you up to, then? Tantric yoga for one? Come on. I know you're just going to be sitting on your couch drinking three-day-old Pinot watching *Game of Thrones*." How does he *know*? "I'll be there at seven."

"How—"

"And Amy?"

"What?"

"Wear something nice."

CHAPTER 21

Of course, the time I actually don't want a babysitter to be free, Arielle is one hundred percent available. This is pretty inconvenient, as not being able to get a babysitter at such short notice would have been a stellar and very plausible excuse for me not to go out on this date. But that's not how it went down. Arielle got here twenty minutes ago and now Matt's standing at the front door, staring.

I can't actually believe what I look like right now. And from the way Matt keeps looking at me, neither can he. Well, he said dress *nice*, didn't he? As soon as I got off the phone with him, a due-diligence audit of my wardrobe confirmed that I wasn't in possession of anything "nice." Having given up on the whole having pride thing a long time ago, I threw myself at Lizzie's mercy and, seeing as giving me a complete and utter makeover was something she was actually interested in doing, she hooked me up. I told her I was going to my college reunion and she believed me. Let's hope she never discovers that I attended college for all of one year before dropping out—and in London at that. The fact that I lied to Lizzie underlines the truth, of course, which is that I'm doing something tonight that I certainly shouldn't be. The first lie has been woven.

I have to say, the transformation is rather dramatic. I'm in a slinky blue dress with some helpful underwear beneath it. My hair has been excessively pulled at with a flat iron until it's lost its usual halo of fuzz. I'm wearing very expensive makeup.

"That's more than a dress. That's an Audrey Hepburn movie," says Matt. I'd forgotten his slightly annoying habit of quoting movie lines at the times when I'd like him to actually be genuine.

"Get home before midnight, Mommy, or you'll turn into a pumpkin," says Violet, who is, of course, entranced by my transformation.

And what exactly do I think I'm playing at, dressing up like this and going out on a date with my ex? I'm getting a glimpse, that's what. And then I'm going to walk away. If I can't have the life, I can at least get a good look at what it is I'm missing out on. No one can argue that I'm not entitled to that. I want to see it up close. I'm hoping that I hate everything about it. And if I love it? Well, in that case the memories will just have to last me a long time, won't they?

Matt and I are whizzing along the freeway in comfortable silence. Maybe he's saving the big conversational download about Peter's future for over dinner. My brain's so busy drinking in the decadence that is the inside of his Porsche, I'm not sure I'd be able to concentrate on a conversation anyway. I'm a sucker for a leather interior. The most luxurious thing about the Honda is that it smells fruity. And that's only because Billy recently decided to smear half my strawberry lip balm over the backseat. As we pull up to the restaurant, I get a zip of anticipation through my stomach. Matt just happened to mention on the way over that the executive chef—a friend of his—is putting together a special tasting menu just for us. He also told me this place has recently been awarded two Michelin stars. I'm officially excited.

As soon as the Porsche comes to a stop, the valet runs to open my door for me. I can't remember the last time someone opened a car door for me, or any kind of door actually. I swirl my legs to the side in perfectly clamped-together unison. No one will be getting a flash of my lacy underwear tonight. Not unintentionally anyway. I didn't say that! Seriously, though, that's not what tonight's about. Besides, the fact that I flat-out fail the pencil test these days is reason enough to conceal my body from anyone who isn't legally contracted not to run away from it.

I gracefully extend one leg toward the sidewalk and then rise up to my new height, complete with four heel-added inches. I feel like a supermodel. Matt comes around to join me, and we start to walk toward the restaurant. I'm already having the time of my life and we haven't even gone inside yet. We're almost at the ramp when two guys on skateboards, who've been flying down the sidewalk for the last few seconds, clatter to a noisy halt right in front of us. Suddenly we're inside a blinding cloud of flashing light, surrounded by the sound of camera shutters opening and closing multiple times—I didn't know a camera could be so loud. Within two seconds the photographers have taken off again.

However, it's too late for me—I'm officially losing my balance. Lizzie's heels are surprisingly easy to walk in, and they fit so snugly that up till this moment I've felt like a surefooted goat climbing the side of a mountain. But now that I'm four inches taller, my whole center of gravity is in a different place. It had been shifted forward as I walked toward the door, but with the skateboarder ambush I had to make a sudden shift back, and the move was too quick for me to compensate. As I watch Matt halfheartedly chase after them, my arms are doing huge, rapid backward windmills, hoping to grab on to anything, *anyone*. On my third staggering step backward, my heel misses contact with the sidewalk; I list to the side and fall flat to the ground. My cheekbone smacks hard onto the concrete.

For a second, everything's numb, and then in its place the hard ache of pain comes rushing in. Instead of crying, I close my eyes. When I open them again, I note that I'm face-to-face with a small green shrub.

"Hello, shrub," I try to say, but my mouth seems to be clogged up with tiny stones. I just ate gravel. Literally. I start to spit the stones out of my mouth. At least I hope it's gravel and not my teeth. Just when I'm beginning to wonder why no one is helping me out, I feel a lift under my armpits and suddenly I'm sitting upright. A man wearing a well-tailored suit appears to be the one who sat me straight.

"Are you okay?" he asks.

I try to talk; a bit more gravel has to come out first.

"I think so. I hit my face on the ground." Someone comes rushing forward with a glass of water. I take a sip. I'm not so injured that I don't notice that the glass is very thin with a rim so delicate you could bite it in two if you wanted to. I'm almost back to enjoying myself here.

"Can you stand?"

"Yeah," I say, and start my shaky ascent upward. Before I get all the way to standing, I feel a release of liquid in my nose and a torrent of blood floods down my face, dripping right onto the middle of my/ Lizzie's dress. Oh, great. That's going to go down like a cup of cold vomit. Matt comes jogging back down the street and speeds up to a run when he sees me stumbling around, bleeding.

"What happened?" he snaps at the maître d', as if it were all his fault.

"I'm sorry. Gwyneth Paltrow was supposed to be coming in tonight with her new guy. They must have thought you were them." Matt seems mildly pissed at this information. I know why—he thought the paps were for him. I, meanwhile, am elated that someone could have mistaken me for Gwyneth! Yup, officially back to having a good time again. I feel a puff of relief that at least we won't have to worry about the images surfacing anywhere. Once they figure out it's just little ol' me, those pics will be trash bound. I revel in the exclusive insight of how annoying it must feel to be in the constant eye of the media. My nose appears to have stopped gushing, and apart from a square lump I can feel rising up on my cheekbone, I'm in pretty good shape. I've dealt with worse and gone on to do more demanding things than eat dinner before now. The dress is a darkish blue, so the blood isn't too noticeable. Let's do this!

"Come on, Matt, let's just go inside."

"Are you kidding me?" he says.

"Er, no. I'm fine. I just need to clean up a bit and I'm good to go."

"You're injured!"

"It's just a tap to the head."

"You need to get ice on that."

"So I'll put some ice on. Inside." What is his problem? I don't know why, but suddenly I can see my glorious evening slipping out of my grasp.

"We're not going inside, Amy. You're a wreck."

"I'm fine." From behind me I hear the valet opening the car door. Wait! Don't I get a choice in this?

"Come on," says Matt, guiding me by the elbow into the front seat. "We'll come back another time."

No, we won't. This was my one opportunity and now it's gone. Peter would never let me walk out the door looking like this for a night on the town with my millionaire ex. No one who had any interest in holding on to their wife would. It's like Cinderella got a black eye on the way to the ball and then wasn't allowed inside the palace because she looked too rough.

This is not fair!

Matt takes off driving pretty fast and he shoots by the on-ramp for the 110.

"You missed the freeway," I say.

"I'm taking you home."

"Well, you're going the wrong way."

"I'm taking you to my home." *Oh.* "It's not far. We can get you cleaned up and have a minute to talk before I have to hand you back over."

I consider protesting, but seeing as I'm not the one driving, I don't think it will get me very far. Plus, it must be said, I am a little intrigued to see his fancy house. We make a left on a nondescript street and start to climb. Then we start to wind. Within about thirty seconds we've left the urban sprawl of an American city and have entered the south of France. I'm starting to enjoy myself yet again. The windier and narrower the road, the more my spirits lift.

"How does anyone ever get out of this rabbit warren in the morning?"

"It's not exactly a bunch of commuters living up here."

Welcome to the Hollywood Hills. We slow down outside a nothing-special black iron gate. He punches in a code and the gate rolls back, revealing another steep incline. I think all this incline/decline business would actually get on my nerves after a while. I suddenly wonder what Kimberly's going to think about Matt bringing home his beaten-up ex-girlfriend. Does she even know I'm his ex-girlfriend? I never did find out about the presence, or lack, of my legendry in the Colburn household.

"What are your kids' names again?" I ask, subtly reminding Matt that his family resides alongside him inside his fancy home.

"Jessy and Asher. The nanny will have them down by now. Kimberly's at a retreat. We'll have the place to ourselves."

That sounds ominously presumptuous. And why is it that the people who least need an exotic retreat are always the ones to get them? Most people would consider Kimberly's daily life a retreat from the real world—what on earth is it that she needs to retreat *from*?

Finally, we get to the top of the slope and I see it, Matt's home. This is how Elizabeth Bennet must have felt the first time she laid eyes on Pemberley: *this could have been mine.* It's huge. It's architecturally beautiful. A mass of glass boxes piled one on top of the other. Every light in the place is on, illuminating the whole spectacle like a dollhouse on display. I'd be worried about people looking in and seeing me in my underwear, but I suppose it's not like anyone can just walk or drive by. Considering we're right in the middle of Los Angeles, this place feels surprisingly isolated.

"I guess you don't care much about the size of your carbon footprint." I hope that didn't sound as snarky as I'm feeling. We drive up toward the garage. One of four garage doors starts to rise as we approach. It's completely soundless.

"Actually, this place is pretty eco-friendly. All the bulbs are energy efficient, and we get most of our power from the solar panels on the roof."

"Still, doesn't help matters if you leave all the lights on." I pout.

We enter the house and I try not to stare at everything. This place is a shrine to modern living at its most perfect. And it's so neatly ordered, I can't believe that anyone lives here. Let alone two kids. I know Matt's watching for my reaction. I'm not going to show him even a flicker of the explosion of admiration that's going on inside my head.

"Where's her retreat?" If I'm looking through the window into this life, I may as well get the full picture.

"Bora Bora," he says. "She always goes to the same place with her sister. She says she couldn't get through the year without it." Oh, *please*. Matt opens up a door to reveal a bathroom the size of my living room. "I'll bring you some ice," he says.

"Make sure it has whiskey surrounding it."

"Got it."

Twenty minutes later all traces of blood are removed from my face, my mouth is gravel-free, and I've held an ice pack to my cheekbone for long enough to satisfy Matt's inner nurse. We're sitting outside on one of the decks by the pool. I'm sipping on one of Matt's posh whiskeys and I feel completely relaxed, probably for the first time since I gave birth to Billy. The trees above us are strung with rows of soft fairy lights, and Matt's lit a collection of oversize candles at the center of the table. The surface of the pool looks like it's covered in dozens of tiny lights floating on lily pads. Below us the nighttime hills edging the canyon roll out over the landscape. The air is soft and still and exquisitely silent. I feel like I'm queen of a kingdom. I don't want to talk about Peter. I don't want to talk about anything. I just want to capture every moment of this so I can close my eyes and replay it anytime I need to.

"What are you thinking about?" asks Matt after a while. I always used to be the one who asked him that. He'd usually answer me with a strained "nothing." He's changed. A lot.

"I'm thinking about Kimberly," I say, because I am. I've thought about her quite a bit since our meeting. And now, seeing her palace, everything that she has garnered for herself, I'm thinking about her some more. And wondering aloud: "Why her?"

Matt stretches himself out long on the seat. My question seems to have made him more comfortable rather than less. It's like he's been waiting for me to ask it ever since I met her. The mellow lighting, the whiskey on an empty stomach, the shared loveseat, the bang to the head, the new turn in conversation—we're on dangerous ground here. Regardless, we press on.

"She's nice," he says.

"That's it?"

"You were never that nice."

"With me you sacrifice a percentage of nice in exchange for smart."

"Nice trumps smart. Pretty trumps nice. That's the order it goes in: pretty, nice, smart."

I should act horrified to hear something so blatantly backward. But in all honesty, it's something I've suspected of men all along. At least he's being honest.

"Except nice got boring," he says into his whiskey.

"At least you're left with pretty."

"You're pretty, Amy."

"I'm pretty today. Normally I'm a straggly haired fashion disaster."

He curls his fingers into the hair around the nape of my neck and gently tugs. He knows that move makes me helpless. Are we really doing this? I turn in the seat to face him. I've missed his face. I didn't even know how much I missed it. It's something I must have known all along, without knowing that I even knew it. Buried knowledge.

"To me, you are perfect," he says. And the way he says it, with such gruffness to his voice, trying to compensate for the emotions hurtling through his body, I know that he means it.

And right in that moment, nestled in the top of our kingdom on the hill, he feels it so intensely that I start to feel it too. The love buried under the rubble that is the ruins of our relationship has fought its way out to the air. And it's taking its first deep breath in ten years. The effect of the whiskey has suddenly drained from my body and I'm cold all over. He still has his hands coiled in my hair. We're both stuck, staring into each other's eyes. And then it's completely obvious: we love each other. We never stopped.

Matt pulls my face forward till our lips are barely apart. This would be the moment for me to pull away. Everything up to now has been silly games. *This* is deadly serious. This is how lives get changed. This is how I lose Peter forever. Now that I'm right in the middle of the moment where the choice actually needs to be made, I'm not so sure I want to lose him after all.

And then Matt kisses me. This time there's no pulling or pushing away. No more thought to who or what I might be losing. No care to who in the hell might stumble across us. No one will stumble across us. Because we're in our own private universe. It's a universe where we're both twenty-seven and anything is possible and life is carefree, even though we don't yet know it. He pulls me all the way into his body and holds me there tightly. I can feel his lips are shaking. I don't think I have legs anymore. If he were to let go of me now, I think I'd just vanish into the ether like a will-o'-the-wisp. I consider telling him to stop, but I know he wouldn't listen. I'd only be saying it so I could say afterward that I tried to stop it. I tried to put the cork back in the bottle—it just wouldn't go. But we're not stopping. Because we know that when we do, we'll have to take our first breaths in a brand-new world. And we'll have to admit: everything's changed.

CHAPTER 22

So everyone thinks I'm flying to Urban Monocle's headquarters in Chicago today to talk with Tim Rowney about managing the quality assurance lab at their LA roastery. Over the trajectory of my life I've learned that the best lies are the ones that include the most detail. This one's detailed enough that anyone outside the coffee world who hears it won't want to know anything more about it, in case they accidentally die from boredom while listening. And the advantage of this is that when Peter tried to question why I had to be gone for a whole week, I started talking about bean density and the best way to measure different degrees of water activity and his eyes glazed over and I won. I got a week off. No further questions. He'd only been back from his course about four minutes before I walked out the door, so him being freshly detoxed of anger was also probably working in my favor—or else he might have put up more of a fuss.

I arrive at check-in just a few seconds after Matt. Perfect timing. Our lives have already stepped into a pattern of synchronized coordination. I wonder if he'll sweep me up into a full-body embrace then and there and kiss me hard on my mouth just like he always used to. I get closer and am about to go in for the embrace when I see he's talking to himself. Has the strain of an impending affair sent him over the edge already? And then I notice the white wire hanging down from his head like his ear is wearing a tampon. He's on the phone. He waves hello as we get closer and then stands awkwardly beside me in line, occasionally raising his eyebrows toward me in acknowledgment. Not exactly the big beginning to an illicit week away that I was imagining.

Eventually, after I've checked about two months' worth of Facebook updates, he finishes his call.

"Sorry about that," he says. "Work."

"Right."

He gives me a chaste hug and a peck on the cheek. I look at him quizzically. This was not the same tone we were employing last time we met.

"Paparazzi," he says, and gestures over his shoulder. I don't see a soul there, but I'll take his word for it. "Hello!" he shouts into thin air. I jump a bit, as do the elderly couple standing right in front of me. "Mike! What's up?" He's on the phone again. This time he wanders off, walking in disorganized figure eights all around the area so that I'm forced to shuffle both his and my luggage forward as the line progresses. He finds his way back to me just before we're about to check in.

"Sorry."

"It's okay. I expect you've got a lot of wrapping up to do to extract yourself for a week."

"Extract myself?"

"From work?"

"Oh, right," he says, looking at me like he's suddenly remembered he forgot to turn the oven off.

I'm about to try and clarify with him that he actually *is* intending on extracting himself from work in order for us to have some time to figure out what's going on here, when his phone rings again. Apologetically I hand over the tickets and passports to the agent, who processes them all with a disapproving eye. I'm not sure whether she's disapproving because Matt's still on the phone, or because he's left me to haul the bags onto the scales, or because she just *knows*. Whatever she's disapproving of, I'm right there alongside her. This phone call is a particularly long one and it takes us all the way through security—with a quick break for the phone to go through the scanner—and up to the moment of boarding itself. In fact, we are the very last couple to board as Matt is determined to talk right up until the moment the agent threatens to shut the gate. Only then does he hit "End" on his call, like it's no big deal at all.

"Matt!" I growl at him as we finally get ushered on board, and he pulls his phone out of his jacket and starts firing off a text message. "You have to turn that thing off." We make it to our seats. Thankfully, we're in first class so we don't have to do a walk of shame through the entire plane.

"Sir, I'm going to need to ask you to set your cellular device to airplane mode for the duration of the flight," says a smiling and impossibly pert flight attendant who's just popped up out of nowhere.

"Of course," says Matt, still rapidly texting. "I'm doing it right now," he says as he continues to text. I'm sitting next to Matt, quietly dying. At my postmortem the coroner would be pretty quick to pinpoint the exact cause of my death: terminal embarrassment. Just as the flight attendant's bright red smile threatens to freeze in place, he switches off the phone and puts it back in his pocket.

"I don't know how Kimberly stands it!" I say as the plane's engines kick into motion. And then I remember how she stands it: she's happy to put Matt first, second, and third. And I could never do that, which is why Matt and I broke up and he and Kimberly got married. "And how is Kimberly?" I say. I don't know whether I'm feeling competitive again or curious, but all of a sudden I kind of want to talk about her, to find out what really has gone so drastically wrong in their marriage that he's decided to bow out for a week and skip off to Barbados with me.

"She's fine. Same as ever. Boring as ever." I give an infinitesimal shake of my head. I wonder how Peter would describe me if the situation were reversed. "Don't feel bad for Kimberly. She's had a wonderful life. It could have been your life, but you were too busy running off, trying to fix the third world. She was there and she was persistent. She grew on me."

"Like a cunning fungus up a damp wall."

"Are you comparing me to a damp wall? And what about Peter? What's he made you into?" he asks.

Breadwinner. Second-class parent. Adulterer. These words all come to mind, but I don't utter any of them. I am aware that lying to my husband and then scooting off for a week away with my ex is pretty disloyal. Unacceptably disloyal. However, I feel that comparing him to fungus, or a leech, or something else uncomplimentary would just be crossing the line. I mean, the line's already been crossed, but saying mean things about him to the guy I'm cheating on him with would be like crossing the line and then pulling down my pants, squatting, and peeing upon it. And I'm trying not to let my brain even think about how terrible a mother this little illicit trip makes me. This is the first time I've got on a plane and left my children for nothing to do with work. Is it really *that* bad a thing to do? Sometimes people do this. Sometimes parents take a vacation somewhere nice . . . just not normally while lying to the father of their children about it. I should stop trying to sugarcoat it: I am an excuse of a mother. And just as I was beginning to get the hang of it too. I put my head on the window and watch Los Angeles passing by below. My kids are somewhere down there, missing me.

The world's pertest flight attendant walks back through the cabin, and Matt stops her to order a whiskey. I'm possibly back to admiring unadmirable qualities in men here, but somehow proactively ordering a drink makes him seem so confident and cool. So decadent. I'd never dare do that. Once when I was on a flight, my mouth was so parched that the only way I could stop my lips from sticking to my teeth was to apply a thick coating of lip balm about every eighteen seconds. Did I push the call button and ask for a beverage? I did not. These days I always bring a bottle of water on board with me. Peter never drinks alcohol. No beer. No wine. No spirits. He didn't do the drinking thing in high school (just to be contrary), and as a result his taste buds missed out on some crucial formative years. Now he can't stand the taste of it. I've tried making him all kinds of jazzy fruit cocktails to get him interested, but no—he just doesn't like it. Every time I drink a glass of wine in front of him, it feels a little awkward. On the upside, I have a built-in designated driver.

The flight attendant brings Matt his drink and he smiles in thanks. Her smile back has a bit more oozy warmth to it than is strictly warranted. She's not flirting—necessarily. It's just that one of Matt's smiles will make you emit sudden warmth—even if you didn't know you had any to spare. That's how he's gotten as far as he has in life. He's utterly determined to achieve his ambitions—the same as me, but the difference is he's learned how to make people feel good about giving him exactly what he wants. It's more than merely being charming. He makes people feel like they just stepped into tropical sunshine. He makes problems melt away. Wouldn't you like to bask in a tropical sunlight that melts all your cares away and has you thinking that everything is possible? Everybody wants a chunk of that.

"How are you doing?" he asks, turning to face me.

"I'm okay." Better now that he's turned his attention away from his phone and the flight attendant and has focused all his sunshine on me.

"You sure?" he says, smoothing my hair back behind my ear. There's no way he could smooth Kimberly's hair behind her ear; it's way too big and bouncy. It'd just ping right out again and they'd be back exactly where they started.

"Yeah. I'm thinking about the kids."

"The kids will be fine. Kids are happiest when their mommy is happy," he says. I wonder if he's considered how *unhappy* the mother of *his* kids is going to be when all this finally comes to light.

"What are we doing here? Really?"

"Let's just give ourselves a couple of days at least before we start worrying about all the implications and complexities here. We'll work it out. People work this kind of stuff out all the time. For now, I just want to enjoy you. I've missed you."

"I've missed you too," I say, and lay my head down on his shoulder. It's comfy here. I could stay like this all the way to Barbados. I just might.

"Are you still worrying?" he asks after a moment.

"Yes, I'm a human being."

"Please. Just relax. We're going to have some wonderful days together here and then we'll figure all of this out. It'll be just fine, I promise. It always is in the end."

I'm about to tell him that it's the journey from "here" to "just fine" that's worrying me more than our potential for reaching a happy ending when he kisses me. And for about five seconds there's a tidal surge of emotion in my chest and I kind of forget about everything. It's like I can actually feel every molecule of love I ever had for him trickling back into my bloodstream. He kisses me once more, this time softly on the nose. And then in my favorite gesture, he rubs his hand over the top of his head. Look at the man. He is gorgeous. He's not making it difficult for me to develop some pretty serious feelings here.

"I've got to say. I'm a little jealous of Peter these days," he says, leaning back in to kiss my earlobe. "He has you whenever he wants you."

"He doesn't generally want me."

"Oh?"

"Well, it's hard, with the kids and stuff." Our red-lipped flight attendant is glancing over now as Matt starts to work his way down to kissing my neck. He suddenly stops short. *What? Wait!* I was enjoying that.

"You know why I'm most jealous of Peter?"

"No?" Could it be because he got to spend the last decade with me? Because he got to marry the woman of your dreams? Because I bore his children that should have been yours?

"Because he's so damn talented."

"Excuse me?"

"That script of his, the Irish one. It's so fresh. Unmessed with. He's free to write things like that. Real stuff. He's a real writer. He's not trying to pretzel his act so it meets the target demographic requirements and includes a lead that'll appeal to a global audience. He can just write. He's so free. And I'm in handcuffs."

"Handcuffs?"

"I'm just a brand, Amy. I don't know if I actually have any real or good ideas anymore at all. Everyone just sits there and says, 'Yes, yes, yes, Matt. Whatever you say, just make us the money.' It sucks. You know what I did before I left?"

"Lied to your wife about where you were going?"

"I floated this extra-crappy idea for a reality show. Just to see what the reaction would be."

"What happened?"

"They all fell for it. That's what that flurry of phone calls was about—everyone trying to get in on the 'great' new idea. Except it was a sack of shit that I just made up on the fly."

"What's the idea?" I ask. Maybe he's being overly modest.

"Storm into some office building somewhere and offer a worker one million dollars to walk out of their job then and there—providing they do an entertaining resignation."

"Okay."

"And then as soon as they get outside, we tell them there is no million dollars. It's just a setup. And then film their reaction."

"That's god-awful. I think you could even get sued for that."

"Exactly! It was meant to be a bad idea. But no one said a thing! When I get back, I'm firing everyone who said they liked it."

"A little harsh maybe?" Is he in the habit of setting people up like this, I wonder?

"I'm like the emperor wearing the suit of invisible clothes. Except there's no one to tell me I'm naked!" I look at him. Where has the honey-sweet man of two minutes ago gone? He's insane right now. "There's no one to tell me when I'm naked!" he repeats again, louder. I think he's actually trying to get a rise out of people by shouting the word *naked* in first class.

The red-lipped flight attendant makes her way over. We're about to get in trouble.

"Sir," she says, the smile in place as ever.

"Yes?"

"I'm so sorry. This is completely unprofessional of me, but I just had to ask . . . Could I have your autograph?"

"Of course," he says, all signs of bolty-eyed insanity melting away. He's instantly back in control, the savvy Hollywood producer. "And may I ask what your name is?" he asks, in a tone with an unacceptable level of flirt to it.

"It's August," she says, melting like chocolate left on the dashboard in the very month of her namesake.

"That's my favorite month!" he says.

"How can it be?" I object. They both look at me, and it's pretty clear they've completely forgotten I was ever there. "It's way too hot."

"So what are you working on right now?" she asks, like she really wants to know the answer.

Matt can barely get the words out quickly enough. "I'm working on a new reality show, actually. We go into someone's office and offer them a million dollars to quit their job, as long as they do it in a totally crazy way that means they could never go back afterward."

"Awesome!" she says.

"And then when they get outside, we tell them the whole thing's a setup. There is no million dollars!"

"No waaaay!" She laughs. "That's crazy!"

I think Matt's found his audience demographic. Good God, in what other city would a flight attendant, or *anyone* actually, recognize a producer? None. It's a pretty solid bet that August's got an IMDb page. I excuse myself to use the bathroom. Hopefully by the time I get back she'll be doing something useful, like holding the vomit bag open for someone who's drunk too much first-class champagne. Our seats are about as far away from the bathroom as it's possible to be in first class, so I decide to dive behind the curtain and use the ones right there in economy. But from the sounds within you don't have to be Sherlock Holmes to figure out that one contains a hefty man suffering from either a stomach flu or the worst case of food poisoning ever, and the other contains a person who is dead. Or maybe they're just taking the world's longest and most silent shit. After twenty minutes I give up and head to the bathrooms in first class. I get within five paces and hear some couple—probably not married from the sounds of ecstasy coming out of there—joining the mile-high club. I give up. I can sit on it till Barbados. I make my way back to the seat. Matt's not there. Probably taking a royal tour of the plane, giving out autographs. It should be Matt and me in the first-class bathroom joining the mile-high club. Instead, we've skipped the whole fun "having an affair" part and have gone right into complaining about work and tolerating each other's flirtations. We've gone right back to where we left off ten years ago. It's very boring.

I slip my bag out from under the seat to grab a novel I've got stashed in there. As I ease the book out, I see it's got a Post-it attached to the cover: *I'm ready to hold your hand.*

It's from Peter. It's always been a teasing point/pet hate of mine that he's never held my hand. I'd go to hold on to his and he'd bat mine away. Embarrassed, I guess. It used to upset me. My parents always held hands anytime they left the house. I just thought it was normal—what married people did. And then eventually I got used to not having my hand held and just stopped bringing it up. There were bigger problems to solve. Now he says he's ready to hold it. He's asking for another chance. He's kind of saying he'll do it right this time. He's saying he's ready to be a man, to be a real husband. Maybe I'm reading too much into one sentence. Nevertheless, I'm instantly swamped with guilt.

What am I doing here?

CHAPTER 23

Two days of pure luxury later, and I've remembered exactly what it is that I'm doing here. I'm getting more of that glimpse. And I'm starting to see how it could all be mine.

When Matt and I first got together, we spent two whole weeks in Barbados. It took us about twenty minutes of island time to realize we loved everything about the place: the transparent bright-blue waters, the Old World architecture, the modest lushness of the countryside, the easy nighttime breezes. All we talked about, in the spaces of time when we weren't frenetically "doing it," was how amazing it would be when we had a place of our own here one day. This, of course, was the "one day" when we'd have tons of money. Well, that fine day certainly came around for Matt Colburn, because his place is spectacular. Apparently, we're nestled away somewhere on the west side of the island. That's all I really know about our location and all I really care to. When we pulled up outside this place—inside his "Blu Sofisticato" Maserati GranCabrio—he told me he bought this house thinking about me and hoping that he'd bring me here one day. However, I suspect that was actually a big pile of pig shit. This house has all the markings of "Kimberly bought it," or if not her, then some impersonal global real estate agent twice removed from any real thoughts on what Matt actually wanted in a beach property.

Don't get me wrong, this house is beautiful. Extremely decadent, and I'm sure it was very expensive, but not a thing about it says "Matt." It's nothing like his house in LA. The only way I can think to describe the décor is "fussy French," and the place is just so, so *big*; I've no idea why they bought a house this size for just the four of them. The dining table sits sixteen! It's just too large. If you're about to step into the pool and suddenly remember you forgot your sunglasses back in the bedroom, you are screwed. Well, not *screwed*, obviously, but you are looking at a good seven-minute round trip to go and retrieve them.

No well-meaning-but-marble-and-granite-loving designer has had their way with the gardens and patios, thank God. They are more or less neutral in décor, just some white floating linens and loungy-style furniture, and that's where we're spending most of our time, bobbing along in what I've been told is an infinity pool. The water in the infinity pool is somehow exactly the same shade as the turquoise sea, so if you stand a little ways back from the edge and squint a bit, you can't tell where the pool ends and the Atlantic begins. It's truly magical.

The last forty-eight hours have been somewhat hard work considering that illicit extramarital affairs are supposed to be at least a little bit fun. However, I'd say we've probably reached the point where perhaps around seventy percent of the magic of our past relationship has been recaptured. Maybe sixty-five. The crux of the issue is that I'm just not one of those carefree types who can temporarily forget about the larger picture. I can't just close my eyes and enjoy the ride without constantly analyzing what we're doing. I'm not Kimberly. This gets Matt a little worked up—he's completely content to not think about the reality part of it at all, which you can go ahead and file under "Definitely Ironic." Let me give you an example: I am no longer using the living room, not even to walk through on the way to the kitchen. Matt, however, continues to use it and thinks I'm completely nuts for not doing so. When we first arrived and Matt was giving me the grand (grand) tour of the place, we walked into the living room and on top of the piano, inside kid-decorated frames, were photos of Kimberly and the kids. They weren't a bunch of perfect professional shots like Kimberly has on her Facebook profile. (Yes, I friended her for nothing more than the purpose of having a good dig. If I'm going to be a villainess, I may as well embrace it.) They were literally snapshots of family vacations. The kids decked out in snorkel gear looking like dorks, everyone standing at the foot of a stunning waterfall, Matt and Kimberly smiling over ironically flamboyant cocktails. Knife-in-the-heart kinda stuff.

It's not unusual for someone to have pictures of their family in their vacation home, of course, and there's no logical reason that Matt should have hidden them or got someone to take them down before we arrived, but seeing those pictures rattled me. And when Matt went to put the pictures away, that upset me even more. How disloyal is it that he would hide pictures of his perfect family because they bothered the woman who was potentially going to rip that family unit in half? I told him as much, to which he said I was being "overly dramatic," but the pictures remained in position—and ever since then I've avoided that room. It's not that great a hardship, as there are plenty of other places to hang out in this McMansion of the Caribbean, but it must be said, every time I go in the kitchen via the dining room rather than the living room, I feel a stab of guilt.

The other major issue has been the pretty-much-continuous stream of work calls, texts, and e-mails. He even has a fax machine in the kitchen that somebody sent part of a script through the one time he didn't respond quickly enough for their liking. We had a talk and he unplugged the fax, shut down his laptop, and agreed to only check his phone once a day. He let me know he wasn't happy about it, and I told him that as I'd left my family behind for a week to look at what was happening between us, he should respect that and give this situation his full attention. I could tell that no one had spoken to him like that since we were last together. I'm not sure whether he loved it or hated it.

And so finally, at two days in, with work and family distractions forcefully pushed to the background, we're getting some time to figure out "us." So far that's consisted of a lot of peripheral discussion whilst coyly wrapped around each other like a two-headed octopus floating in the shallow end of the pool. There has been no sex. That was my idea. But just because no one's taken their clothes off yet doesn't mean we aren't intimate. Our brains are getting slowly back on the same wavelength. Tuning back in to "Matt and Amy." We're starting to chatter again, just like we always used to. Matt's an expert at small talk, always happy to come join me on one of my whimsical "but what if" rambles. With Peter, it's all big-scheme planning and full-on discussions about life, kids, work. I've missed silly chitchat. The idle patter of two people just speaking their own internal monologues out loud. No filter. We dropped the filters sometime yesterday.

"Would you offer up the grounds for communal farming purposes or would you barricade the gates and just try to survive off your own vegetable patch?" I ask.

"Communal farming purposes, probably. It depends."

"What does it depend on?"

"What the other people on the island have to trade for the use of the land."

We're earnestly discussing hypothetical survival tactics in the event we were stuck on the island of Barbados forever. Our completely plausible backstory is that there's been a massive global earthquake, the island of Barbados has become untethered from its roots, and has floated off into the middle of the Atlantic. There's no point in trying to get home, because California is now an apocalyptic wasteland and everyone we know is dead, plus all the pilots and yacht captains on the island have died after an outbreak of typhoid fever. It's incredibly sad, but we've made our peace with it.

"Trade for, like, a cow or something?"

"Exactly. Or women."

"Women? What would you need women for?"

"Repopulate the island, of course."

"What about me? Can't you repopulate the island with me?"

"I would if you'd let me," he says, running his hands firmly around my butt and down the back of my thighs. Oh Lord, I have no one to blame but myself for that segue. "We could start right now. I might actually be able to think straight about our situation here if we just got the mating part out of the way." He slides his hand into the bottom of my bikini. I pull it out again. And now there's a rather unsubtle lump in his swim trunks. I'm torturing him. I'm torturing both of us. I gently nudge my arm under his and bring it back up to the surface of the pool.

"I'm concerned that I might not be glamorous enough for you," I say, hoping that a sudden distraction works as well on adult men as it does on children.

"Amy, you're beautiful."

"You know I don't have even basic feminine-grooming skills. I've no idea how to use a heated eyelash curler, and honest to God I don't know where people go to buy fancy event dresses that don't look like they were designed for drag queens."

"You know how to do high-end when you want to. You were all dolled up the other night for our dinner. You looked great."

"I had help. A lot of help. What if I had to come to a premiere or a viewing with you? People would wonder why you were bringing your landscaper along."

"A viewing?"

"You know, when people view the movie before it comes out."

"Do you mean a screening?"

"Maybe."

"I don't care if they think you're the gardener. I'll tell them all you do a great job trimming my bushes," he says, kissing my neck rather hard and grabbing my hand and pulling it down toward his trunks. Distraction hasn't worked. This is definitely edging toward something here, and unless I get out of the pool right now, I don't think I'm going to be able to muster the willpower needed to halt it.

"What about your mother?" I say.

"My mother?" Matt instantly breaks away from me.

"Yes, your mother. She loved me the first time around, but I'm sure she'll despise me now that I'm gearing up to make her grandchildren play parental ping-pong."

"So what do you want? Should we get back on the plane and forget any of this ever happened, because of what *my mother* might think? What are you trying to do here, Amy?"

"I'm trying to slow this down," I say, backing away. "It's not that I don't want to get physical, Matt. I actually really, *really* want to do that."

"So let's do that," he says, moving through the water toward me again.

"I can't."

"Why not?"

"Because of science."

"Because of *science*?"

"The moment we have sex, my hormones are going to make my body pledge eternal allegiance to yours and I'm not going to want to let go, ever. That's how the female body works."

"Baby, I won't want to let go of you ever either."

"It's no big deal. It's just oxytocin, but the minute those compounds get released into the bloodstream, I won't be able to make clearheaded decisions anymore. My body will be making them for me."

"Such a romantic way of putting it."

"I still don't know how you feel about me. We haven't talked about any of that. I haven't heard the words from you."

"What words?"

"Those three words, Matt. They're not that uncommonly spoken."

"It's a bit soon for 'I love you,' isn't it?"

"*A bit soon for 'I love you'*? Why would I put my entire life at risk for anything less?"

From underneath a towel on one of the loungers comes the chirp of a distractingly loud cricket. Matt glances over, bothered.

"What's that noise?" I ask. Something's not lining up quite right here. The loud cricket chirps again.

"Sounds like a cricket or something," he says. He looks guilty. We independently bob around in the pool for a few seconds or so, both lost in our own thoughts. Slicing through the silence, the obnoxious cricket sounds again, twice.

"I need my hat. My scalp is starting to get burned."

"So go get it," he says.

"It's in the kitchen. You get it for me," I say. I'm not sure what's going on here, but the second he's gone I'm checking under that towel, as I'm pretty sure that what's under there is not a loud and repetitive insect.

"Okay, I'll get your stupid hat," he says with a faux sigh, and starts making his way toward the edge of the pool, incidentally in the same direction as the chirping towel.

"Other side of the pool, buddy boy."

"What?"

"I want you to leave via the other side of the pool. And then I want you to go inside and get my hat."

"Ballbuster."

"Philanderer." He doesn't laugh at my joke, just takes off at a not-that-relaxed pace toward the house.

The second he's inside I launch myself out of the pool, run over to the lounger, and throw back the towel. There lies his phone. The chirps must have been text messages. He's supposed to have this thing switched off. I pick it up. The last two texts were from Kimberly. It's a series of emoticons, which I'm guessing are supposed to symbolize love and general satisfaction within a relationship. I type in the PIN Matt used for everything back in the day. Still works. His bank PIN is the reverse of mine. I took it to mean that we were meant to be—at one point. I'm beginning to think that I read too much into things. I scroll back to where it seems that the current conversation kicks in.

Kimberly: How's the biz trip going?

Matt: Up and down. Missing you guys. How was fat camp?

Kimberly: Shit. I only lost two pounds. I've got to lose at least ten.

Matt: Why?

Kimberly: Because I'm overweight.

Matt: Says who?

Kimberly: Dr. Tawa.

Matt: She's full of crap. To me, you are perfect. ;)

That's his last text: *to me, you are perfect.* And after that the onslaught of emoticons from Kimberly. I instantly sort the upset in my head into four specific sections:

1. "Up and down." What's that supposed to mean? Is he complaining about the chaste and complicated nature of our affair to his wife, even though she doesn't know it? That's just inappropriate.

2. "To me, you are perfect" is what he said to *me* just before he gave me the Kiss That Changed Everything. How could one person consider both Kimberly and me to be *perfect*? We are complete and polar opposites. And also, if he's even considering leaving his wife for me, why on earth would he be telling her that she's perfect? Obviously, he must think she's defective in some pretty substantial areas or else why is he here with me, trying to get my bikini off in the infinity pool?

3. Seeing "To me, you are perfect" written out has just reminded me that this is not in fact some romantic line that Matt created in the moment, inspired by nothing but the strength of his emotions for me and the soft white candlelight. No. It's from a movie we watched together a decade ago. It's what some guy flashed on a cue card at Keira Knightley on her doorstep while stating that he was too honorable to consider having an affair with her. Again, I'm pretty sure this falls somewhere on the irony spectrum.

4. The winky face. He stole a line from a movie, used it on two women, but the worst crime of all is the stupid winky face at the end. It just lowers the tone. What does it even mean?

I agreed to come on this trip, was persuaded, purely because of the strength of his passion for me. Because of what he said about me being perfect to him. I thought that I was going to be able to truly and absolutely connect with another human being in a way that I hadn't in years. But now I see it in HDTV clarity: I'm just a symptom of his middle-aged crisis. He doesn't want me. He wants twenty-seven-year-old me. He's not looking for something real, he just wants to escape from his own reality. Jesus Christ.

Just for kicks, I check the next text down. It's from an unnamed number. It simply says: *Dinner when you get back?* I click on the message and am confronted with a headless image of a pair of awkward, tiny breasts. I am instantly so mad I feel the entire top of my body rush with angry, warm blood. Whose boobs are these? There's nothing else in the message chain. I look closer at the pic. It appears to have been taken in a harshly lit bathroom. Just at the bottom of the image there's a thin line of blue waistband. I know that blue. That's JetBlue Cabin Crew Blue. He fucked that flight attendant. That's who was banging in the first-class bathroom: August and Matt.

Right.

Matt's coming back from the house now. He's marching pretty fast with my hat scrunched up in his right hand. He can see I'm reading his phone. He's furious. Well, I'm about to top it.

"Looking for this?" I say as he gets within earshot, and deftly drop the phone into the pool.

"Goddamn it," he says, and dives in after it. He emerges thirty seconds later, phone in hand, and after a quick rub of his head (don't find that gesture so attractive now) he pulls the case off and starts trying to figure out how to get the phone open.

"There's nothing you can do to fix it," I say. "You'll just have to buy a new one."

Matt suddenly sighs and makes a big show of taking his fury down a few notches. He's probably wondering whether I threw his phone in the pool because he'd broken our agreement to keep phones shut off or because I've actually managed to get in there and see all his awful secrets.

"I'm sorry. I know we said no phones. It's just that Asher's had a slight fever and—"

"I saw the picture of the tits."

"What tits?"

"Don't do all that. I know what you did. In the bathroom."

He pauses and I can almost hear his brain assessing the risk of trying to continue his denials against the risk of being candid about what he's done.

"Amy . . . I am so, so sorry. It was just a physical interaction. It didn't mean anything."

"Wait—isn't that what you're supposed to be saying to your wife *about me*? We haven't even started anything yet and you're already cheating on me."

"Amy. It was just a random fuck."

"*Excuse* me?"

"Honest to God, it was practically one step up from jacking off. It didn't mean a thing at all. I haven't been with Kimberly since you and I kissed, and then you wouldn't do it till we came away and I just . . . I just lost it for a moment. She was there. She said yes."

"So you're saying this is my fault?"

"I don't know. Kind of?"

Why am I even having this conversation with this man? As Violet would say, I am "wasting up" my time.

"Never contact me again," I say.

"Amy—"

"Stop it. Do not try and justify any more of this or Kimberly hears everything."

"Okay," he says, instantly cowed by the fact that I might tell his wife.

He stands there in silence, soaked, holding his phone in his hand, waiting. After a moment I realize that what he's waiting for is for me to leave. He isn't even going to make a gesture toward trying to change my mind.

It's suddenly incredibly clear where I stand in the placement of things. Somewhere way below his work and his wife, probably only a couple of steps up from Bathroom Boobies.

* * *

It takes me less than two minutes to pull all my belongings together. I move quickly, not that there's any real need to. It's fairly obvious that he's not coming inside anytime soon to try and stop me. I turn my phone on. No messages. That's a good thing. I go through Matt's jeans pockets. Yup, just where I thought they'd be, the keys to his Maserati. On my way out I walk directly through the living room, ease up the lid of the piano, and shove the snapshots of his family inside. *Good luck explaining to your wife where those photos with their irreplaceable frames have gone.*

I take the coastal route across the island to the airport. This island is still so beautiful to me, despite what's happened. It's tearing my heart in two that I'm leaving this place so soon after I got here. Perhaps it was actually Barbados more than Matt that I was so excited to get back to. I let one more tantalizing white-sand beach pass me by before I make the decision to pull over. I'm not going back without spending at least a bit of time on one of these heavenly beaches. God knows when this opportunity will ever come round again. As I pull my bag out from the front seat of the car, I wonder how such a pretentious vehicle could have made me feel like a slinky Bond girl when I first got in it. Looking at it now, it just seems like a silly blue Batmobile.

I dump my bag on the sand, strip my dress off, and head out into the water, car keys in hand. As soon as I get waist-deep, I hurl the keys out into the luminous blue sea. Instantly gone. Over. That may have been a juvenile gesture, but it definitely felt good. The water around me is so clear that if it weren't for the soft, sandy bottom, it would be just as if I were back floating around in the pool. All my anger and indignation toward Matt seem to have followed his keys out to sea, and now I feel nothing. Just empty. What have I been doing? How could I get angry with Matt for cheating on me when I was planning to inflict that same pain on Peter? And what I almost did to Peter would have hurt far more than what Matt did to me, because Peter actually loves me. I don't love

Matt. I haven't genuinely loved him in years and years. I just mistakenly felt entitled to try on his lifestyle for a moment.

Well, it clearly didn't suit me. It's time to go home.

It's not till I'm in the back of a minivan taxi that I check my phone again and see that I've missed a call. It's from an LA area code, but I don't recognize the number. There's no message. Just as I'm about to put the phone back in my purse, it starts ringing again from the same number. I'm about to hit "Decline" when a small voice reminds me that I am—despite all my evil acts—still a mother. Which means that unless you know for a fact that it's CarMax on the other end calling about the unpaid car loan, you pick up. You always pick up.

"Hello!" I say with an edge of fear in my voice. I've suddenly scared myself into thinking the worst. I surely deserve it.

"Amy?"

"Yes."

"It's Roth."

My brain's empty. My mind flips back through the days and weeks, and then I remember.

"Roth from Bean à la Bean?"

"Y-es," he says. "Roth" is a pretty unconventional and cool name, and he probably takes great pride at not being confused with "Roth from Wells Fargo" or "Roth from LensCrafters." "It's Roth from Bean à la Bean. And I'm calling to see if you still want a job."

CHAPTER 24

I wake up to Billy's freezing feet making contact with my shins. How he manages to have such acutely cold extremities in a place where it's eighty degrees most of the year, I'll never know. The rest of his body is bundled up into a ball, and he fits pretty much in the space between my knees and my chin. Kind of like an extra-large maternity bump. He's taken to sleeping in the big bed with the rest of us recently. And why not? Of course I say "recently," but it's only been since I broke the news to the kids that I'm going back on the road again. Possibly for months this time. And you needn't think that Violet took the news any better than Billy. You know when some people swear off the carbs and then one day decide to start chowing down on the Lay's again, and their body weight instantly doubles? Take that idea and apply it to the fluctuating emotions of a three-year-old girl. I can't even get in the car to run an errand without it triggering one of her epic meltdowns, and she's right back to creeping in beside me whenever I try to take a shower. She's terrified. She's devastated. And so am I.

Turns out Jasmine grew a pair of eyes and found out the truth about Roth and the nanny. Roth told me that they tried to work things out, but in the end they just couldn't get there. The way he explained it was that ultimately neither of them wanted it badly enough to be able to motivate themselves to do all the work necessary to fix it. She left, and her father's money left with her. Without the artificial buoy of pop-in-law's cash holding things up, the accounting books of Bean à la Bean are pretty much sunk. Roth needs the Yayu. He offered me my old deal back and here we are. I'm booked on the three o'clock flight to Addis Ababa this afternoon.

However, as the morning light slowly fills the room and I look at Violet strewn across the bed—her pale face even paler than normal; her chubby, sweet lips slightly parted as she lets out a teeny-tiny snore—I'm not sure I can do it. How can I leave them? I could barely bring myself to do it in the past, and now that I know them and love them more deeply and fully than ever before, how can I? How can I physically leave them behind? I think the pain of it might actually kill me. But what else would we do? The savings are gone. The unemployment benefits won't last forever. The credit cards are bursting at the seams. The house is a heartbeat away from being repossessed. We're down to one phone and one vehicle. After Barbados, unsurprisingly, Peter has not been invited to return to Colburn Entertainment. He told me he left a few messages for Matt that were never returned, which he alleges is Hollywood Morse code for *Your services are no longer required*. I'm not sure if he's telling the truth or not—I know he didn't want that job. But after everything that's happened, I'd be a nervous wreck over Peter working alongside Matt anyway, so I'm not pushing it.

All in all, we are in dire financial straits. On the plus side, we do have the sleeping-in-one-bed thing down. Maybe we could just lug our mattress down to the railroad tracks, sling up a tarp, and join our local homeless community. I shouldn't even jest. Not taking this job would be the first step toward that actually happening. And how could I ever risk that? How could I risk my children's future, their safety? How could I risk them being hungry? But at the same time, how on earth am I supposed to leave them?

This first trip back to Africa is going to run into weeks. Then I've got a quick stop home before turning around to fly out to Colombia for another epic trip. Roth had to lay off his other buyer in order to afford me, so I'm going to be running around the world covering a double workload till the Yayu starts paying its way and Roth can afford to bring on an additional buyer. The kids could be in middle school by then. They'll already be completely different people by the time I get back from Africa. I touch my nose to the top of Billy's head and try to subtly wipe my flooding tears onto his hair so they don't touch his face and wake him up. My throat feels like someone's got it in a clamp from the strain of holding back the floodgates. I try to flip on a mental video recorder. I want to keep every millisecond of this moment alive so that when I'm gone, I can teleport myself back here and make believe that we're together again. I squeeze Billy's sleeping body into mine, trying not to panic. I cannot afford to fall apart today, in any sense. This will be my last moment with my babies for weeks and weeks. I hear Peter softly knocking around in the kitchen, and before long the foreboding smell of bacon creeps into the bedroom. I only get another thirty seconds before my repressed snuffling rouses Violet. She blinks open her huge eyes, sleepy at first, then within one second they engorge with accusation. She sits up.

"Why are you crying, Mommy? *You're* the one who's leaving *us!*"

I give Billy's limp body one final long hug. This is the end. From here till I leave it'll be a manic blur of last-minute packing, followed by a gut-wrenching good-bye. This final hug marks the end of my time. It feels like it marks the very end of their childhood. I kiss the top of his silky hair, press my cheek to his head one last time, and sit up.

In the corner of the room I see the new kitten squatting right in the middle of my open backpack.

"Inkie, no!" I yell, pulling him off and running to his litter box. We make it just in time.

The doorbell rings. I glance at the clock. It's already later than I thought.

And so the crazy begins. I can see from the kitchen that it's Lizzie at the front door and she's got a blanket in her hands. Looks like the one Banksy used when she gave birth in our closet. Turns out Banksy—as mysterious and subversive as her artist namesake—was actually a girl. Even after Lizzie's helpful makeover, things haven't been quite right between us. Especially since I shrank her dress while trying to get the blood out. But you can't ignore it when the neighbor's cat gives birth in your closet. And since then we've been more or less back to normal with each other, both of us on our best behavior.

I open the door. Inkie immediately makes a bolt for freedom. I pick up his tiny black body with the top of my foot and drop him back inside the house. I slip out the door, closing it behind me. Who's going to make sure Inkie doesn't run off into the street when I'm in Ethiopia? Let alone feed the thing. I give that poor kitten two weeks at the most. I realize I'm standing out on the porch in my pajamas. They're my most uncool pair (and believe me, there's stiff competition for the title), covered in small snowflakes and dorky-looking penguins in top hats. I notice I'm not looking much worse than Lizzie, though, who's in gray sweats and an off-white T-shirt. She's not wearing a bra, and I think there might be a pimple brewing on her forehead.

"Here's your blanket," she says. "I cleaned it."

I should hope so. That thing was covered in cat placenta last time I saw it. In fact, I'm not even sure I want it back at all. Though thinking on it, Inkie might enjoy it seeing as he doesn't get to live with his mother anymore. I decide then and there that the human race is just cruel. What's the purpose of this worldwide obsession with separating children from their mothers?

"Thanks," I say, gingerly taking back the blanket.

"Off to Africa again today, then?" she says, except for the first time ever she refers to my working life without any overtone of judgment or undertone that she's likely to call social services on me at any given moment on account of me being the World's Worst Mother.

"Yes," I say. "Unfortunately." I honestly don't know whether to count myself amongst the fortunate or unfortunate anymore.

"I wish I could give Daniel that gift," she says. Her face looks very different with all the pious taken out of it.

"What gift?"

"The gift of being able to stay at home with Odessa."

Record scratch. Is she saying she wishes now that she was the breadwinner? If she's trying to be nice, it really isn't working.

"You know, you might feel differently about that if it was a gift you actually had to give." I am not in the mood to listen to her indulge her silly little fantasies about how neat her life would be if she could pop off to some hipster media job every day and have Daniel at home wearing his own version of The Apron whilst whipping up batches of cake pops. This woman should spend less time saying ridiculous things and more time advising her daughter to keep her fingers out of her nose.

"Maybe I'd enjoy it. Maybe I'd hate it. But I do wish . . ."

I stand there in my unhip pajamas, waiting for her to finish her train of thought. Last-minute packing be damned, I have the feeling she might be part of the way to a self-realization here that working mothers are not selfish harridans intent on destroying the very fabric of our society and I want to hear it.

"I wish I could contribute."

"But of course you contribute." I'm not making it easy for her. I'm going to make her spell it out. Loud and proud. I've been waiting for this moment for five years, and I'm not going to ease the words out for her.

"I mean, financially. I wish I could contribute in that way."

"Oh," I say, as if the concept had never occurred to me. "Well, didn't you do something with fashion before Odessa was born?"

"I was an art gallery assistant," she says.

"Couldn't you do something like that again?" Unless perhaps there's dagger-to-throat competition for gallery assistant jobs in LA? I honestly don't know.

"I don't think it would help much."

"Why not?"

"I mean it wouldn't help as much as we need. Daniel lost his job."

Now, I don't remember what Daniel does for a living specifically. Something to do with financial legalese. He tried to explain it to me once—back when we used to do neighborly barbecues, back before Billy peed on his Hush Puppies—but he lost me at "master netting agreement," and I've carefully avoided getting anywhere near the subject ever again. Whatever the job was, it generated enough dough to float the huge mortgage on their five-bedroom Pasadena Craftsman and fund at least one skiing trip a year, as well as frequent getaways to their second home in Del Mar. I expect they'll be feeling the loss quite keenly. This is my big chance to crow, to start a lengthy monologue on the pitfalls of relying on a man to earn your money for you. However, Lizzie looks so beaten, I don't have the appetite for it. And besides, our family is not exactly a shining and gracious example of how to do it right.

"I just wish I had your kind of earning power. I wish I could carry my family like you can. This has happened and there's nothing I can do. I'm helpless to *do* anything."

I wish I had the answer for her. But having just dragged my family through the hell that hers is about to go through, I can't say I've learned anything about how to survive on no income. The only thing I've learned is how much and how deeply I love my children, which isn't really a helpful revelation seeing as now I have to fly thousands of miles away from them. I've learned how to be a mother. But sadly, so sadly, that's a job for which you just don't get paid.

"I'm so sorry." What else is there I can say? "I'm sure Daniel will find something soon."

"Right," she says, and continues standing there on my doorstep. All of a sudden she looks tiny, standing there in that off-white T-shirt. "So Odessa had these." She hands over a pair of scissors. They're bearing my ever-sassy "Amy's Kitchen Scissors" label. I notice the blades are now extremely rusty. "I'm sorry. I don't know how she got hold of them. I found her trying to cut off one of the new kittens' tails."

"Oh God."

"I know."

Again, this would be a wonderful time for me to extract some level of revenge by asking her if she's considered speaking to Odessa's pediatrician about a child psychiatrist referral, but right now I don't have the time and I don't have the will. I can tell this woman is mentally beating herself up worse than I ever could. I'll leave her to her work.

"Lizzie, I've got to go," I say, and crack open the front door.

"Of course," she says, and steps back off the porch. A second later she leaps back up and pulls me into a hard hug. After a moment I hug her back. She stays in the embrace probably about five seconds too long, and just as I'm starting to feel completely awkward she whispers, "I'm sorry."

And then she's gone, hurrying back down the street. As she heads in toward her house, she starts to run. I think she may be crying. This, of course, does nothing to help my own fragile emotional state. Crying can be as contagious as a hearty yawn, and as I close the front door and dive into the shower, the vice clamp is back around my throat. I think it's going to be staying there for a while.

The next two hours slip by at warp speed, just as I knew they would. Just as they have dozens of times before. And then the backpack is fastened, the taxi's at the curb, and there's nothing left. There's no more time standing in between this moment and the one when I walk out the door, away from them for days, weeks, and then more weeks on end. I open the front door and signal to the driver that I'll be out in just a minute. And then I turn back. The moment is upon us.

"Where's Violet?" I ask. I can't leave without saying good-bye to her, despite the punch to the gut that I know it's going to be.

"I don't know. She's probably in her room," Peter says. I'm surprised she hasn't been glued to me like normal this morning. Maybe she's old enough to have figured out how to sulk.

I pick up Billy and wrap his body around mine. He nuzzles his head into my shoulder and holds tight. We stay there, and then I give him a quick pat on the shoulder and carefully lower him down. He looks back up at me. He's angry. He's resigned. He's only five years old, for goodness' sake.

"I'll miss you, Mom," he chokes out, and then runs for his bedroom before we can see that he's crying. No slammed door today. Just the sounds of a small, sad boy crying into his pillow. Billy's never said he's going to miss me before. I feel the clamp close tighter around my throat and my heart. I stare after him.

I can't do this.

"Peter, you've got to sell *Draker's Dark*."

"What are you talking about? Matt said it was poorly written and commercially unviable."

"Matt's only one person."

"He's a pretty knowledgeable person."

I'm going to have to tell him. Now. *All of it*. With the taxi meter running.

"It's not true what he said about the script."

"That's nice of you to say, but—"

"He lied. He knows it's good. He told me."

"He told you it was good?"

"Yes. It *is* good, Peter."

"Then why did he—"

"Because . . ." Here I go. It's literally now or never. "He's jealous of you. And because he wanted to sleep with me."

"What?"

The driver honks. Can he not see we're having a crucial conversation here?

"Just keep the meter running!" I yell down the front yard. "Don't let Matt stop you from trying to sell this screenplay. Because it's good. And I need you to sell it so I don't have to do this anymore. I don't want to miss my children's childhood."

"Did you *sleep with him*?" He's livid.

"Matt? No." He doesn't need to know about the Kiss That (Almost) Changed Everything or the trip to Barbados. At least, not right now. The meter is running after all. "He's a manipulator, Peter. I think he set you up to fly off the handle in front of me that day in the writers' room. I think he set it up for you to be out of town for a week so he could try to get closer to me." I'm waiting for the furniture to start flying. I'm waiting for the rants, for the *I knew it*s and the *I told you so*s. So far he's quiet. "It didn't work, Peter. We're still here. We're still together. I love you."

Peter's wrapped his arms tightly across the top of his chest and he's staring directly at me, breathing in and out very slowly.

"Peter, are you okay?" The crazy heavy breathing is scaring me much more than the normal screaming and yelling. Is he gearing up for something huge? Is this what a nervous breakdown looks like?

"I'm doing the Turtle."

"The Turtle?"

"It's a breathing technique. Do it with me."

And so I do. And for the next few minutes we both stand there with our arms wrapped across our chests staring at each other, silent, breathing. His inhales and exhales start to become very long. In, two, three . . . out, two, three. I find my breath wanting to fall into sync with his, and so I let it. Why not? My only briefly self-conscious moment comes when I realize how lacking in self-consciousness I am. We're both right in the middle of the moment. In the now of it. Breathing together. Looking directly at each other. I feel more married to him than I ever have. It's not the kids, or the mortgage, or the letter of the law that binds us together—it's this. This true connection that we have, that we still have, buried under all the layers of fossilized stress.

Eventually Peter lowers his arms; I follow.

"Kind of ironic that the minute we do this is the moment I'm walking out the door."

"Don't go," he says. "Send the taxi away."

"Don't say that to me." The clamp, which had started to ease off during the Turtle, is moving into a death grip. "You know I have to go." He knows it. I know it. It doesn't mean that we don't wish it wasn't so. He pulls me into a hug and kisses me firmly on the top of my head. For the first time in a long time, I feel safe. And loved.

"I'm sorry about Matt," I say.

"It's okay. It's done now." I'm suddenly extremely glad I threw Matt's phone into the pool. That I threw him back to Kimberly. This is where I'm supposed to be, with Peter. I look up at him and he kisses me. And it's a real kiss. Not a "two kids later in a flailing marriage" kiss. It's a kiss that makes me wish that the taxi wasn't due for another half an hour.

"You have to figure this out, Peter. You have to sell your screenplay or do something. I can't miss any more of this. Any more of you and me."

"I'll work something out," he says. And I believe him. For the first time ever, I believe *in* him. Because if he can conquer the indignant anger that's been running wild through his body like anarchy all these years, solving a chronic unemployment problem is just a step away. And compared with what he's already solved, it's a simple step.

"I've got to go," I say. I'm already running late. If we get into traffic on the way to the airport, it could be a disaster at this point.

"I know," he says, not letting go.

"Where's Violet?" I ask again.

"Probably in her room," he repeats. "Let's go and look."

And so we do, holding hands. She's not there.

"I'll check the backyard," I say. We let go of each other's hand and Peter heads toward the front of the house calling her name. I go out the back door. Inkie tries to follow, but I toe him inside the house again.

"Violet!" I yell. Where is she? The side gate is closed and locked, and she's not on the side deck. She's not on the back deck or in her playhouse. Not hiding behind the trash cans. The back gate is locked too. I determinedly keep my breathing under control. There's no reason to go anywhere near panic yet. All the gates are locked. There's no way she could have gotten outside the house without us noticing. I do a thorough check of the garage just to be sure. Nothing. She must be back inside. Peter's probably found her already. That taxi driver must be ready to throttle me.

I let myself in through the back door to find Peter standing alone in the kitchen. We look at each other.

"Find her?" he asks.

"No." I shake my head. We stand there for a couple of seconds, staring at each other. Is this the official moment when we're supposed to start panicking? Wordlessly we pass by to check each other's work. He heads out the back door and I start ransacking the house. I can feel the sharp edges of panic start to jostle inside my chest. I go through every room, beginning at the front of the house. I pull the contents out of our closets, I upturn furniture, I empty out boxes, I yank dishes out of cupboards, I pull storage containers out from under beds. Nowhere. She's nowhere to be seen. I hear someone screaming her name.

"Violet! Violet!" Billy's staring at me, and I realize that it's me who's screaming. I've gone from relatively normal to batshit crazy in the space of about six minutes and can you blame me? She's not here.

The doorbell rings. I stop upending my shoe collection and run to the front door. Someone must have found Violet wandering down the street and brought her back home. It's the taxi driver. I hold back the urge to scream *fuck you!* at him.

"What's going on?" he says. "You're going to miss your flight."

"I've lost my daughter." Saying it out loud makes it bone-crushingly real. I can feel the blood falling away from my head in one quick, cold wave. I think I'm going to faint.

"What do you mean you've lost her?"

"What do you goddamn think I mean?" If I were the taxi driver, at this point I'd doff my cap, if I had one, get in my cab and drive back home or to the cabbie depot or wherever it is that cabbies go when they're not cabbing.

"How old is she?"

"She's three."

"Did you call the police?"

"No. Not yet. I mean . . . Do you think I should?" Is it that real? That serious?

"I'll call them. You keep looking," he says, like he's done this a thousand times before.

Suddenly I feel completely negligent. More so than any other time over my catastrophic motherhood career. Of course I should have called the police by now. What was I thinking? Peter runs in through the back door and into the living room looking hopeful.

"Anything?"

I shake my head.

"I'll walk the block," says Peter. "You stay here in case she shows up."

And so I'm left. Standing here in the "do nothing" role. The "stay here in case she shows up" role. It's ridiculous, what's she going to do? Saunter in the front door holding an ice-cream cone she just picked up on her way back from sightseeing in Old Town? She's gone! She's missing! She's not going to voluntarily come back. She has to be proactively *found.* The only thing that stops me from running out the door is Billy. If there's some kind of *Chitty Chitty Bang Bang*–style kid snatcher in the area, I have to stay and protect him. I can't lose both of them. You see how I've gone off the deep end here. Well, wouldn't you?

After what seems like an inappropriately long time, the cops show up. They walk way too slowly up the front yard, take their time walking in the door and introducing themselves, and then start asking me a thousand questions. It's all I can do to stop myself from screaming at them: *stop asking me questions and go out there and FIND HER!* She could be miles away by now, and you're asking me what color her Strawberry Shortcake nightgown is? I don't know! It's got Strawberry Shortcake on the front—isn't that distinctive enough for you?

"And you're sure she was still wearing her nightgown the last time you saw her?" asks the male officer.

"Yes."

"Even though it was nine a.m.?" says the female officer. Don't judge me right now, woman! Do your job.

"Y-es." I swear she gives a miniraise of her eyebrows. If I didn't need her to find my daughter right now, I'd punch her square between the eyes.

After a moment the male officer goes outside and starts talking to someone on the radio. Another cop car shows up. At last. Something's happening. Peter returns from his search. He's covered in sweat.

"I can't find her."

"The police are here."

I glance at the clock. It's noon. If we find her within the next two hours, I can still catch the evening flight out. I stop short. What is wrong with me? As a person? I hear a cop knock on Lizzie's door and explain the situation. She sounds shaken as she replies that she hasn't seen her. I can just imagine her pulling Odessa tightly against her body, thinking that her problems may be bad but all of a sudden realizing that nothing is as bad as it could be. I can give her that today at least.

Billy, Peter, and I sit there in cold, horrified silence as the minutes tick on. Minutes that Violet's not here. The police go through every nook and cranny of our house—even more thoroughly than I did. They come to the same conclusion: she's not here.

More cops arrive. I'm on the last fringes of being able to hold it together. Before too much longer there's going to be an ambulance arriving instead of endless cop cars as I'm going to be the one having a nervous breakdown. The taxi driver sticks his head in the front door.

"Still nothing?" he asks.

I bite back the snarky retort that yes, she was playing with her pink Girl Lego in her room the whole time and all these people walking around looking like police are just part of a costume party we spontaneously decided to throw. The Lego sets were a gift from my mother, by the way. I'm not sure why having a vagina means you can't just use the same multicolored Lego pieces that boys do, but what do I know? Having misplaced my second-born, I feel like I have even less authority to speak on any parenting subject than I normally do.

"No," I say. "I'm sorry. I should let you go. What do I owe you?"

"I'll stay," he says. "I'm involved now."

He takes a seat on the couch right next to Billy. It doesn't seem right to ask him whether his meter is still running. I'm trying to decide whether this is extraordinarily intrusive or unbelievably supportive when I hear it: a small girl crying. And I think it's Violet. It's not just me imagining things, as Peter leaps to his feet. He hears it too. The crying's coming from outside and Peter beats me out the front door.

Daniel's on the sidewalk outside our home, and he has Violet wrapped around him. Her nightgown is immodestly hitched up around her hips, and I thank God she was wearing underwear when she went to bed last night only a split second after I thank God for her safe deliverance. Daniel's always looked a bit like a Gap model, but dressed in Levi's and an old T-shirt, with two days of beard growth, he looks like an all-American hero.

She's found.

Somehow I beat Peter to her and grab her little body out of Daniel's arms.

"Where was she?" I ask, half-hostile. We haven't got the full story yet. What on earth was she doing sequestered away in their house?

"I found her in our tree house," he says. "She was sleeping. I thought I'd check up there, because we've found Billy camping out there before."

The fence. We never fixed it. This is all my fault: the millions of cop cars (which are already starting to dissipate), my completely traumatized family, the certain escape of Inkie, my missed flight, the taxi driver's wasted morning. Violet snuggles into my body and I clasp her right back. What would I have done if I'd lost her? I'd have died. But she hasn't been lost. She's here. I have her. At least for the moment.

"Thank you, Daniel," I whisper, resting my head on hers.

The police finish up the rest of their paperwork and everyone clears out pretty fast. Everyone except the taxi driver, who's standing there, waiting for direction. I check the clock. If we leave like *now*, I can make this evening's flight, which means I won't miss my internal flight to Jimma. And it's important I don't miss my internal flight, because Getu booked that for me (flights are less than half the price when booked inside Ethiopia); it's going to be super difficult if I have to reschedule it, because Getu has one phone on the farm and he never answers it. Yes, that was poor planning on my part, but Roth is supremely anal about costs right now and half price is half price.

Peter and I meet each other's eyes. He knows it. I know it. I've got to go.

"Violet, honey. Mommy has to catch her plane." I kiss the top of her head. One last kiss.

I brush my cheek against the soft skin of hers and then hand her over to Peter. She doesn't fuss. I think she's dazed by everything that's just happened. I'm not going to wait until she figures out exactly what's going on and screams the place down. The taxi driver is already starting the cab back up. I give Billy one more hug. Peter and I spontaneously touch heads, closing our eyes. We breathe. This time it means something. Our Hawaiian kiss has returned. None of us says anything. We're still too stunned for "good-bye."

I start my walk down to the taxi. Violet suddenly catches on to what's really happening.

"No, Mommy. No!"

I keep walking. There's nothing to be gained by going back. With that last kiss I made the transition from mother to coffee buyer. Logic reigns. There's nothing more I can do for her. She won't be calm for hours. Perhaps even not quite right for days. And none of us will be fully whole until weeks and weeks have gone by and I return again.

"Mommy, just one more hug!"

I keep walking. Tears flowing down my cheeks now. How can I stop them? I don't go back, because it's never one more hug. I'll never be able to give her enough hugs to plug the pain of this separation. Just one more won't help. It'll be as useful as one more ice cube thrown into a heartily burning house fire. I open the taxi door. *Don't look back.*

I look back. It's a mistake. They see I'm crying. I never cry at good-byes. Both children immediately kick it up a notch. Violet strains against Peter, holding out her arms to me.

"Mommy, don't go!" yells Billy. I get in the cab quickly. I'm too traumatized even to wave.

"Drive," I say. The cabbie pauses as if he's going to ask me if I'm sure I want to do this. "Just drive," I repeat. And he does.

Straightaway I want to ask him to drive around the block and come back. Just so I can give her that one last hug after all. But I don't. Because I know if I come back one more time, I'll never be able to persuade myself to leave again. And so I just keep on going.

Why?

Because I have no choice.

CHAPTER 25

It's been raining hard and solidly now for around half an hour. I was pretty wet with humidity and general sweatiness before the rain started, but now I'm saturated. I keep my eyes firmly on Getu—as I have been doing all morning—as he deftly cuts a path through the foliage around us. There's no pathway beneath our feet—we're walking directly on a twisted mass of undergrowth. It's kind of like walking on a springy mattress covered in vines that are trying to catch you around the ankle. I'm not certain, but I think the rain's beginning to let up a little. My pants are tight around my waist—apparently I gained some weight during my work hiatus—and that's not doing anything to add to my general comfort right now. Out of the corner of my eye I see something large and black land on my forearm. I brush it off as quick as lightning and keep on walking like it didn't happen. That's why you wear long sleeves in the forest.

Luckily, this rain only started after I picked up my new samples of Yayu this morning. There's no way I'd have been able to identify any kind of plant varietal in this downpour. I'm right about the rain letting up; a few seconds more and it slows to a patter. And then it's gone as quickly as it began. Within thirty seconds the humidity and the heat are back, and my drenched clothes start gently steaming. So now you see why I've never had much use for mascara. The birds start their singsong again, the crickets their chirping, and the forest is alive once more. The forest is an extremely noisy place. You'd be disappointed if you'd come all this way looking for silent solitude. A swarm of flying insects rushes through the canopy above. The way the sunlight catches them makes them look like enlivened particles of dust. I suddenly remember that I forgot to renew my yellow fever vaccination before I left. Oops.

"Hey, Getu," I say, and he stops. "Wait a second. I've spotted something."

He doesn't say a word. He's used to these frequent stops by now. Sometimes it takes us half a day to get back to the farm. The coffee trees in this forest grow wild, and there's just an explosion of varietals all mixed in and growing together. This forest has the biogenetic diversity of central London at rush hour. Every time we come out, I see a coffee tree with a leaf size and color that I've never seen before. I take a clipping from the new tree, zip it into a plastic bag, and put it in my satchel next to my recent haul of Yayu beans. I'm cataloging all the new varietals I'm finding to try and get an understanding of the range of diversity in this forest. It's astounding. I've counted thirty-seven new coffee trees so far. And I've only been here three weeks!

My MO from Roth is to find Getu's Yayu and confirm that it's rust resistant, which I've done. But I've also been digging a little bit into *why* it's rust resistant. I've been driving to Jimma University most days to do a deeper dive into the molecular structure of the bean and see what makes it so different from the other trees. The lab there is pretty basic, but I don't need much more than a microscope, storage, and some enzymes. The research is going well so far. Slow, but well. I've identified seven polymorphic markers that seem to make this thing more inclined than the other trees to be disease resistant. I haven't quite figured out the special DNA sequencing that makes it completely immune. But I'm getting there. And why am I doing this research? Because it's important.

And because this is *my* discovery. And because no one else seems to be doing much about the problem, and because this could potentially save a whole industry. It's vital work in every sense. I must say, I don't much like driving back and forth on that crazy rutted road to Jimma. However, having said that, the drive's been getting a bit livelier recently due to my growing number of carpool buddies. Every time I see a woman loaded up like a packhorse—schlepping grain, firewood, et cetera.—if there's room in the back, she gets a ride. After I stopped the first time, word spread, and now I'm something of a community bus service. They're all pretty grateful for the ride in Getu's old VW, and don't seem remotely bothered by the lack of a working radio or air-conditioning.

It feels good to be back in Africa. I've missed it. Life's more real out here. Even the air's alive. Charged. There are just fewer barriers between you and reality. There's always a lightness to the scent of the forest just after it has rained. The air is soft and it smells fresh, green, pure, natural. Everything is lush and dripping with liquid: me, the trees, the vines. On our way out to find the Yayu this morning, a gorilla crossed our path and that seemed as normal as walking past a tomcat back home. I'm about as up close and personal as you can get with Mother Nature right now. And I love it.

As we leave the cover of the trees and head back to Getu's farm, I see there's still a heavy layer of mist lying over the valley, even though it's getting on toward noon. The hills are covered in trees for as far as I can see. I've never known a place to be so green. It's not so far from here that the earliest fossils of modern humans were found. Some say that Ethiopia is the cradle of all humanity. The place on earth where our story began. As if God touched his hand down on Ethiopia's red soil and said, "Begin. Flourish."

You'd think that now that I'm hanging out in this Garden of Eden, I wouldn't have much trouble forgetting about the life I left behind in Pasadena. Or at least pushing it to the back of my mind most of the time. Not the case. That hard good-bye has haunted me for the last three weeks. I didn't even stop crying till we touched down in Addis Ababa. That was like *a day* later! I miss them. Life has a bleak hole at its center without them. But sometimes—not that it's in the cards—I do wonder what I would do if, out of nowhere, Peter figured out a way to make enough money so I didn't have to do this anymore. Finding the best coffee in the world, bringing it to "civilization," and working with these farmers to try and drag them and their families out of poverty—that's what I do. As I discovered, without this job I'm just a clueless mother who's still wearing Old Navy when she should clearly have moved on to Banana Republic at this stage of her life. Could I really ditch all this for a part-time job in a coffee shop and sincere conversations about junior soccer leagues? And now, of course, there's the research. I've been searching for this rust-resistant varietal all of my career. And now that I've found it, there's work to be done. Big work. As it is, I have to leave the coffee forest next week to go down to Colombia and it's just too soon. I need more time here.

As we approach the farm, I breathe in the scent of eucalyptus and charred coffee beans that permeates the air around Getu's house. The beautiful brown-and-white chickens are running free and wild, and the family goat is standing nearby, seeming to await our return. Getu's wife, Hanna, is working in the vegetable garden alongside their three sons and two of their daughters. She's beautiful, like so many of Ethiopia's women are. Her whole body is elegant and elongated; her cheekbones are high and wide, her nose looks like it's made from the same fine porcelain she serves her coffee in, her eyes huge and clear, her hair naturally wild. If she lived in New York City, she'd have been model scouted by now. Maybe when the scouts get tired of exploiting eastern European women, they'll find their way over here.

I watch them all digging and weeding in their garden; they work so naturally together. I envy Hanna with all my heart. Here she is, working alongside her children in nature's paradise, while mine are thousands of miles west doing goodness knows what—days of travel away should they need me urgently. This "uncivilized" woman is a much better, closer parent than I could ever hope to be. And her kids are just fine. They learn everything they need to know about their world by working right at her side. They're always clean, fed, cared for, loved. They're happy. Their whole family is happy. They're together. Why can't I have this?

Rahel, Hanna's youngest daughter, comes racing out of the house toward her mother. They both look at me and start waving. Rahel sprints over.

"*Ilmo,*" she says, out of breath. That translates as "son." Somehow without another word spoken I know that Billy's on the phone. I dash back to the house and grab Getu's cell. The thing's supersized, complete with a pointy antenna on the top. But it works.

"Billy?"

"Mommy!" He sounds excited and distressed all at once, and my heart immediately breaks in two.

Screw it. I know in that instant, from that one word, that I'd give it all up in half a heartbeat to be with him. I'd condemn the whole world to never drink another cup of coffee again if I could only hug him tight right now.

"Billy, my lovely. Why are you calling?" He knows he's only supposed to call outside of our weekly calls in an emergency. Calls from the United States to a cell phone in rural Ethiopia are not cheap.

"Mommy, I miss you," he says. And my devastation is complete. How can I do this? "When are you coming home?"

"Not for a while yet, sweetheart." I thought I might have time to stop home before Colombia, but it's not going to happen.

"Mommy, I have to tell you something bad that I did."

The mind boggles. What's he done? Set the neighbors' tree house on fire? Given all of Violet's dolls a crew cut? Snuck onto a cargo ship headed for Nigeria?

"What is it, sweetie?" I'd forgive him more or less anything right now.

"The reason Daddy's writing career is over. It's my fault."

"What did you do?"

"I e-mailed Daddy's script to that man he didn't want to see it. And then the man was mad, and now Daddy can't make money writing anymore." So that's how Nico got *Draker's Dark*.

"Sweetheart, you sending an e-mail is not the reason that Daddy can't make any money writing."

"But I wanted him to stop so that he'd look after us again and you'd go back to work." *Um, jeez, thanks, Billy.* "But now you've gone and I wish I hadn't done it, 'cause now Daddy can never make any money and you can never come home. And it's all my fault. I'm sorry, Mommy." Billy starts crying, and whatever remnants of my heart are left crumble away to dust.

And then I decide: *I'm not doing this anymore.* I'm not living another day without my children by my side. This stops. Now.

"Billy, where's your father?"

"He's out. We're at Lizzie's." Oh my God. He's making this call from my unemployed neighbor's house!

"As soon as he comes back, tell him you called me and tell him what you told me about Nico."

"Okay."

"And then you can tell him that I'm coming home."

CHAPTER 26

I'm woken by a gentle but firm touch on the shoulder. I pull up my eye mask to see the Air France flight attendant smiling down at me. She's perfect. How is it possible to look so pulled together and immaculate toward the end of a long-haul flight? Maybe there's a secret flight attendants' lounge on the plane where they all go to get restful massages and have their red lipstick flawlessly reapplied by an in-flight makeup artist. Otherwise, how could it be possible?

"Madam, we are approaching our descent. Please fasten your seat belt."

I oblige her and she moves on. Or should I say, floats on. I can only imagine the bedlam that would ensue if a bolt of *Freaky Friday* lightning were to hit the plane and she and I swapped lives. God knows how a woman accustomed to living a life of calm within the clouds would cope when thrown into the utter insanity that I'm sure is going to greet me as soon as I touch down at LAX.

My mouth feels vile. That last glass of airplane white wine was not a good idea. I'm not the kind of woman to keep a compact mirror handy, but if I were, and if I were to look in it, I'm sure I'd look a state. It's been a hell of a journey. I've been moving infinitesimally in the right direction with each flight for about two days now. And this is my final one. It's no quick feat to spontaneously travel to the States from the depths of Africa. I flew from Jimma to Addis Ababa to Saudi Arabia to Berlin to Paris (don't ask) before finally getting on this flight to Los Angeles. As well as not looking good, I'm pretty confident I don't smell that great either. Both my clothes and I are still covered in a layer of dried sweat and forest rain. After I hung up from talking to Billy, I started moving and I didn't stop. I was worried that if I paused to take a shower or change clothes, my impetus—fueled by nothing more than my crazy—might have been lost.

And maybe a pause in the impetus wouldn't have been such a bad idea. The fewer miles between Los Angeles and me, the more excited I've become at seeing the kids, but the more frantic I'm getting about what the hell our family is going to do. Roth was furious, of course. He'd pretty much staked the survival of his company on locating that bean. I still can't believe I did it. And I can't believe I stood my ground and didn't tell him Getu's location. It's still my find of the century. It's about all I've got standing between my family and their starvation. The information's valuable, though I'm not quite sure how I can make it pay. Especially now that I've decided never to be parted from my children again. I honestly don't know what we're going to do in the immediate future. We'll have to sell the house straightaway. Luckily, the market's come back and I bought that house before prices went insane, so if we make a quick sale, we can live off the equity for a while. A few months anyway. But then what? Should we move to Oregon and grow pot for cash? Start a commune? Should I try to persuade Peter to take a Chippendales job after all? I wonder if I could go back to college and finish off my botany degree. Not that the world is crying out with a need for botanists right now. I could always take my research on the Yayu to Monsanto or one of the other evil conglomerates. The *money* they'd drop for the DNA sequencing to a rust-resistant Arabica! But could I do that? Realistically? I'd feel about as comfortable handing

Violet over to Woody Allen for the afternoon so I could go for a spot of light shopping in downtown Manhattan. In other words: it'd probably work out okay, but why on earth would you take the risk with something so dear to you?

We land. Through the haze of jet lag and shitty plane sleep, I make my way through passport control and then customs. The minute I step out into arrivals, I see Peter. He's alone. I'm immediately all-over cold with nerves. I don't know which reaction I'm more terrified of: a furious tirade or him dismissing my whole flight from paid employment with a distracted "It'll be fine." Because I'm pretty certain it won't be fine. I've burnt my bridges with Roth. And the coffee world is tiny. Everyone will have heard what I've done by now. Some of the more enterprising among them will be on the next plane to Ethiopia, combing the coffee forests for the discovery. They won't find it. I've known Getu for eight years and I'm the only buyer he trusts. He's been burned before, and badly. He'll keep the whole thing secret until I tell him otherwise. He knows I'll handpick someone to work with him.

Peter doesn't see me at first. He looks bored. And then he spots me. And his reaction tells me exactly how he's going to take this: he's over the moon. He somehow looks younger, infused with the good stuff. He pushes his way through the chic French tourists and sweeps me up off the ground, squeezing me till I think I'm going to break, or at least pee myself. And then we're kissing. And it's the kind of kiss that has my fellow passengers rolling their eyes at the girl with the oversized backpack being greeted by her boyfriend at the airport. No one would take us for lukewarm married-with-children right now. We look young and in love. And I feel young too, despite the two nights of airport sleep. I feel like I could do anything if I've got him on my side. Maybe this was the right choice.

"You've really gone and screwed it up this time, haven't you?" he says, that dopey grin still on his face.

"Kinda," I say. "Where are the kids?"

"With Lizzie. I wanted you all to myself for a moment," he says and goes in for a second, more thorough, kiss. Good Lord. It's beginning to dawn on me that his deliriously joyful reaction may not entirely be owing to me bailing on my job and crossing two continents to be reunited with him. I pull out of his second rib-crusher. "What's going on? Why are you so happy? Aren't you concerned that we're going to have to sell the house and move to a hippie commune in Big Sur?"

"Will they have weed at the commune?"

"Yes, they farm it. That's how the whole thing's funded."

"Awesome. Will we be partaking in free love too?"

"No."

"Damn," he says, looking genuinely bummed. I punch him in the chest. I can pack a pretty good punch when I want to and he's winded for a second.

"Jesus, Amy."

"Sorry," I say. I'm not sorry. He's keeping something from me. I didn't call Peter from any of the airports. And believe me, I had plenty of opportunity. I was afraid talking to him would be like jumping into an icy-cold plunge pool of reality. But seeing his reaction to all this, I wish I had called; I might have saved myself a whole heap of anxiety. "Spill."

"I think I've sold *Draker's Dark*."

"What! How can that be possible?"

"Nothing's confirmed yet," he adds quickly.

"What happened?"

"You remember how you told me that you'd purposefully withheld the information that your ex-lover had been pestering you for sex?"

"That's not quite how I put it, but yes, I remember."

"Well, after you told me about it, I sat on the info and did nothing."

"Why are you telling me this?"

"I thought you'd be pleased?"

"I am. Kind of."

"I did nothing *until* I saw that they'd decided to show a rerun of *Real World Vampires* on Fox last week at eight p.m. Prime time for a rerun of something that was as interesting as a bunch of chewed-up cardboard the first time around. I was incensed! I did the Turtle for like two hours straight, but it didn't work because I was just so mad that something as trashy as *Real World Vampires* gets to be broadcast to the nation. And the man who created that shit gets to approach my wife for sexual favors when I never get to have sex with her. It's not cool."

"So you were mostly mad because Matt's trashy-but-successful show was getting a prime-time rerun."

"And because he'd been coming on to you." I give Peter a doubtful look. "Honestly, I was mostly mad at him for being a sex pest. Really—eighty percent of the anger was because of that."

"Are you sure it wasn't more like sixty/forty?"

"I'd say seventy at the very least. Seventy-five by the time I was driving over there."

"You went over there?"

"Of course. I wanted to deck him."

"Oh my God! Did you actually hit him?" I feel a flush of inappropriate excitement.

"I had all intentions of hitting him."

"So what happened?" I ask, a little deflated. Don't get me wrong. I'm not suddenly all in approval of my husband's anger-management problem; it's just a little more exciting when he's foaming with anger in the name of defending my honor.

"When I got there, he was having a meeting with the head of production for Lionsgate."

"Oh."

"I know. Kind of awkward. So instead of beating Matt up, I gave the producer my elevator pitch."

"You had an elevator pitch ready?"

"I didn't really have it ready, but I did make one up on the spot. It was a bit longer than the standard elevator ride. But he liked it."

"He did!?"

"This exec has green-light power, Amy."

"Is that like some kind of fun superpower?"

"It means that if he likes a script and it's not ludicrously expensive to make, he has the sole power to put it into production."

"Oh my God!"

"I know! I'm going over to Lionsgate tomorrow to pitch it to the committee. I know I'm going to sell this one."

And I believe him. I have to. Because I know that in about an hour from now I'm going to be back together with Billy and Violet. Violet'll attach herself around my neck like an orphaned baby orangutan; Billy'll be reticent at first and then will come in for a long snuggle and a story. I'll ruffle my fingers through his extra-thick hair and tolerate his stone-cold feet on my shins. We'll be back together.

And Peter had better sell this goddamn script, because this time, whatever I have to do to make it work, I swear I'll never, *never* be parted from my family again.

EPILOGUE

I honestly don't think there's a truck in the entire world—certainly not in Ethiopia—that has enough suspension to be able to cope with these insanely bumpy mountain roads. My body's been shaken so much recently that every time I step out of the truck and I don't collapse into a pile of jiggly jelly, I'm surprised. I'm considering buying a motorcycle so I can at least try to steer around the worst of the ruts in the road.

So I expect you're wondering what the F-word I'm doing thousands of miles away from LA once again. Peter's big sale of the century fell through. *I know.* The deal crumbled into a thousand tiny pieces before he even got to the pitch meeting. The producer with the fabled green-light superpowers had gotten an earful from Matt and a couple of other producers about what a nightmare Peter is to work with, and after Peter had tried to call him about five times, he got a short, sharp e-mail from the producer's PA saying he was no longer interested in pursuing the project. Peter didn't throw a fit or a tantrum upon the news, or try to storm Lionsgate's offices in order to change the producer's mind. He just fell into a dark, quiet depression. The kind of depression I'd never witnessed before. No moodiness. No passive-aggressive remarks about the importance of not leaving a residue of toothpaste around the sink after brushing one's teeth or pointed suggestions for the right way to stack the dishwasher. No more hours spent in the garage with nothing but his laptop and pee bucket for company. He slept during the day. He watched trashy TV at night. He didn't eat a whole bunch. It had become clear to him what should have been clear years ago: Hollywood had locked her doors to him and put the key in a high-up place that he'd never grow tall enough to reach.

And what was my response to all this? I didn't waste a minute. The moment I heard the script sale had fallen through, I put our house on the market at just under value. It sold fast—just like I knew it would. It broke my heart to sell, but I did it anyway. I had the world's biggest garage sale, packed up a few boxes for shipping, got us all inoculations (my yellow fever booster included), handed Inkie back over the fence to be reunited with his mother, called Getu, and booked four tickets to Addis Ababa.

I know.

The first few months were the hardest. They were really hard. All four of us cooped up in two rooms at the Holiday Inn for weeks while I negotiated land-lease agreements with the local government, and then worked to get the shack that passed as a house hooked up to the electricity grid. At least it had a concrete floor. We were grateful for that when the rains came in. And then with the rains came pneumonia for Violet. She pulled through it. I almost didn't. And then, just as I thought I was going to fall apart mentally, Peter came back from wherever his depressive state had taken him, and haltingly, day by day, we became a family again.

In a huge surprise to both of us, Peter quickly developed some pretty impressive "man" skills and started slowly patching up the shack till it became quite livable—and then became a home. Getu and I, along with a crew of locals, planted up the land with the Yayu. So far the trees are doing very well. They're sturdy little things. It'll take about five years for them to fully mature. Until then we're just picking what

Yayu we can from the forest next to Getu's house, where it all started, and exporting it back to Bean à la Bean in the States. Roth went from hostile to extremely amenable during that first conversation when I told him what I'd got stored up and ready to go. He could barely get his contrite apologies out quickly enough. He's paying well for it, though, not that it'd be any other way with me at the helm. I know what this stuff's worth. Of course, the bigger expansion—and the really worthwhile money—should come along when our miniplantation is mature. Until then? Let's just say it's a good thing our overhead is practically zero.

However, in another Peter triumph that I didn't see coming, he sold a novel! He wrote some folksy type of thing about a family of clueless Westerners who move to the coffee forest of Ethiopia to try their luck running a coffee farm. You can probably see where he got the inspiration. The book sold quite well, and the BBC—which hadn't heard about Peter's bad rep in Hollywood—is currently kicking around the idea of developing it into a miniseries.

I glance at Billy in the backseat. His head's resting easily against the window. Riding inside the world's rattliest truck doesn't seem to bother him at all. To him it's as relaxing as a beautiful African lullaby rocking and shaking him to sleep. I'm not getting a motorcycle. How could I lose my lab partner? Billy and I have been riding into Jimma together to work on the DNA sequencing at the lab. The work's still not near done, but I'm making great progress. Billy's fascinated by the whole thing. He sits right by my side as I stare down a microscope for hours on end. Sometimes he gets on with his schoolwork, sometimes he requests a peek down the microscope, sometimes he conducts his own "experiments" with test tubes. He's a changed boy, no longer a ball of pent-up emotion with too much energy for a relatively small suburban backyard. He's engaged. He concentrates. He listens. He smiles a lot. He hasn't asked to see an iPad since we moved to the farm. Why would he? He has a whole forest as his playground. It's not all play for Billy, though. We pick up his special box of educational stuff for expat homeschooled kids once a month when we go into town. He's already reading at a third-grade level. Getting him this far this quickly is my proudest life achievement without a doubt.

Violet? She's blossoming too. The pneumonia changed her somehow. She became calmer, older, less given to screeching and screaming to have things her way. She's forgotten all about Disney princesses and wouldn't know what to do with a Bratz doll if she came across one. Instead, her make-believe games have her in the starring role of intrepid explorer—she tells Billy he's the pack mule, carrying her special science equipment, and he's happy to comply, braying away. All traces of her illness are gone. She runs, she climbs, she chases after wild animals (I should probably put a stop to that). She mixes mysterious leaves and half-grown vegetables together in a clay pot and declares herself a magic jungle chef. Every day is a biology lesson.

It's six o'clock, and the landscape is starting to think about darkening. I'm glad I've made it back home in time. Those passes are no place to be after nightfall. As I pull up the truck, I see Peter is sitting on the porch. He's burning a kerosene lamp—the electricity must be out. It's spotty at best. He's pounding away on his typewriter; he gave up on computers a while ago. The whole thing looks very turn of the century. The lack of electricity in the house seems to have had a directly inverse effect on the amount of electricity within our relationship. These days there seems to be so much more time and mental space for plain ol' getting down to it. Besides—what else are you going to do after the sun goes down, the batteries for the radio go flat, and the candles burn out?

I can see there's been exactly zero progress on the guesthouse. Peter must have been in writing mode today. My parents—who were super concerned when I revealed that I was spiriting their grandchildren off to the wilds of Africa—came over recently to visit, and what they saw completely turned their opinion around. Dad's knees eased up the minute he was out of the English chill, and when Mom qualifies for her county council pension at the end of the year, they're considering moving out. Or at least spending some of the year here, anyway.

I don't see Violet anywhere. That doesn't send me into an instant panic like it used to. She'll be around. Antagonizing the wildlife, I'm sure. That girl's not happy unless she's driving something or somebody crazy. Most often me. Yup, there are still times when I want to throttle every member of my family—even here in paradise.

Am I crazy for doing this? Maybe. At no point during this transition did I stop to ask myself if this was actually a good idea. I just acted on instinct and kept on moving till we were situated in this new life. Was I terrified like I've never been terrified before when Violet had a fever of a hundred and five and the nearest hospital was a six-hour drive away? Absolutely. Do I worry about another Rwanda? Ebola? All the time. Do I think this is the best thing I've done as a mother? Without a doubt.

I open Billy's car door. He wakes up and gives me a dozy gap-toothed smile. He lost his first tooth this morning, right at the front. It's the first "first" I haven't missed. The sun's crawling quickly down behind the trees. Night is approaching. It's time to go and put Billy's tooth under his pillow to see if the tooth fairy's going to pay him a visit.

It's time to go and be a mom.

ACKNOWLEDGMENTS

Thanks to Todd Burke for accompanying me on my coffee journey, and all the journeys. I know some of the stuff I drag you through isn't much fun, so thanks for showing up in equal parts for all of it. Thanks to Robb Lanum for his take on faucets and foot fungus; to Kerry West for her portrait of Africa; to Rowena Escalona for the magical chats; to my readers Fiona Pearce, Ellie Cobb, Andrea Stein, and Linda Molnar Hines; and, of course, to the Kerley crew back in Kent.

Thank you, thank you to Laura Longrigg, my wonderful agent, who started everything. You simply rock it. And thanks to Ethan Ellenberg. If I haven't told you before now how happy I am that I have you in my corner, let's get that in black-and-white right now: I am *so happy* I have you in my corner. Thank you to Miriam Juskowicz and to Robin Benjamin for your wonderful edits and for just "getting it." A huge thank-you to Caroline Upcher, who saw a tiny flicker of a flame and decided she'd have a go at getting it burning properly.

And, lastly, to the two minipairs of Thunder Feet who inspire me to try harder every day: I love you *big* (not small).

THE BIT ABOUT THE AUTHOR

 Virginia Franken was born and raised in the United Kingdom. She graduated from the University of Roehampton, in London, with a degree in dance and worked on cruise liners as a professional dancer before changing tracks to pursue a career in publishing. Virginia currently lives in suburban Los Angeles with two kids, a dog, an overweight goldfish, and one bearded dude, in a house that's just a little too small to fit everyone in comfortably. She gets most of her writing done when she should be sleeping. This is her first novel.